2020 Collection: Short Stories

Petrina Binney

Dear Debs, Hope ya like the book. Check out page 256. Love, Petrina x

Published by Petrina Binney, 2020.

This is a work of fiction. Similarities to real people, places, or events are entirely coincidental.

2020 COLLECTION: SHORT STORIES

First edition. July 28, 2020.

Copyright © 2020 Petrina Binney.

Written by Petrina Binney.

'A Can Of Worms: A Short Story of Love and Lies', first published, 28th January 2020

'It's The Landing That Hurts: A Short Story of Disaster', first published, 28th February 2020

'Desperately Seeking Spinach: A Short Story of Obsession', first published, 28th March 2020

'If This Were A Swedish Film, We'd Already Be In Love: A Brief History of Fiona', first published, 28th April 2020

'Love Letters To The General Public: A Little, Widespread Romance', first published, 29th May 2020

'The Good In Goodbye: A Short Story of Revenge', first published, 28th June 2020

'The Desiccated Ingénue', first published, 28th July 2020, in this collection

A Can of Worms: A Short Story of Love and Lies

THE TROUBLE WITH KEEPING a *lot* of secrets, of course, is the terrible certainty that, sooner or later, something desperately important is bound to slip out.

I need to perfect it. I don't want to scare her off. I don't think I could bear it if I lost our afternoons together.

A small muscle dances below her left eye and – just like that – I'm lost.

She seems to know I'm staring and thus, she pushes her glasses up her nose. It's a thing she does. There are lots of things she does. This is one of my favourites: the slow, delicate slide of the glasses up to the bridge of her nose. As if she can hide behind them. She'll clear her throat in a moment. It will sound like music. Like slightly phlegmy music and then, she'll smile and I'll forget myself for a moment. Sometimes, you only need to see a trace of smile to know a person inside out.

The frames are tortoiseshell. They suit her. Perhaps it sounds condescending – perhaps it is condescending – but I don't think most people really know what they're shopping for. Whether it's glasses or anything else – it's as if they've never seen themselves. They'd make just as good a choice if they grabbed the last pair in a closing down sale, but not her. I think she knows her face.

I wonder if she knows how frequently I think about her mouth. Her lips are full. Deep red, like Shiraz.

If I'm honest, I've never been all that good on red wine. I'm learning. It's a process. Usually, I make a face. Last time, I wound up taking off my blouse in the bathroom and not quite getting it back on properly. Still, it was only me and the Channel 4 news, so I don't think it really matters.

Her eyes are perfect clouds. They see everything, know everything. She has a good nose. Not dainty, but not the sort of thing you'd have to warn people about before they walk in the room. There's no doubting what it is.

It's definitely a nose.

Her chin is dimpled; there's a little groove there that she touches with her pen when she's thinking.

Her skin is soft.

I imagine.

I don't know.

It's not as if I've leaned over and stroked the woman.

But it's important to note all these small details. These are the things that will mean something if there's ever a hostage negotiation, or if the world turns upside down. She'll be able to communicate with me via the smallest of movements. If it comes to it, I'll remember what she looks like when she's worried or considering her options. I'll know whether to send chocolates or police officers.

Or, in smaller ways, on Saturdays, I'll be able to tell her: *you're doing that thing you always do when you're* – whatever she's feeling at the time. And she'll smile as she realises that all her little idiosyncrasies are important to me because – well, of course they are.

She probably wouldn't be so adorable if there were actually terrorists threatening her toenails, but I would know there was a problem just from the way she slides the pen into her top pocket. From the way she curls her fingers round the arm of her chair. From the angle of her eyebrows, I would know.

It's one of many things I can't tell her. Not just yet.

I've whispered it to myself in the dead of the night. She means more to me than I do. Which is only fair, because I love her.

I know.

It's a revolting sentiment, even at the best of times, but there it is: love. I find it usually makes people feel rather uncomfortable, like an unexpected tickle on the soft skin just behind the knee. The kind of tickle that can only mean that a rather confused wasp has flown up your trouser-leg. In seconds flat, there'll be a mad dash to casualty and a lifetime of hearing about appropriate clothing choices from various aunties, who only turn up at Christmas, but have an opinion on absolutely everything. Love, as a conversation piece, is painful and frightening. I try not to think about it.

It's quiet in here. I know I should tell her something that's real.

"I'm worried that I'm a compulsive liar," I tell her.

That'll do. And, for the time being, everything is all right because I'm noting her little behavioural ticks and I'm being honest with her. Kind of.

I do worry that I'm a compulsive liar. Maybe I'm not *actively* worried. I mean – I can see that it's worth worrying about.

I think that counts.

I admire those people who can say anything, actually *anything*, and not worry about causing offence. I like that. I wish I could be like that. To just speak my mind, to say it all, would be liberating. More, it would be exhilarating. At least, to begin with. But I can't help thinking that it would become unutterably dull after a while.

I think, if I were hand-on-heart honest, I would feel like a bank manager. Like a bank manager who hasn't been laid in fifteen years. Like a bank manager who hasn't been laid in fifteen years and breaks wind on the front doorstep so as not to upset the dog.

It would be very limiting. Very...

"... in particular that worries you?"

Her voice is like a woodwind instrument. It's textured but precise, polished but reedy. There's a hint of every fee-paying school she's ever attended in her voice. It's like an ache. She probably had a horse called Binky. I expect she had pen pals all over the world. When she was young, she must have sorted through their stamps and kept them all in an album. It's in her voice that she drinks cocktails, not from a can, but mixed by hand. She puts kale in things. She holidays in sand and snow. She is refined. She is glorious. But I wish she wouldn't talk when I'm thinking.

"Jacqueline?" She tilts her head as if I've already said something extraordinary.

"I just..." I'm guessing how I should finish this sentence. "It's difficult."

She smiles. It's only a small flicker but it'll do. It's a step in the right direction anyway.

I make a small noise in the back of my throat. She seems impressed. I don't exactly know what she's going to make of it, but that's hardly my business.

I have nothing to say right now.

She's very good at what she does, I'm sure of that. There's a clock up on the wall a little way behind me. She hasn't looked at it once. I like that. I like that she's just here with me and that time, as a concept, no longer matters. She just sits behind her leather-covered desk, with its fine gold stitching and the bust of – whoever he is – and the special mug that sits, neglected, from one afternoon to the next.

Because a mug is friendly. A mug says, '*You can talk to me.*'

I suspect she's more accustomed to bone china, but she indulges in a mug so that the others don't feel uncomfortable. I think she must realise we're past that point. We're closer than the charade of what may or may not constitute acceptable chinaware. But we can't really talk about that. Not yet.

She pushes the glasses up her nose again as she frowns at something in her notebook. It's nothing I've done. Can't be. I've been on my best behaviour. Maybe it's her own handwriting that eludes interpretation. There'll be a *J* that might be an *I*, or something like that. Sometimes, she writes something down and I wonder what she thinks of me.

There's a lot of thinking happens in this room. It's really quite exhausting.

Minette doesn't realise that my whole week is a run-up to our afternoons together. It's rather challenging, finding the right words, keeping her on my side but getting closer. Getting her to actually see me.

Once, she asked me how I was feeling, 'in myself'. I didn't want to tell her I'd rather be in someone else. It was still early, and she might not have taken it the right way. But I knew what she meant. She's noticed. I've been going to the gym. I'm practically toned. Almost in shape. *A* shape, certainly. The lighting has to be right for me to look like I'm making actual progress but she's noticed.

To be fair, I don't really care about physical fitness. Not mine, anyway. But I thought it might be important to her – healthy mind, healthy body, that sort of thing. And you can't expect these things to just fall into your lap.

Unfortunately.

So I filled in all the paperwork, started a payment plan, and now, I spend three nights a week with Leah.

She's irrelevant.

Don't bother to remember her name because it won't come up again.

Don't get me wrong – Leah's all right, for what she is. She's just – not my most important thought.

"Compulsive liars," Minette says, "tend to keep people at a distance. The lies act as carefully constructed barriers to keep other people from seeing the liar for who they really are, or who they are afraid they might be. Would you say you have a fear of intimacy?"

See, what she's done there is she's taken a can of worms and started knocking it against a fucking rock. She doesn't see the irony of asking someone like me such a personal question. I've already told her what I'm going to do. It's as if she doesn't listen.

"I'm not afraid," I tell her.

Now, that's almost true. Actual skin-to-skin intimacy doesn't bother me at all. She could find that out for herself quite easily if she'd just get out from behind the desk, but I don't think I care for this conversation. It's liable to get out of control and that way – madness lies.

A small thought dances on the periphery but disappears when I try to look at it directly. Apparently, it's not time for that yet.

I see her watching me over the top of the tortoiseshell, ignoring her latte and thinking about what she's going to have for dinner. I see her. Thinking.

Leah tells me that I need to feel the burn and keep going. To push myself beyond the extremes of what I believe I can do and carry on. She says, unless I pass out, I'm not pushing hard enough. But she has to say that. It's her job. And Leah doesn't make me feel this way. Which is a shame. But there's something rather distasteful about someone who's prepared to sweat with or without company.

Minette is something altogether different. She's slim but there are curves, thank God. She's dark, with soft curls and curious eyes. She's older than me. Perhaps forty-five.

All right, I'm being kind. She's probably fifty. She sits in her nice office with its picture window, a large leafy fern (which I think is plastic. It's not dusty, it just looks a bit – like it could be), and her bust of – whoever the hell he is.

And I want her to know. I want her to know me. I want her, on so many levels, but most of all – I want her to know that, with me, she is safe. A woman should be cosseted, I'm sure I read that somewhere. I mean, actively cosseting a person sounds like an extreme sport and, God knows, I wouldn't want it done to me, but... Whatever, I want her to know that she is loved.

"I think I need a new job," I hear myself say. Didn't realise I was going to speak but it's not jarring. I often catch myself unawares. Still, I should have practised this bit. This chat could go anywhere. Down unexplored avenues that I'm not certain really fit with the person I'm pretending to be.

She could have me.

There are secrets.

I want to tell her.

I can't tell her.

How can I tell her that my heart leaps when I see her? When I think about seeing her? When I think about...

"Is there something else you'd rather do?" she asks.

Don't say it. Don't say it.

"Erm..."

Don't. *Please*, don't.

"Well..."

I don't know how long she's been a counsellor for. She has a lot of qualifications on her wall, but with that swirly writing they use on certificates, half of them might belong to someone else. When I first came here, I told myself they couldn't all be from the internet and so far, she seems to know her stuff.

"I always thought it might be nice to be a travel writer," I muse.

I would hate it.

She must know I would hate it.

All those people... and airports... It would be awful. Even the thought makes my throat go tight. To be surrounded by tourists, with strings of greying, peeled skin clogging up their fingernails as they search for the right currency and the language for a lager and lime: it would be hell. Besides, I'm not one to stand in a queue, checking my pockets for my passport, my tickets, my money.

I'd need my mum.

I'd get mugged. I know I would. And how can I tell her that the snap of an airport-security latex glove has never really done it for me?

Unless that's what she's into. In which case –

She'd never tell me that.

No. She knows I won't become a travel writer. She must know. I wouldn't make it to Heathrow. She'll start laughing any second now.

"You're still young," she offers. "You could enrol in college. Maybe do a few writing courses, or..."

I don't hear the rest of it. I don't need to. If she thinks I'm still young, she must have been watching me quite closely. She must have made an assessment of my age by checking me out, at least a little.

Maybe a lot.

Maybe despite herself.

Maybe it's simple torture just looking at me.

"How does that sound?" she says, finally.

It's in her notes.

Of course, it is. She knows I'm twenty-eight because it's in her notes. Damn.

"I can look into it," I tell her.

She knows I won't. I'm sure she does. It's different if you're with someone. Then, you wouldn't feel so adrift. It's got to be better when you know you won't just get swept along in the riptide of someone else's baggage claim.

No, I won't look into it. There's no point. I get travelsick on the second floor of Fenwick's.

I already know I'm smiling at her. My face has conspired with my thoughts to paint her a picture that's not ready to be seen.

Her hair looks glossy, like she's never used the same towel twice. I want to touch it. You don't have to tell me. I know I can't. Even if I were to rise from my seat and make my way towards her desk, she would frown out her puzzlement, push back against the floor, and wheel her swivel chair back towards the wall before I could reach a single strand. Even though it would mean the world to me. Even though it would probably hold me for another week. Even if she can't, won't, mustn't...

"So, how are you feeling?"

"I like a poppy-seed bagel," I shrug.

Why am I saying that?

"Why do you say that?" she asks.

I'm thinking of breakfast, the morning after. The morning after everything changes and we can stop pretending.

It doesn't take much to get me thinking of food but the thought of making breakfast for her, watching her twist in the sheets as the milk float chugs down the road, and the bin men call out to each other, as the streetlights make way for a pimple of sunlight: it's bliss. Just the idea of her in the morning, her glasses on my bedside table, her clothes dotted along the staircase, her underwear on the windowsill, gives me a bubbly feeling round the waist.

I feel weak.

"Jacqueline?" She's reminding me she's still there.

I should change the sheets before she comes back. I can't expect a woman like Minette to cope with a cotton-poly blend. She's made for satin. Or silk. I'll have to remind myself to check out new mattresses online when I get home. Perhaps it's a good thing that this relationship is taking so damn long to get off the ground. I may have to move house.

"Jacqueline," she tries again. There's a firmness in her voice. Not sure how I feel about that.

"You see..."

But I have to think about this. I don't want to overreach. It's a big step. I don't know that we're ready for it, and I don't want to push my luck.

Then again, we have to start somewhere. Getting my name right feels like as good a place to start as any. Unless it's too much for her...

Of course, it's these tiresome little details that keep us in our seats. Before anything further, I want to sweep everything off the desk and put her in place of all the paperwork and the books that go unread. I want to knock the bust of bronzy onto the carpet and unbutton her blouse. I want to hear the sounds she makes as she falls away from her own accountability. I want her to have nothing but instinct.

And me.

Obviously, me.

There's very little point in any of this without me.

Then again, it could be an experiment. If I don't ask her to use the name I keep for friends and could-be lovers, then nothing will happen. All manner of things might complicate and damage the structure I'm trying to build – that each of us, secretly, builds around herself to stay protected, or connected to other people – it might all be destroyed. But if we don't take the chance when it so readily presents itself, nothing will happen at all.

That's right. I'm sure, that's right.

It's like a secret conversation we're having. A conversation inside the one we're having out loud. If she says 'yes', then it's going to be okay. Maybe it means she knows and, perhaps, she even approves. If she says 'no' – well, I don't know what I'll do. Still, Leah says it's important to set out our intentions and stick to them.

Okay. I'm going to ask. I am. I need to think about how to ask her to... "Would you call me Jaxx?"

The question falls out of me, as inevitable and startling as a sigh. It's out there. I've said it.

And for a moment, there's nothing. Something deeper than silence. The office, the window, the world, all disappears. I'm not sure either of us is really there anymore. It's like I can't even hear my heart beating. Maybe it's stopped. Maybe I'm dead. I wait to see the change in her facial expression. If I'm dead, she'll surely make a face.

"Of course," she smiles and makes a note.

She's going to call me Jaxx. It's like I can hear angels singing.

"It's J-A-X-X," I tell her.

She pulls her lower lip into her mouth, like she's considering a new flavour.

"Double X," she remarks.

I can't tell if she's impressed or not.

"One of them is a kiss," I blunder. "I'll let you choose which one."

She puts her shoulders back.

Oh, God. I'm an idiot.

She breathes through her nose.

I'm an idiot.

"We've talked about this," she says, and in this moment, I *want* to die. Right here and now, beside the potted fern, which may or may not be real, with the bust of whatshisname looking down at me with his narrow eyes and bald, shining head. I suspect he's a doctor. Maybe a hero. Probably dead. They're usually dead, aren't they? His could be the last face I see before the world goes dark.

"Just a joke," I shrug. I laugh – a little too warmly, a little too long. I'm probably making her nervous. I'm making *me* nervous. Time to change the subject.

Think of something.

No, I can't die in front of the plant. Plastic or not, it's wrong to die in front of shrubs. It upsets the natural order. They should always die first.

Say something.

"I was going to say..."

Not that. Not yet.

"I can recommend someone else," she says, "if this is getting too much...?"

"No. No, it's fine," I hurry. "I was just thinking about – I say silly things when I'm nervous."

That is something of an exaggeration. It's just that timing isn't really my forte. I worry about saying the wrong thing, about saying too much, about scaring her off, because I haven't quite tapped into that whole 'timing' thing.

"And..." My voice has dropped. Good lord, I sound quite serious. I almost don't care if she's impressed. I am. I sound good, strong; like a superhero, hands on hips and secret identity. And then: "I have some important stuff to do later on," I confide. When did I start whispering?

"Would you like to talk about it?" she asks.

She has the most beautiful eyes I think I've ever seen. Hazel-blue, like the sky right after a storm. Perhaps a storm at sea, and – yes, she's waiting for me to say something.

"Oh, it's..."

It's like free fall. I have no idea. Maybe that's why I've never had the mind for learning another language. Free fall in English is more than enough. From one word to another, I don't know what I'm going to say. Maybe that's why the stories feel so important. I can plan them. The words might be a surprise, but the general direction is known. Like when you speak to a friend. You know where you're going, but the words just come out the way they do. But to do that in another language – I don't know how anyone manages it.

Like, if you think back to when we learnt French at school – it was supposed to be conversational French, but no one actually talks like that. They couldn't. It would be obscene.

If you met someone in a bar and they told you their name, where they lived, that they had blonde hair and would like a ham sandwich, you'd think they were barking. But that's because, with language lessons in school, you're learning the words, not how to *think* in another language.

In the meantime, I owe her an explanation for why I'm too busy to see another therapist. And I have no idea what I'm going to...

"It's just that I need to... Well, I need to get something for... It's a present. For my... cousin's bar mitzvah."

And, just like that, I'm Jewish.

I'm going to have to remember that.

It occurs to me: I really should have a series of cue cards, or a notebook like hers, to remind me of the pertinent details of my life. At least, of the life I've told her about. We'll move closer to the truth, I'm quite sure, when the fiction and everything else falls away but – first things first. It's important to stay the course, to find the right order. The words can't just tumble out as one long phrase because that would be – well, intimidating, probably.

In the meantime, as far as Minette is concerned, I'm a Jewish, emotionally stretched, possible-gym-bunny, who says silly things when she's preoccupied. Which is pretty good. There are worse things to be and I'm only *some* of those.

She's sensible. Minette. She's very organised. You can tell from the state of her office. Not a speck of dust, not a single cobweb. I like the way she moves. She holds her keys tightly in her fist as she approaches or leaves her car. Like she's ready to defend herself.

I need that kind of influence around me. Someone who thinks about things, about how dangerous the world can be, who doesn't shy away from it but doesn't take unnecessary risks. Then again, how many of us really understand the risks we take?

How many of us would listen even if we could be told?

I wonder if she has an emergency backpack, in case of nuclear war or global internet crisis. Planes might drop from the sky, looters might take over the suburbs, but Minette would be sitting under her dining room table, in her well-secured home, with a larder full of baked beans and enough freeze dried coffee to wake the dead. And because of her years as a therapist, nothing could shock her. At least, I hope not. She may be the most capable person I'll ever know.

I need to know her better. I need…

"Are you coping with the cravings?"

Oh, and I've just given up smoking. That was the other thing.

Definitely need a chart of some sort.

"Fine, yeah."

She doesn't know that if all I had to look forward to was the bus to and from work, and the microwaved, rubbery roulette wheel of office-lunch – could be bad chicken, could be good ham, neither sight nor smell will provide a clue – I'd find it very difficult not to start walking other people's dogs. Just to get me out and about, in the fresh air, with a healthy occupation, and the nods of my fellow walkers.

Not ham! Definitely not ham.

Jewish now. Must remember.

Somehow, I know my thoughts would slither back to the way her tongue plays at the corner of her mouth when she's trying to find the right word, but at least I'd have company if I became a dog walker.

"I…" I stop myself.

"It's all right," she comforts me. Even as I make her shuffle for reasons she may or may not understand, she does what she can to make me feel better. God, she's wonderful.

"I just really like talking to you."

There. That should do it. Okay, she's probably feeling sorry for me now. Like I'm some sort of bleeding heart in an advert, but it's better than her palming me off on another therapist.

I wonder how long it will be before she realises that these sessions have to end, not because I'm blurring the lines, but because there are no lines for people like us.

"Taking intimacy off the table, then..." she says.

She's amazing, picking up her earlier train of thought. She has no idea how many ways I've already had her. In hotels. In broom closets. In the ad break in *Corrie*. All in my head, of course. I know that.

The thoughts are still in their dreamy, incomplete form, because they're locked in my imagination.

But that's where we keep all the best things. On the inside. Got to keep them safe. And so, we lock the dreams away, with our PIN numbers, awkward first kisses, public bouts of explosive gastroenteritis, and the other things we just won't speak about.

"Are you all right?" she asks, and that's when I realise I've been humming the chorus of *Tradition* from Fiddler On The Roof for nearly two minutes.

"Yes, sorry. I'm here." Totally redundant phrase. Don't know why I've used it. She knows I'm here. I'm booked in. Regular appointment, Friday afternoon, six weeks and counting – building up to something special. I can't blame her for not knowing how important our relationship will be. She's all the way over the other side of the desk and what with her being so short sighted...

"In our last session..." Minette begins, but she can stop there. I know what happened, and frankly, it was difficult. More than that – it was distressing. And it was my fault. I suppose.

We talked about my feelings around my family.

In truth – because why not dabble a little with the truth – my mother convinced me to book the first session. She'd talked it all over with Dad, she told me and – well, her reasons really don't matter. I'd been debating just cancelling it over the phone.

But, as the day drew closer, I realised that would be rude. So, I was just going to come in and apologise to the receptionist. Make something up about a work-based emergency, and not bother to rearrange the appointment for another time. Because it was an emergency and I wouldn't have time to grapple with my pockets and then, flick through my diary, looking for a better time. Pretending there was something actually in my diary.

I'd make my excuses and head for the door. I'd employ a hurried pace, but it would be dignified. Just because I was heading for a nightmare of paperwork and spent fire extinguishers did not mean I would get there red-faced and sweating. And besides, I didn't need a receptionist thinking I couldn't cope. I had it all perfectly arranged in my head.

But I was running late. It had been raining and, one thing and another, I was late. The storm was dripping across my shoulders when I blundered through the front door and I really wasn't expecting to be shown straight into her room, but there she was. Minette. Writing up her notes or jabbing at the crossword, I hardly remember. All I know is – I saw her – and everything shifted. She asked me what I hoped to achieve from our time together and... I'm not in the habit of shocking myself but it just slipped out.

I know it shouldn't have.

But, once said, I couldn't take it back.

"So, how are you feeling now?" she asks.

"I'm okay."

There's a flicker in her eyelid. She doesn't believe me. "The grieving process takes time," she soothes.

I'm sure she's right. She's studied this stuff and I...

"It must have been very hard – to have lost both your parents so suddenly."

I close my eyes too tightly. There are little green-blue spots behind my eyelids.

"It's all right, Jaxx. You're safe here."

I feel awful.

"It was an accident," I stumble.

They're in Basildon.

"I..."

She thinks they're dead.

"It's just that…"

Because that's what I said.

Then again, people can be dead in Basildon. *They're* not, but that's not why we're here. Not anymore.

I'm blinking too much but I can hardly tell her now, can I? I don't even know how that conversation would start. Going into therapy because your mother thinks you're a chronic underachiever seems a little thin. And probably Freudian.

Maybe bronzy is Freud?

When she asks me how I'm coping, it feels as if I have no skin. I don't know what to say. The lies are wretched and the truth brings no comfort. I try to say nothing but that never works. I feel dizzy. I'm blinking too much. That's a thing that I do. Often too much. It's like heroin, blinking.

I suppose, if I'm honest with myself, I really didn't think we'd still be talking about them all these weeks later. Perhaps my answers haven't quite rung true. Maybe that's why we're still raking over the whole mess, but I have had rather a lot on my mind.

I wonder if she wears thongs or girl boxers.

"It's important, Jaxx, to connect with your feelings. To allow yourself to feel."

Thongs. Definitely, thongs.

"This is a safe place," she's trying to placate me. "You can tell me anything, that's what I'm here for."

And just like that – it's all business. I can't think about the shapes she makes in the shower, or the faint smell of gardenia that hangs in the air. I can't think about any of that now because she's gone and mentioned my parents and I'm supposed to be in mourning.

I've been doing my best, mimicking the heartache that comes up in hospital dramas. There's usually a tragedy in there somewhere. And, soap opera or not, some of them are pretty good actors.

And even though I know I will rot for the things I've said, I think I'm doing quite well with this. It's a gift I've always had: having feelings that aren't strictly mine. You wrap a baby in a blanket, and I can feel the fabric on my face. You tell me about a broken leg, and I can't help but limp. I just needed to stay with her for a while and it was the first thing that popped into my head.

And now, I'm in a 'safe place'.

My thoughts, such as they are, have turned into a putrid puree of thwarted lust and the desperation that comes from trying to remember daytime TV tragedies while stopping myself from humming.

Well played, Minette.

"You can say anything here, you know that," she says.

I nod, but neither of us really believes that.

She thinks I don't know why she says things like this, but it's glaringly obvious. She's a professional. She does things properly. By the book. She can't have me – even though I want her to – she can't have me sitting here, thinking about sucking on her earlobe, making her eyelids flicker and her breath come in ragged bursts because – I'm 'suffering'. And she has ethics. I'm lucky I don't have to deal with any of that. Not full-time anyway. I give the appearance of a strong moral compass because I have to. For her. And besides, it's part of the adventure. At least, it has been. But not just lately.

"Do you find it difficult to make friends?" she asks me.

"Of course not," I say. I sound sulky. I don't know when that happened, but I sound like I'm in a proper mood. I don't like this tone of voice. I can't think it'll do me any favours. "I have friends."

God, it sounds like I hate them.

I think I've been in love once or twice. I know now that it was nothing very serious. It felt real at the time because – that's what liars do. Real liars. They let you believe whatever is necessary as long as it suits them. As soon as it doesn't, they block your number and walk away, as if it was *you* who had the problem. But it was never you.

Of course, I thought it was real. It felt real. But I suppose, if it had been, they would have loved me back. Or noticed I was there. Perhaps they would have been pleased about it. No. It wasn't love. It was – something to do. A distraction. *It*, not *I*.

"That's good," she nods at her pad. "I'm pleased."

"Can't be unexpected though?" I offer. "Everyone has friends. There are serial killers with fan pages online, you know."

"Do you think friends and fans are the same thing?" she ponders.

Briefly, I wonder if she's actually qualified.

"No. I don't have fans." Somehow, I didn't expect to hear the disappointment in my voice. "But that's fine," I blunder. "I wouldn't know what to do with them if I had any."

I'm trying too hard. It's not like me.

Anyway, I don't have fans but 'friends' is a relative term. I have people I talk to. I have people I talk to about her, about what she was wearing, about the sound of her voice, about what I wish she'd been wearing. I talk about her constantly. And I talk to Leah. I might not like her very much but I talk to her.

Whatever it is, I bet that Minette's underwear is black. In my head, she wears black underwear just – not for very long.

"But you have people around you?"

"Yes."

"That's good," she says, but it's in the wrong context, so it does nothing for me.

Why would she suggest my seeing another therapist? I suppose, if I did see someone else for my issues, multitudinous and artificial as they are, there wouldn't be such a conflict of interest. She wouldn't be a figure of authority anymore. Maybe that's her point. If she were no longer my therapist, she'd be free to date the living daylights out of me.

I can't have another therapist. I don't want another therapist. She has no idea how long it took me to save up for this. The first session was a gift – to sort myself out. And then, I saw her.

My parents were more than happy to believe it would take more than one session, but I can't keep asking them. They're calling the first four sessions my birthday and Christmas presents for the next year, and I'm doing all the overtime I can stomach. To be here. And cover my gym membership. But mostly, it's so I can be here. Just sitting, spending an hour in her company, just thinking about her legs beneath the desk and her mouth above it. I wonder if she bobs her foot under the desk. It's a sure sign, foot-bobbing.

It's a shame she doesn't do clutter. There's nothing below the surface for her foot to knock against. I can't hear whether or not I'm making her uncomfortable, whether or not I'm making her wonder about me. I don't know if her foot is conspiring with her thigh to send a little quiver beneath the silk. Maybe her foot is going to sleep, or maybe it's unfulfilled passion, but without a knocking noise, I have no way of knowing if anything's happening at all.

And I know what she'd say if she knew what I've been thinking. She'd tell me that I've formed an attachment. An understandable, but fruitless attachment, because she listens to me. Because she appears to take an interest and, in a world where I might struggle to tell the difference between friends and fans, and I have no parents to steer the ship, that must mean a lot to me. But it's not the same. It's my mind she's interested in. Nothing else.

But the mind is surely the best place to start.

She has no idea that, in the days between our meetings, I spend whole afternoons, just sitting in my cubicle with the same three walls and the percolator burping down the hallway, and I... it's not as if I fall asleep. I loll, a little. I fall over the edge of a daydream and picture myself creeping over to her side of the desk. She rotates her chair and kicks a thigh over my shoulder. There are no words in the daydream.

Neither of us needs to speak. She just – leans back in her chair and closes her eyes and I am everything.

"And your grandmother, how is she?"

Well, that's terrific.

Just terrific.

Of all the thoughts I was prepared to entertain, Nana wasn't in my top fifty.

"She's fine," I breathe. I sound bored. She should know from this tone to change the subject.

"We talked, didn't we, about how to best move forward?"

That's better. I nod because we did.

She brushes her hand against the soft contours of her jaw and I melt. She smiles absentmindedly and I hear the fabric stretch as she crosses her legs under the desk. Still no knocking. "And do you think you're ready to talk about some of your plans?"

"Yes," it comes screaming out of me.

I mean – I can't tell her about my *real* plans. Not the *real* ones. But I need her to understand how much these sessions mean to me. I need to be improving, just not too quickly. Got to get the humming under control. And I'll have to think of a decent reason for the sudden reappearance of Mum and Dad if she ever comes round for Sunday tea, or game night with the family.

"I think I'm getting better," I say. Oh, that's good. I'm proud of that. "Don't you think I'm getting better?"

I think is the great opener. It suggests that I could be wrong and probably am. I could *think* that I'm a millionaire. The question is, am I?

I'll save you some time. Millionaires don't eat noodles. I don't know what they eat. The poor, presumably.

But – *I think I'm getting better* – dangles the carrot that I might be. Equally, I might not be. I don't pretend to be an authority on these things. And playing down one's special skills and expertise is, also, highly attractive. I'm modest. Perhaps I need building up a little bit. Perhaps she could be the one to inspire me to greatness. These should be the thoughts that cross her mind, not mine, but it's a start.

Getting better – means it's a process. It's not finished. *I'm* not finished. We can't call it a day just yet. There are probably months and months of sessions still to come. I am a work in progress. I could become a masterpiece.

She smiles, and for a moment, I don't notice that she hasn't answered my question. "I'm pleased," she offers, finally. "Although, there's…"

"No quick fix," I finish it for her.

I've heard it before. Not from her, but she seems quite pleased that my expectations of emotional wellbeing are sufficiently tempered. These sessions could last forever because recovery is not something to be rushed. But I think that's true for most things: if it's going to be lasting and real, it's got to have a solid foundation.

She writes something down and I wish I could just catch a glimpse. Just a tiny, little look over her shoulder to tell me what she's thinking.

But if I were to ask her out, she'd look sad. Whether for me, or for her, I can't guess, but I can see that semi-pickled look inside my head. I would hate to see that expression rush across her face, pulling it all down, especially if I'd caused it. I wouldn't make her unhappy for anything.

I am here for the joy of things. The wonder and the splendour of it all. I'm not here for the horrors and the tempestuous rumblings of the world. I am here to make her realise how wonderful things could be. Even as she tries to fix me. Even as she tries to help me make peace with my feelings because – even though, there's nothing really wrong with them. For the most part.

I wonder if I'm really going to say it.

"You know that having feelings isn't wrong, don't you, Jaxx?"

I'm just looking at her now. Any time spent looking at her is not time wasted. I nod to make the moment last.

"Feelings are only natural," she goes on. "It's how we deal with them that matters."

"I thought I might get a takeaway tonight." Well, say what you will but I'm proud of myself. That was pretty daring. "Maybe a Chinese."

She's writing something down.

"Do you like Chinese?" I ask. Good tone of voice, I'm using. Very close to nonchalance. Now, if I could just control my face. There's an ache in my cheeks. I look too eager.

"Hmm..." which I think is rather lacklustre as responses go. It strikes me that she's very closed, for the sort of person who's supposed to be all about feelings and their proper expression. I don't like to think of her bottling things up. It's not healthy.

"Maybe Indian?" Okay, I know I'm pushing it but she's not exactly giving me anything to work with here. "Have you tried that Indian place on the High Street?"

"Not recently," she says, and even though she suddenly sounds far away, it's as if the world has started turning again. I don't remember why it stopped but now we're having a conversation, like adults, like lovers-almost, about what we're going to have for dinner.

I dare myself.

I have to.

"I wondered," I take a breath. Timing is everything. "I wondered if it was too soon for me to start seeing someone. Romantically, I mean. What do you think?"

She leans the notepad against her knee and looks to a spot beside the potted plant. "Well, I don't think you should rush into anything."

Knew it.

She wants me.

I don't know why she can't just say it.

Okay. That's a lie. She can't just say it for the same reason I can't just say it.

"Anyway," she says, but I'm not paying attention anymore. I'm wondering if we'll have a summer home in Italy, or perhaps a place in Cornwall. Somewhere with weather. Somewhere rugged, I fancy, with howling winds and no neighbours to make noise complaints or rattle at the door to ask if our power has gone out because they haven't had a working kettle since half past nine in the morning.

Of course, we shouldn't rush into it. She's quite right. I'm no stranger to taking my time. I raise an eyebrow to myself. I am shameless.

For now, we should make the most of these moments together, when we both know what we're really saying but neither of us is actually saying it. Because we can't. If one of us breaks the silence, then perhaps the whole thing will be spoiled, like a bag of apples at the bottom of the fridge. It should be complete and perfect, unsaid, unsullied, precious. The words would only interfere with the feeling that crackles like electricity between us. It is painful and obvious, and threatens to slide me straight off my chair.

We'll just spend these silly hours, looking at each other, talking about deep, important things.

Me: getting better.

Her: watching me do it.

I've brought her a hundred terrors over the last few weeks. It's easy enough to find things to talk about. They print them in the papers every day. It doesn't have to be anything genuinely apocalyptic. Although, of course, I've dabbled.

Nuclear annihilation had seemed like quite a fertile subject, but given my total inability to do anything about who might press the button, and what might happen to the world outside the window when they do, we decided that I should stop trying to control the things over which I have no power. I say *we* decided. *She* decided. I agreed because I was looking at the skin where her neck becomes her shoulder, so I wasn't really listening.

It's a strange space she occupies. With the others, I mean. She uses her words, precisely. Like she's plucking the correct lines from somewhere on the back wall. She makes people better, by talking. It's a rare gift, that. She creates a sense of calm and stability – just with words.

"Did you get a chance to…?" she begins.

I don't answer.

I'm thinking about how I look.

I imagine I'm making my eyes look soft. *Kind*. It's important – to look kind. It probably matters more than anyone really says. And so, I soften my looks.

A sudden thought makes me wonder about eyeballs in the summer, when the weather get too warm, when the tears threaten to spill and mix with the sweat – yes, even in England, the sweat, and I want to look away, to look out of the window, to smooth the liquid from the corners of my eyes. Even as I wonder, with the icecaps melting, if it's going to get so hot that eyeballs start popping on the High Street.

She looks concerned.

Me, looking sexy, might look more like *Me, having a stroke*.

I watch the movement in her blouse that comes quite gently with every breath. The steady, sexy rise and fall, the desperate need I feel to peel away the pretence with my teeth. And she'll just sit there, opposite me, posing her questions, making her notes, and probably doodling in the margins of her notebook.

I wonder whether she's sketched my face into a corner of the page. I'd be surprised if she hadn't. I'd make an excellent subject. Dark eyes, one might assume soulfulness and warmth from a single glance, so long as it's not a glance in which I'm thinking too much about eyeballs.

I've been using a new conditioner and, even though my hair still feels as rough as a farmer's thumbnail, it looks like liquid. Like it's ready to run off my head. Which is exactly what I was going for.

She's looking at me.

"I'm sorry?"

Well, that'll have to do.

"I asked how you were getting on with the meditation tapes."

"Great, yeah," I nod. "Don't know why I didn't start it years ago."

I haven't listened to them.

Well, there's no point, is there? Sitting around and breathing – I don't need a CD to tell me how to do that. I'm doing it now.

And I don't quite trust meditation, as a concept. I mean, I have as much time for floating around in a bubble of serenity as the next girl, but I can't escape the idea that... Well, what if there was some sort of mind-melting advertising crowbarred in there somehow? Like, I might suddenly and inexplicably develop a taste for Brie. No earthly inspiration for it, no real need to dissect it as a desire, but on some level, perhaps I'll know – the Brie people did it. They'll have paid top whack for an advertising spot in some overpriced meditation tapes so that overwrought housewives in Surrey, and small-time seductresses in Essex, can fill up their shopping trollies with Brie.

Maybe this is the sort of thing I should bring her as a problem...

"We spoke about your taking up a hobby," she reminds me.

"We did." I don't feel the need to expand on this.

She smiles.

I don't know why she has to smile like that. It starts as a flutter but, quite rapidly, it starts to feel like a new bruise. Like a bruise before the colour. There's an ache. I'm not sure smiles are supposed to do that.

"Are you all right?" she asks. "You look a little flushed."

I can't say I'm surprised. "It feels like... everything's moving too fast. I... I don't know if..."

"It's a panic attack," she tells me.

It isn't.

"Just try and focus on your breathing," she advises. And suddenly, she's in front of me. Crouching. Cupping my hands together, teaching me to breathe.

I don't say anything.

I can't.

She looks me in the eye. She breathes at me.

It's all too wonderful. I think I'm going to pass out.

She uses her calm voice. It's like she's taken a whole bottle of tranquilisers. It's slow and soft and... every day should begin and end like this. With the quiet concern in her eyes and the breath heaving out of me.

Everything goes quiet as she returns to her seat.

It's a good while before she says anything. Then: "You were telling me about your hobbies."

I wasn't.

"Do you want to tell me more about them?"

"Yes."

Oh, but that's a whopper!

There's an eagerness in her eyes that betrays us both. "Whenever you're ready."

It's like she's trying to kill me with longing.

"Hobbies, yes. Right." I nod for a little while, but she seems to want more. "Bridge. Chess, euchre. Line dancing. Fencing, that sort of thing."

She doesn't realise I'm just listing hobbies. I'm not naming activities in which I actually take part. What kind of preoccupation is line dancing, anyway? I can just imagine trying to catch the bus in a check shirt and spurs.

"Problem is..." I am, I'm going to say it. "A lot of these things need more than one person. So, I was wondering..."

"What about gardening?" she asks quickly.

Now, she's thrown me there. I wasn't prepared for — "Gardening?"

"Maybe something small. Perhaps a box of herbs on the windowsill, you wouldn't need another person for that."

Spanner. Big old spanner in the works and I'm going to have to tread lightly. A little more lightly. I'll have to stop stomping my feet in any case.

"Maybe I *should* take a little more time before I start dating." I pause. I can actually hear myself doing it. It's like I'm waiting for a taxi. "But I don't want to cut myself off from the world, do I?"

"I don't think there's anything wrong in meeting people." She nods. "That's part of life. But you can talk to people without it turning into something romantic. You know that, don't you?"

I don't hear anything else. I'm wondering if she's a dog-person or a cat-person. I'm not sure how I can sneak it into the conversation. Looking at her, she could be a cat-person, but I hope not.

If there were to be a dog, it would have to be something large. A gundog of some sort. I can't picture her with a Shih Tzu. She deserves to be striding out of some huge country estate, with knee-high leather boots, a big hat – fluffy, Russian, faux fur, and a big, soft-eared dog, padding along beside her.

Yes, I think it's a dog.

A toy dog would never keep up and, with a cat, the outfit would be all wrong.

It's easy – talking to her. If there's something worrying me, I know I can tell her. Even if it's something that I'm not worried about, I know she'll listen and treat it with seriousness it – well, not the seriousness it *deserves*. Obviously. But the seriousness it *would* deserve. If it were real...

Of course, politics is the most dangerous and dull of subjects for any conversation between two adults, almost drowning in desire, so I try to avoid it. I can't guess her political affiliation and I feel no great need to offend her. And besides, we don't tend to talk about anything that's real. Maybe that's what keeping the words inside. Maybe that's what's keeping it... perfect.

In fairness, I have other things to think about. I have to choose what I'm going to wear. I have to think about whether my perfume is too strong. Whether the issue I've brought for her attention is really worth her time.

I'm aware that she's asked another question.

This is always a challenge.

She's frowning now. My silence is saying more than I need it to.

"How do you mean?" I ask. This is a good staple. Perhaps she knows that I haven't been listening, but she doesn't let on. She's classy that way.

"I asked if you'd considered taking some time off work," she nudges.

I hate my job. I hate what it does to me. I hate that it robs me, daily, of energy that could be better spent on my recovery, and getting this woman out of this office and into a hotel room. I hate my colleagues. I hate my customers. I hate the girl who checks her text messages while hovering over the coffee cups. I hate my boss and his smug little goatee. I hate everyone and everything that isn't in this room, right now. And I'm not totally swung on the bust of whatshisname. That said, he's still better than anything out there.

I hate everything.

"Maybe," I say.

"Have you been doing the breathing exercises when you feel constricted?"

"Yes."

I don't feel constricted. I feel – everything else – but not constricted.

Almost everything else. Still, there's time.

It occurs to me: I'm only really myself when I'm here, with her. Minette, sitting only a few feet away and me, wondering if she makes sounds in her sleep. If she snores. Not a deal-breaker, but I'd like to be prepared. I wonder whether she cries out when she has a nightmare, or if she even dreams at all.

I do. I dream all the time. Sleeping or not, it makes no difference. I dream constantly. Not just of her. I know other people. I just… prefer her.

It's easier to concentrate when she's nearby. Like she's my lucky charm. I like having her near me. I know she has to be professional and, I'll be honest, it's a drawback, but I think we can get through it.

Maybe she finds it hard to trust herself around me. Maybe that's the problem. I don't say it's my magnetism, although, clearly, it is. Okay, I know I'm not a rock star, but I also know there's something here. Because there is. Because I can feel it.

I suppose it's the lack of reciprocity in this relationship that really annoys me. She can ask me anything, and she does, because that's why we're here. To get me well. But I can't really ask her anything in return. It makes the whole thing lopsided.

There are things I long to ask her.

But I know what will happen. I'm not ready to tell her how I feel. It would come out messy. A shuffle of words. A spillage. It would be awkward and embarrassing and, let's face it: it would probably sound as if I have a… Like I'm…

But there's no reason to play this as anything less than it is. This is real and powerful and – the problem is with other things.

The world is a dangerous place. I don't think I could bear the look on her face when I tell her. If I tell her… that it's all a distraction. All of it. Cornwall and the cottage and the dog and even her underwear – it's all lovely but it's keeping me from what I should be saying.

Irony is complicated but I know that's what this is. I don't suppose anyone else would have noticed.

Sometimes, you just get a feeling about someone. Perhaps you catch a glimpse from across the street, from behind a bush, from behind a parked car... There's usually crouching involved, but you just know.

It's knowledge. It goes beyond a feeling.

Sometimes.

Recently.

Three weeks ago.

And that's the trouble. If I tell her, as I know I should, then I have to tell her everything. Not just about him, but about me, about why I was there.

In some ways, I think she might be pleased. I'll take the credit – I've worked very hard. Keeping the secrets close. There have been exaggerations. My parents are fine, I can get them on the phone if need be. Perhaps they'd back me up and say that I'm all right, really.

Perhaps they'd do that.

Lord knows, I could keep her away from my mum and dad until I come up with something to explain their unexpected vitality and relative limberness. Then again, plenty of people don't care for their in-laws, or for their child's choice of life mate. Maybe I'm saving everyone all that palaver by keeping them in their separate corners of my life.

Maybe I could ask Leah to tell her how hard I've been working – improving myself, and such. Other details, small things, might fade from her memory in the fullness of time, but I would need to tell her why I was outside her house.

It's not that bad. If anything, I'm more of a side issue here. Barely even that, in fact. I was just curious.

But she might not hear me out. She might call the police or insist on my leaving before I've had a chance to...

Not sleep with her. I don't mean sleep with her.

I don't *just* mean sleep with her.

Naturally, I long to ask her if she's really read all the books on her shelves, if she realises the clock on her cooker is four minutes out, if she'd like me to remount her bird feeder because the squirrels are having the best of it. But I need to tell her about him.

It all comes down to timing.

I watched him from the corner as he opened the latch on her gate, as he trundled up the path, as he cradled the package under his arm, carefully, lovingly. As if it belonged to him. I watched as he turned the parcel over in his hands on the porch, as he examined the label. He had a look on his face... It wasn't as if he was checking the address. Any idiot can do that and not use their eyebrows half as much. He was – it was more like he was wondering: *who's this from?* Or, *what do they want?*

It was unnerving. Even as I stared, with only the sound of my own heartbeat and the wet leaves at my fingertips, my skin went cold. I felt weak. *I* felt weak and he wasn't even looking at me. He was too focussed on what was happening in her life. In her post. As if it had anything to do with him.

It's not that I'm jealous. I know how it sounds. That's why I can't say it. I doubt she'd let me get this far if I were speaking out loud.

I was only – I was checking on her.

It's not as if I was going to knock on the door. I certainly did not imagine that she might smile in the doorway and invite me in. That tea might make way for bubbles, in the bath, in the glass, might pave the way for candlelight and fluffy pillows...

Frankly, it doesn't matter what I might have thought.

I watched him. As he rocked right up to the doorbell, pressed and straightened his shirt. I watched him. As he cupped his hands around his eyes, and looked through her front window.

Maybe I'm not giving her the credit she deserves. Perhaps she could handle it. Perhaps she already knows. But that's why we have to talk like this. I don't want to just throw this at her when she might not be ready for any of it.

I can't be sure, of course, but I suspect he's the sort of guy to pocket the odd parcel. Nothing conspicuous, nothing for keeps, just a little something, here and there, simply so he can post the 'Sorry We Missed You' note through her door and come back some other time. Perhaps for a signature or just to look her in the eye.

Maybe, if he does keep some of the deliveries back, maybe he thinks that it brings her closer to him. That he has something of hers on his nightstand. That he can read her name every morning, drawing her in by reciting her name as he brushes his teeth, as shaves his stubble, as he pulls the plug from his bath.

Maybe he's made a shrine out of her envelopes.

He doesn't know, but I see him. I know what he is.

Because I watched him as he looked through her window, as he got up on tiptoe. I saw him, as he slinked around the side of the house, as he shuffled up to her back door. I watched him as he checked the handle. As he lifted a plant pot on the patio and frowned to himself.

I smiled, quite alone, but I smiled. Minette's no fool. She doesn't leave a key outside the house because she knows not to invite disaster. My lady isn't quite mine, but she's hardly stupid.

And even as he came back to the front of the house, and clambered back into his van, shaking his head and thumping his steering wheel with the flat of his hand, he didn't notice me.

Even if she would hear me out, I have to wonder whether she would take me seriously, given all the stories and half-truths I've told the two of us for all these weeks.

I know I should be able to trust myself. That the words will come out, in the right order, because they always do. Because that's how it works. I take a breath, and the words just come.

I know I have to tell her.

I must.

I will.

I...

She should know so she can take steps, make a complaint, have him removed from the route and put on a list, put into prison, fall down the stairs. She should know.

She makes a note on a post-it.

I'd like to ask her out for a drink. The hell with my desire for her. A little drink, loosen the inhibitions and then, perhaps, we can talk about her getting a big dog and a panic button.

There must be a way around it, a way of telling her about him without mentioning me at all. I'm a distraction. I need to be better than that.

I want to tell her something of destiny. I want to tell her that we came into each other's lives because we were supposed to. Not because I'm a whack-job with overprotective parents, and she's a highly qualified fixer of people, because, actually, my problems are irrelevant. I'm here because I stepped through a door and into a world.

It's just... Sometimes, you see someone and you just know. She's here to make me better. I'm here to save her.

"I'm afraid we're out of time," and I believe she means it. I believe she's going to miss me between now and then. Maybe I can send her an anonymous note about the delivery man. Maybe I can pretend to be her on the phone and tell his boss to reprimand him.

"Thank you," I say. "This has been very helpful."

"You're doing really well, Jaxx," she says.

It is the trouble with keeping a lot of secrets. Sooner or later, something desperately important is bound to slip out.

I nod from the door. "Okay. Love you. Bye."

She looks at me and I'm lost.

It's The Landing That Hurts: A Short Story of Disaster

IT'S LIKE A CALL THAT never comes. Hour upon wasted hour, watching the phone, a frown that cracks the face, grinding teeth until they snap, twisting fingers 'til they break, and only then, you see that the line has come unplugged.

It's frustrating.

It's like that feeling when you start to wake up and she's already talking. Perhaps she's even asked a question. Maybe that's what woke you in the first place. The change in her tone, the inflection. I'm not ready, but she's already asked me something.

She might have had the whole discussion, while I snuffle into the pillow and shimmy my way through half a dozen painted dreams.

I'll admit, I've resented it. If she's talking, close up, she can surely see that I'm asleep. She's familiar enough to be in my bedroom, in the dark, in the quiet, and yet – the voice persists. My eyes are shut but now I know – this is not my bedroom.

Doesn't matter how loudly I shout inside my head, my body refuses to obey.

Wake up!

Nothing.

Not a dicky-bird. Stupid body.

Years ago, I had a girlfriend who talked in her sleep. Not quite the same thing as *deliberately* talking to the dreamer, I know, but her chatter-and-sigh would peel open my eyes even as she snored and called out for more pickles.

Now, I don't mean an occasional phrase, a word, a burst of sound: any of that might considered normal or, at the very least, a *cousin* of normal. No, no. She had whole conversations. She did accents. It was like an unconscious theatrical production every night. And in the small dark hours, she would talk and I would tumble out of my dream to deal with – whatever she was saying – because I had no choice.

Of course, what she was talking about meant nothing to either one of us. Even in the morning, over Frosties and buckets of coffee, with my bleary eyes and her well-rested face, I would ask her the importance of Tommy Cooper in her dreams, and she would look at me as if I was insane. And yet, she'd had so much to say about him when she was asleep, when she forced my eyelids open.

The night she cried out, '*Fire! Fire! Leave the children, they'll only slow you down! Run for your lives!*' was worse.

God, I haven't thought about Sadie in ages.

What's happening now is much the same. I can hear it and it annoys me because I'm going to have to deal with it. There's only one thing that's changed.

I can't deal with it.

Also, there's no Sadie, although that is undoubtedly for the best. She was never much for a crisis. She wouldn't manage – this – without making it her own special drama.

She just... There are people who are meant to look pretty and that's about it. Their largest concern in all the world should be their acrylic nails or the way they part their hair. She couldn't deal with the all the man-made fibres in this room, in this bed. God knows, we're better off without each other. I do mean *we*.

Even me. Even now. We'd never cope with this together. She'd be able to wake me up but, dear God, I'd have to hear about it.

There's a noise. I don't know how long it's been there but the gushing, sucking sound has been playing over and over for so long,

I barely remember a time when I couldn't hear it. Right beside me. Over and over. A sound like a plumber who's about to tell me how much it's going to cost to tear out all the pipes, followed by a sigh that might be me.

There's something else.

Not music. Something like dialogue, but it's far away and interspersed with awkward applause and occasional whooping. Maybe a talk show, or the repeats from fifteen years ago from the higher numbered channels. The ones we don't bother with unless there's genuinely nothing on the TV and it's getting desperate. One of those channels no one remembers the names of.

You know the ones.

A suck in, like air across the fillings. A sigh out, like I'm going to live and die on kettle noodles. It takes a while for the word to find me in the dark. I can't turn my head to check for definite but the thought drops down to the soles of my feet and I know I'm right.

Ventilator.

It's too hot in here. Whether it's the sheets or the gown, or the sheets *and* the gown, I don't know, but it's as if all the air has been sucked out of the room. Like I'm living in space. It's a vacuum. No air. Just the black and the spinning and the random sounds that might be blood rushing round my body, and what might be conversations down unknown or half-forgotten hallways. It's like living in a constant shadow. It's like not living. Just listening. And the suck and sigh of the machine beside the bed.

The days have a pattern, like an ugly seventies carpet. It's taken me quite a while to work it out. I couldn't say how many days or weeks because – I've been looking at the pattern, not the numbers, because – why would I look at the numbers?

When the door opens, a nurse, I suppose, whose perfume smells like vanilla, comes in to put a clip on my finger and a cuff around my arm. I can hear the sound of air pumping as the fabric grips my skin.

She scratches numbers into the paper. I hear the Velcro tearing, and what I'll assume is her, sliding the records back into the metal cuff at the bottom of the bed. Then, the door flaps shut and she's gone.

Maybe it's morning.

Okay, fine. I've decided. It must be morning.

Of course, they must have to do this more than once a day...

I'm beginning to see a flaw in my timing system.

The young fella with the bucket comes in – during what I have determined should be afternoons – before visiting time. He makes a particular sound as he cleans. Top teeth over bottom lip, a peculiar sound, like a whistle without the requisite oomph to create a recognisable note; like an obscure B-side from a would-be rock god. The room soon smells of cleaning products and musky, Christmas-gift aftershave, and then, he's gone as well.

Quite often, the family comes. They sit. They talk. Sometimes, they cry. Mum rearranges the grapes. Dad tells her to stop fussing. Caleb asks why they have to drink the coffee from the machine because, he says, it tastes like feet. I lie here, wondering whether or not I'm leaking on the bed.

As much as I recognise my fingers when the nurse reaches for them, I'm not completely aware of my body; not its specific parts, anyway. I feel heavy. I don't suppose I've ever felt so weighty. It's not me, not as such. It's more like a feeling of something solid. I couldn't tell you where my feet are, if my arms are crossed, if my mouth is open. I might be drooling all over the pillow. My period might have started. I don't know. That end of the bed is weird and unfamiliar. I might be bleeding into the sheets right now. Could be. I don't know what day it is. It might be the fourteenth by now. I couldn't tell you how much equipment sits around the bed, or what any of it does. I'm not a doctor. The problem is, neither is she.

Once I realised it was a hospital, I assumed my visitor was a doctor. And from her tone of voice and over-interest in my hair, I decided she was middle-aged. In my head, she was like a watercolour. I couldn't quite see her face but I could imagine her in surgical scrubs, with a gentle, noncommittal smile. Piped lines and an embroidered name over a breast pocket. Poking out of the pocket, there would be a vast array of biros and a torch that looked like a pen. I could see her signing things with a flourish, with a stethoscope looped across her shoulders as she jogged over to theatre and saved lives with a sweep of her hair. I realise I've spent too much of my life watching medical dramas with a plate of noodles in my lap.

She's not who I thought she was.

The door clicks shut. She's just the other side of the curtain. I already know it's her. It's not visiting time. I know it's not visiting time because she's here. She's been bouncing on her heels for half a minute. There's a crunching sound, as if she's flexing the muscles in her neck and something's come loose. There's a semi-humming sound. Like she's doing facial exercises. I can't tell if it's breath-spray or an inhaler, but there's a hiss. Any second now, she'll pull back the curtain, push the trolley through and – yes, here we go.

"There's a whole gang of them out there at the nurses' station," she begins. "They've been asking after you. A fair number of phone calls, so I understand. They've said that it's just family allowed in to visit for now, so they haven't, you know, *seen* you…. but they're thinking of you. It's important you know that. Anyway, I've brought your cards through. I'll read them to you later on, if you like? Maybe? No. Well, we'll see how it goes, eh?"

It was easier to mistake her for a surgeon, with perfect bone structure and a complicated love life, when she didn't talk so much.

Sometimes, a conversation doesn't really need two people to participate so I just wait, which is just as well, because she hasn't quite finished.

"You look so peaceful, sleeping like that. Just like an angel. Apart from the hair. Don't get me wrong. It's a lovely shade of turquoise,

I just think you'd suit brunette better. It would fit better with your eyebrows and lashes. Maybe it's just me."

She tuts to herself, which seems appropriate.

"As if that really matters. I'm sorry. You have very... exciting hair and it's not for me to comment on it. Anyway, it's probably for the best that they don't want to inundate you with visitors. You couldn't have a whole gang in here, anyway. They'd never fit. Not all of them. And you need a good rest, get your strength back.

"Anyway, I got a little bit ahead of myself last time, didn't I? No need to spare my feelings. I should have begun at the beginning. No point telling you about the hairdressing lady who comes in, or even the padre, when I haven't even told you where you are..." She chuckles to herself.

Either she has a very strange sense of humour or she's just really, really uncomfortable. Maybe both. I'll find out soon enough. It's not as if she won't tell me.

"So, you already know this is St. Martins but I don't think I said: you're in a side room, bit more privacy than on the ward. Third floor, so you can see quite a lot from up here. There's a nice view of the park and the cathedral beyond. Well..."

Maybe she's worried about offending me.

"Anyway," she's hurrying now, "there's not much in terms of decoration. Sort of buff-blue walls, off-blue. The sort of blue that's had its best years already. It's not old, the paintwork. I've got the same colour in my kitchen. It was like that in the can.

"What else? Quite high ceilings. It's an old hospital, so the lights are high up. Sharp, but forgiving. Lots of sockets on the wall behind your bed. Locker..."

There's a slight clicking noise as she opens the magnetised doors.

"Not a lot in there. A wash bag and yesterday's newspaper. Oh, shame! Someone's already filled in the crossword."

She closes the cupboard quickly.

"A jug of water. I suppose that's more for the visitors than... I'd have never picked you for a Camilla."

She forces a giggle.

"Just looking at the name over your head. I'd have thought – well, I don't suppose it matters what I thought. Anyway, *Camilla*: makes me think I should change my shoes or cross myself."

It's Cam, I long to tell her. Just Cam. But then again, I really don't think it matters and it's not as if we're friends.

"Curtains. I don't think any curtain in the history of drapery has ever hung as straight as a hospital curtain, do you? I'm sorry. I should stop asking you questions. It's hardly fair and I should know better.

"They seem like a nice bunch, your friends. Not averse to eyeliner, eh? I almost said to one of them, *'You've still got a bit of face showing,'* but you never know how people might take things. I can't bear a scowl. Which is strange because I've seen so many.

"Can't be helped. Some people just aren't very good at working their own bodies, so to speak. And others... say the wrong thing. I do both. Hardly a gift but I don't know what else to call it.

"People get this look. They seem to know you're not deliberately cack-handed, but this expression comes over them, like they're disappointed in you. Even if you're strangers, the disappointment comes shining through. Still, I suppose there's not a one of us who can help their face.

"I don't mean to say the wrong thing. Then again, nobody does, do...? Sorry. Done it again. In any case, I suppose it would be strange – if I went up and spoke to your friends, as if they'd have any clue who I was.

"It wasn't just the eyeliner that told me they were your crowd. They all seemed to be carrying those paper cups of over-explained coffee. You're too young to remember but, years ago, we used to order things in restaurants with no idea what we were getting. Everything came with an indecipherable title. 'Monty's Crab Surprise', that sort of thing. There might have been chilli, there might have been dill – we'd only find out when it got to the table. The key ingredient would make it to the title but nothing else.

"It was a simpler time, I suppose. Of course, more people probably dropped down dead from their allergies. 'Turkey schnitzel with rocket, almond and pomegranate salad': takes the romance out of it somehow. But that's what's happened to coffee. It used to be 'coffee'. Now, it's got at least three forenames and then, you must have your name written on it. As if you're marrying the thing.

"Sorry. This is coming out all wrong."

I'm left to my own thoughts while she struggles with hers. It's an odd situation. I can't say anything like this has ever happened to me because most of us don't speak to people who are asleep. Sadie notwithstanding. She doesn't count. For most of us, it's important to keep the audience awake.

"I heard one of them saying you were an English literature student," she goes on. "I'd offer to read you something but well, I've done one better…"

She's rustling through a bag now. It's like a performance. I feel sure she knows where it is, whatever it is, but she seems to be having trouble getting to it.

"One of them, a girl I think she was, said you'd be missing your Emily. So, I've been to the library. It's a talking book. Well, they don't call them 'talking books' anymore, do they? It's all 'audiobooks' now. Anyway, I thought I could pop it on for you when I go. Now, I wasn't sure if it was Emily Dickinson or Emily Bronte you'd be missing, so I got both. I thought, *if it's not one it's the other*, so we'll just play one and then set the other one going when it's over. I've checked them out for the full three weeks but I'm sure you'll be… Well, I can always get them renewed or… yes. Well, I thought you might like them."

I can't really blame her for talking so much. It's not as if I'm contributing anything to the conversation like: *'Who the hell are you?'* or *'Get out of my room, you weirdo!'*

I just lie here, waiting until I can say things like that, wondering if I'll have those words again, if I'll have any words again. As it goes, I'm more Dickinson than Bronte but the Emily she was referring to will be here as soon as it's officially visiting time. She likes to follow the rules.

"I'll just sit myself down, shall I?" she asks. "I hope you don't mind but it's already been such a long day. My feet are going to... no, they've already started. They're swelling. It's all the walking. It's – I suppose it never struck me before. I needed to feel useful. To people. I hadn't had that for a long time and I knew something was missing. Couldn't put my finger on it for the longest time but once I realised, I knew what I needed to do.

"Don't get me wrong, I love my job. I like meeting new people and seeing the patients getting better. I like getting to know their families and seeing the looks on their faces when I bring the tea trolley. No matter what else is happening, the rattle of the teacups, and the scent of the leaves, does something to them. It's that reassurance. Maybe that's what tea is – a friend in liquid form.

"I'll just pour myself a cup."

I suppose it must be quite a difficult job. There will be patients who are in long term. Some of them won't get better. Some of them won't ever leave this place. Maybe I'm one of them. Too early to tell. Don't want to think about that.

It must be hard to walk these halls and be part of it all, without being a lifesaver. I can't say I've spent any time with medical people but I imagine they can be quite snooty. Then again, wasn't it me who thought less of her when I realised she wasn't a doctor? I would never have thought that was who I... Whatever, man. I have time to work on myself now. Assuming I really need to. Which I doubt. I'm a good person. I send Valentine's cards to the local library.

"I'd offer to make you one, too, but – it'd just sit there. Getting cold. Developing a skin. I can't bear a skinned cup of tea. It's not natural. There's something a little bit tragic about a cold cuppa.

"I must say, I think the rest is doing you the world of good. Whether it's the sleep or the drugs, I couldn't begin to guess but you're looking very serene. Maybe it seems crass but I do think it's important to look for the positive in things. And, of course, this has given you a chance to give up smoking. So, there's that.

"I happened to ask one of the nurses – just making conversation – and it sounds like giving up smoking is all about the threes. The first three days are terrible, but you've already come through that. So, well done, you. Then, the first three weeks can be very difficult – lots of cravings and aches. Totally understandable and, well, you're almost there now.

"After that, the three month mark can feel like a bit of a letdown. You'll have been feeling better for a time but around three months, you sort of – 'plateau'. Her word, not mine. Can't imagine who she thought she was impressing.

"Anyway, I'm sure you'll be awake by then and, well, you'll have other things on your mind, I'm sure. All the telly you've missed and – the weather will have changed. You'll need to hunt out all your winter clothes. I usually keep mine in a suitcase on top of the wardrobe. Of course, it means a lot of laundry to get rid of the musty smell of keeping them locked away for six months..."

There's a pause while she thinks about something that may or may not be in the distance.

"It's so long ago that I gave up, all I remember is how very deeply I hated my husband at the time. Don't worry. I don't feel like that anymore." She pauses. "Divorce can be a wonderful thing."

Now, I don't want to be uncharitable, but if I've been in this bed for nearly three weeks, my concern for her feet is diminishing. Nearly three weeks, and getting visits from strangers, feels a little bit like – if I wake up and she's wearing a 'The End Is Nigh' board, I won't be surprised.

I suppose *she* will be.

"I suppose it depends on whether you're addicted to the nicotine or the behaviour," she goes on. "With me, smoking was always about the rebellion. I don't think I ever cared for it. Not really. I just knew that no one else liked it. So, I kept it up – for twenty-two years. To be fair, my husband was rather annoying during that time and I needed a hobby."

She sips.

"There's a man on the ward who makes little houses out of lolly sticks. He's got a whole village of them in his shed. He was telling me all about them. That's why I wasn't here earlier. He's built himself a town hall to go right in the middle. Anyway, he covered the thing in glue and scattered a load of play sand over it. Since he's been in here, he's just been itching to get home and paint it grey. He says it'll look like a pebbledash job. Sounds like a lot of effort for lolly sticks to me, but it makes him happy. And I suppose it gave me something to think about.

"The man in the bed next to him is having a hell of a time. The kids have left home and his wife's just had a," she lowers her voice, "hysterectomy. They were about to go on their first real holiday when he had his episode. Shame. It's a difficult one. You don't want to be rude, and wandering off has to be well timed, so I stayed with him for a few minutes. Bit of luck, he had a coughing fit so I was able to make my escape. And then, I came here."

I can hear her sinking into the chair.

"See, it's the curse of taking off my shoes. I'll never get them back on without a fight."

Okay, so I basically have a roommate. It's sort of nice. I don't really have to listen to anything she says. Her conversations have a way of circling back around, so even when I miss a bit, it doesn't really matter because she's bound to go over it all again.

Aside from her various travels around the hospital, she tells me about the Specials in the canteen. Minestrone seems to be a favourite. She tells me when the seasoning hasn't been up to scratch. Time moves differently from my part of the room, so I have no idea when it was, but she was quite apoplectic about the state of the tuna salad. Apparently...

"I mean, how can they call it 'tuna salad' when there's no celery, not even a hint of a pickle?"

It's as if she's psychic, though, of course, I know she's not. She wouldn't be in this room if she was.

"It's just tuna and mayonnaise. Nothing wrong with it. I just wish they'd call it 'Tuna and Mayo' rather than watch me dissolve into a puddle of regret in the back corner because – well, it's baby food, really. It's not as if I seek out sandwiches to challenge my teeth. But a bit of crunch isn't too much to ask, is it?"

She goes quiet for a bit. It's almost a relief. I enjoy the moment before I realise it's because I must have a drip of some kind. It's not as if I can't remember how to flex my jaw. It's just that – I don't know if I'm doing it. I want to be aware of my teeth. I should miss food. Crunch. She's right. It's vastly underrated.

"I'll tell you who I saw on the way down the corridor..."

If this was a normal conversation, I'd shuffle in my seat. She doesn't do short stories. There'll be a load of waffle and then a sudden drop. I know this because, although I couldn't pick her out of a crowd, I know her now.

"Mr. Campbell! As I live and breathe, Mr. Campbell!"

It shouldn't be all that surprising, given that he works here, but she's not entirely sure if he's a doctor or a mister. She's decided he should be a mister, whether or not he actually is. He has the eyebrows to be a specialist, so I'm told.

"Of course! I didn't tell you! He disappeared on us for a few days last week and, well, truth be told, no one seemed to know where he'd gone. He might have been in court or on a cruise. Anything seemed possible. It was all very intriguing. He's got that walk. You know the kind. The kind that suggests he might be up to something. I shouldn't say that, him being so high up the pecking order – at least, I think so – but he just has that hint of danger about him. He might have never come back. Might have been having an affair or washing blood out of his carpets. Anyway, he went to the Cotswolds."

See. It's that. The sudden stop. It's not annoying, as such. It's just I wouldn't mind if she paused for breath before moving on to the next thing.

"And the next thing was – I saw Mrs. Simpkins, you know, in Gynae. Poor lamb. She's been worrying herself silly for months that there's something not right in – in the area. I didn't like to pry but it's a terrible itch she's had. Sort of a prickly heat mixed with something like an ingrown – well, to hear her talk about it, you'd think it was an ingrown limb. Anyway, turns out she can't wear manmade fibres anymore."

Part of me wonders if she doesn't get bored, sitting here, with me. With no one else to talk to. Just sitting, looking through the window, trying to think of things to say to a stranger.

"She was proud as punch, naturally. *'From now on, it's silk or nothing,'* she says. As if you say that sort of thing near a tea trolley. Some people have no sense of propriety."

I wish she'd sneak in somebody I know. It doesn't really matter who it is. Just someone. Break up the – well, not monotony. She's been really kind and it's not her tone of voice that does it, I'd just like to hear from someone who knows something about me. Anything, really. Someone who knows not to bother telling me about soup and sandwiches, second homes and possible thrush.

The family will be here for visiting time. They'll bring Emily. But a mate… It would be nice to hear a mate's voice. I'd like to know if they used the tickets or just sold them. We'd been planning it for months. Saving up. Bragging, because – obviously. I never thought I'd see the day I'd be watching Bessie and the Red Notes live on stage. As it turns out, I didn't. I hope they didn't miss it.

"I don't dare look at these medical charts, you know. More than my job's worth."

I can hear her turning the pages.

"It's all numbers and – gosh, you'd want a degree in Latin to pronounce any of the medications. Can't even put it down to a doctor's handwriting, I shouldn't wonder. It could be in block capitals and I wouldn't be able to tell you what you're on. Maybe that's not what I'm here for."

I can't tell if she's referring to her presence in this room with me, or to some great existentialist quandary. Even if I were awake, I don't think I could really engage with either question.

I don't know why she's here. I don't really care why she's here. I appreciate it – in much the same way one appreciates fine art. From a distance. I could do with some time, you know, to miss her.

"Who knows?" I can hear her smiling. "It might not be too long before they can unplug some of this equipment."

There's a moment before she panics.

"Oh, no! Oh, gosh no! I don't mean that kind of unplugging! I just meant – maybe you'll be well enough to… I'm sorry. Maybe you'll be well enough that you won't need so many monitors dotted around you. Honestly, it's like you've got the stockroom of a small branch of PC World stacked around the… Sometimes my mouth gets ahead of my brain. This isn't coming out right. I'm sorry."

My mouth quirks, but only on the inside. I don't suppose it shows up on my face. Maybe it doesn't need to. She's tripping over her words because she's filling in all the blanks. As it is, I don't respond and, I can only guess here but given what I've heard, I suppose silence makes her uncomfortable. As such, she has no choice but to say everything that crosses her mind. It's not polished. It's not precise. But it's hardly earthy. She's just saying what she's thinking while I think and say nothing.

And if she says these things because the silence is too much, perhaps the sight of me is terrifying. Perhaps I'm covered, head to foot, in bruises, dark purple, grey, royal mourning colours, leaking blood beneath the surface, and puffing up my waxy skin. Perhaps she can only guess what I used to look like. Maybe that's why she comments on the hair. Perhaps she imagines she can guess my face, my age, my state of mind, based on the green-blue of my hair and a latticework of bruises.

If I could chip in to the conversation, she'd have a moment to think about what she wants to say. Because that's what everybody does. We all half-hear what the other person is saying while we think about how to say our thing. Some people are more on transmit than receive – I don't mean that. I mean, sometimes, other people's words give us time to consider our own.

It might not be that at all. Perhaps she is naturally clumsy in her speech.

She can't help it, probably. And even if she can, it's not as if she has to elbow her way through the crowd to come and talk to me. Nobody else sees me in the afternoons.

I just... It's unkind. I wish she were important to me. Even a little bit. It's not as if she's a vacuum with – presumably the shape of a woman. It's just that these visits mean more to her than me. Or rather, what they mean to me is a temporary reprieve from the thoughts inside my head. But they always creep back to the fore. Even before she leaves.

They engulf me. I almost see – I don't know what it is – maybe it's nothing.

It's not nothing.

And for a moment, I almost know what it is and then it's gone. I can't look directly at it. It's just on the edge of my understanding and then it's missing. Concrete. Blank. Silence. Not to be recovered.

It's quite limiting.

Maddening. The time inside my head is exhausting. The patterns beneath my eyelids are labyrinthine, broken blood vessels, smell of smoke, ribbons of thought, dismal little flashes like a school disco. Spaces, where I should know something. Voids where I know nothing but the ticking of the clock. She breaks that up for me. With her voice and her words and her slightly simpering concern. There's comfort in her voice. I like it. I just wish I didn't have to rely on it to save me from myself.

This is in danger of getting heavier than I'd like. I hope she says something soon. Something fun. A giggle. I haven't had a laugh in quite some time. Go on, Denise with the teas, give me something to chuckle about.

"I must say, you do look a lot better than you did when you first came in. I can see it now: like the angel of death when they wheeled you through the doors. I suppose it was the shock of the scaffolding-stuff around your head. It's different in films, with fully made-up actors and generous lighting. Maybe it's the absence of a soundtrack. What do you think? A little bit of delicate piano work in the background, might have made it – beautiful, somehow.

"Anyway, the point is, you look quite marvellous now. You know like those women you see on reality TV who've had a nose job? Right in the beginning, they look like they've been hit in the face with a shovel. But after a few weeks, once all the leaking has stopped and the swelling's gone down, they look, well, like they've had a nose job. But only if you'd seen them before.

"I'm saying this all wrong. What I mean to say is – you look marvellous. Maybe there's something to be said for an occasional coma, eh?"

No, I was wrong. I don't need her to talk.

"Nothing personal. I'm sure you were happy with your look before all this but – well, none of us gets enough sleep, do we? I'm sure not. So, maybe there's something in it: a coma.

"And you did take an awful tumble. Practically cartwheeling all the way down those harsh stone steps. Doesn't bear thinking about, really. And then – at the end – a terrible sprawl of broken bones and turquoise hair, surrounded by a puddle of blood. I don't suppose anyone who saw it will be able to shake that image for quite some time. Even hearing about it...

"Of course, it was worse for you. Obviously. Shouldn't even need saying but if it does – nothing but sympathy for you. Just dreadful, everyone's said it. And on a Saturday, as well. Day of the week shouldn't matter, and it doesn't, not really, but all those kiddies – out in town for their back-to-school shopping – going for a Knickerbocker Glory, or whatever they have these days... I don't suppose anyone heard much beyond the screams. And the sirens, of course.

"It's funny the things you think about. Maybe there was a lot of sobbing in the background. Don't see how there wouldn't have been. Just – from the shock. No. It's terribly, terribly sad. Still, you're in the best place and, as I say, you're looking a lot better."

Luckily, there's only so much cheering-up a person can take, or administer, and we must be coming to the end of her visit. She doesn't normally stay beyond a single cup of tea.

"I suppose you were blessed with the weather, really. This time of year, weather on the turn, all those busy people, covered top to toe in duffel of all kinds – I suppose that's how they covered you up so fast. Partly, keep you warm while the ambulance was on its way and partly, to spare the kiddies seeing quite so much of the..."

Either there's some sort of en-suite arrangement here and she's left the door open – which is a kind of intimacy I don't think either of us is really ready for – or she's pouring herself another cup of tea. It's her sighing while she does it that throws me off.

"I think," she says as she settles herself back down in the chair, "that an induced coma is the more civilised sort of coma. I mean, if you had your choice of comas, that would be the one most people would plump for. If they had to. I'm sorry. I'll start again, if I may." She clears her throat. "Hello!"

Oh, wow. She sounds far too perky and she must have been here fifteen minutes already.

"How are you feeling today? I do hope you haven't been too bored all on your tod."

For a moment, there's a crystal silence and I'm not sure if she's slipped back behind the curtain or into her handbag for a sweetener.

"No. No. Oh, I don't think so."

She's changing the channel. She mashes the buttons of the remote control too hard. I can hear the plastic clicking. Whether the batteries are running out or she's used to only-sporadic power, I can't tell.

"I don't know why they leave the television on in here. With the volume down that low, it's not as if you'd get any enjoyment out of it. And what if you were to wake up? Right slap-bang in the middle of a property show, then what? Would you wish you hadn't woken up at all? It's a puzzle.

"I can't bear those property shows," she whispers, "can you?"

I'm not usually up in time to watch them with any kind of regularity. They're all late-morning/early afternoon, and by then, I'm in class or at work, so it doesn't really...

"*'Tarquin makes seasonal chutneys,'*" she mocks.

She's putting on a posh voice. I have no idea who she's impersonating, but she seems quite happy with her efforts. Somehow, I know she's sitting higher up in her chair.

"Yes, *'Tarquin makes seasonal chutneys and Annabelle is a part-time life model. They've decided to have their second come in the Algarve...'* And you just think – how? Is it me? How is that even possible? Meanwhile, the rest of us are on our third day in the same socks."

She slurps her tea before she says it. I already know. There are no secrets here. At least she's got...

"Still, as long as you've got your health, you haven't really got..."

She's floundering. I can hear her doing it. It's like the breath won't come.

"Oh, no. I – I didn't. I mean..."

When I was eleven, I went fishing with my cousin, Freddie. I don't suppose I had all that much enthusiasm for it but he was a prodigy. For a thirteen year old. I remember, he caught this fish, I don't know what kind, and he pulled it on to the deck and it was just – flapping around. Choking. Baking in the air. It was a little while before it went still. I must have started crying because when it stopped moving, he threw it back. God, he was a prick.

I didn't think I'd feel that sense of helplessness ever again. I thought it was a feeling unique to eleven-year-olds. It occurs to me, I've had a pretty simple life, until now.

"Anyway, since I started working here – three months ago? No, it's four. Gosh, the year is just disappearing, isn't it? Well, anyway, since I've been working here, I've started saying my name differently. It used to be Denise. With a short 'i', like De-niece. Now, it's turned into Den-*ees*. It started out as a joke and now it's stuck. *'Here's Den-ees with the teas'* – like I'm on a 1980s game show with a plunged neckline and too many sequins. I've already told you this, haven't I?"

It was a couple of days ago, I think.

"Yesterday. Of course, I did."

Okay. I have no sense of time. No need to rub it in, Den-ees with the teas.

It's become something of a relief when she takes a moment to drink her tea. The quiet is comforting. It's just – sort of nice that there's someone here and we can indulge in – what could be comfortable silence. It's not comfortable, of course, but it feels like it could be.

Maybe in a few more days.

She's grinding her teeth. She does this sometimes and all I can think is: she's probably paid for several of her dentist's holidays. Unless she hasn't. Maybe she has teeth like auction room furniture. Just dotted about in small groups. No uniformity. All different colours. A little worn in places. Teeth like – you could take them home with you today if you could fit them in the car.

"I suppose," she starts slowly. "I should have said all this when I first started coming to see you but, well, you never know who's going to come in and interrupt and it's not the sort of thing to leave half-said.

"By way of introduction, I should probably explain that it's a long and complicated story, with far too many characters and not nearly enough dialogue, but I'll do my best. It's not as if either of us has other plans."

I get the feeling she's practised this bit. Despite myself, I like her. There's something close to adorable about practising a speech for someone who might not hear it.

"It all began about six months ago. I'd just turned fifty-four and I think it's fair to say: my life was in order. Not great, not by any stretch, but I knew where I stood with myself. I had a nice little flat, nothing outrageous, a nice size but easy enough to stay on top of. And two cats, Polly and Percy.

"I don't suppose you'd really notice me in a crowd. I've never been flashy. Probably not the face you'd pick if it was on sale in a shop, but it works well enough for me. My dear mother used to say, *'If you put all the best goods in the front window, you'll never keep the customer inside the shop.'* Not sure she really meant it the way it sounds...

"My life was simple. Empty, I suppose. At least, I can understand how someone outside my life would think it was a little bit dull. Cats, yes, but otherwise, quiet. Don't get me wrong. We all have lousy moments. I don't pretend to be anything special. We could all tell a sad story from time to time. Look who I'm talking to! Of course, we've all got our sad stories. The point is – I wasn't too concerned about it.

"I know a lot of this won't mean much to you because you're still young. We've all been idealistic. I used to listen to the Pretenders, I understand how it is. And although there are the moments – you know the moments – everybody gets them, when the world starts to dim, when it doesn't matter what you do. The ironing pile never gets any smaller, the vacuum cleaner has smoke coming out of it, and there's nothing quite so enticing as a family pack of cheese dip and a freshly washed index finger... Well, I was having one of those days.

"My birthday had been and gone. No cards. I thought I might have heard something this year but... Life isn't always what we want it to be. I paid my gas bill. I suppose the call might have come through while I was on to British Gas but, seems unlikely, really. Bit of a nonday, truth be told. So, I took myself out of the house. Seemed like the right thing to do. I found myself walking to the Wimpy."

She pauses for a moment and I wonder if that's the end of the story.

"Sorry, glancing through your cards – I hope you can forgive my eating meat. I know I'm one of the last, but there's something a bit special about a Wimpy.

"You've got a card here from someone called Phoenix. Can't tell from the handwriting if that's a boy or a girl. Doesn't really matter, of course. They suggest going out for a curry, when you're feeling up to it. I envy you that. I've never been much for spicy stuff. I won't eat anything hotter than me – so that leaves me with beef and gherkins.

"Anyway, getting back to Wimpy. They've got that special sauce. I don't know what's in it. I don't need to know what's in it. The lettuce is always crisp. Like it's been flash frozen. It's a once in a while thing for me. I cook. I'm a good cook. No reason you'd know about that, but I am. But it's different when you're on your own. No one juliennes a carrot if there's only them there to see it. No, I do cook. I like to cook. But I make myself *earn* a Wimpy.

"So, I'd got through my birthday, basically unnoticed, and I decided I'd earned my treat. I was just standing, waiting in the queue, already decided what I was going to order, where I was going to sit. I don't eat in the street. There's something rather uncouth about eating outside, unless you're in Italy. It's a theory, nothing more. I've never been there. I just think there'd be something rather sophisticated about picking at an olive platter, somewhere in the sunshine, a bottle of wine and dark glasses, flipping through a well-worn paperback, pretending to read.

"It's not quite the same when it's a burger in a paper napkin, in the rain, madly swatting seagulls out of the way and trying not to drown.

"Anyway, there I was, in the queue, just admiring the pictures over the counter and…

"It was like – when you see an actor, on the television, and you know them from something, maybe years ago, and it takes you the rest of the afternoon to remember their name. Or what you saw them in. Or both. Well, anyway, it was like that, but in real life. It was only brief but I knew.

"I don't mean like, *'I'm going to marry him.'* I don't even mean that feeling you get when you don't *recognise* someone but you feel a connection to them, which is, I suspect, something to do with past lives or cheese-dreams from three o'clock in the morning but there was something there. Something undeniable. More than reality. Bigger than anything else and just on the edge of my line of sight but sometimes, you just know when someone belongs to you.

"I don't think I'd ever had anything like it before. I never felt that way about my husband. I think I read it somewhere – *Falling is easy. It's the landing that hurts*' – I've never stopped thinking about that. It was a few years after the wedding when I read it and I just knew: I'd made a dreadful mistake. What we had wasn't fireworks or constant, throbbing excitement, but I thought that was normal. But if the landing is supposed to hurt, then, I should have been more devoted to him. I should have been devastated by the idea of his leaving. I certainly wouldn't have packed his bags or booked his train ticket. Someone overwhelmingly in love doesn't do things like that, I don't suppose.

"Maybe I shouldn't burden you with all this. Maybe you couldn't care less. Maybe I might as well be talking to this cup of tea. Trying to work it out from this side of things is... complicated.

"She'd only been gone a few weeks, then, but I couldn't keep looking at him. Across the kitchen table. His face, practically melting into his cornflakes. Both of us, wondering if she'd call. If she'd write. If she'd just – come home one day, suitcase at her side, ready to talk. If she'd forgiven us for whatever she thought we'd done. Because it doesn't matter what you do, you're always to blame.

"He said something about Birmingham. *Maybe she'd go to Birmingham*. I don't know. Dads and daughters have their own sort of relationship. Maybe she'd already told him where she was going to stay. Maybe he knew more of her college friends than I did or...

"But I couldn't keep looking at him. Everything else was simple enough. The divorce should have been traumatic, I suppose. They usually are, when you hear about them. Not mine. It wasn't a relief, either. It was just – a piece of paper and the end of things. But I suppose I always wondered if he'd call me, when he found her, *if* he found her.

"Of course, he never called. Last I heard, he'd married some woman up in Wolverhampton. Good for him. I can't imagine my Keith living in a house with that accent but it's not for me to decide these things for him and he's hardly *my* Keith anymore.

"Anyway, I had my mother, and he had his new wife and I suppose we just went on with our lives because that's what people do. Sometimes, you don't get a choice. Sometimes, the decision is taken for you. From you. Whatever it is, people move on, the world keeps turning and before you know it, you're fifty-four years old, watching the reflection of a fat woman in the mirrored pillars of Wimpy, trying to make yourself believe you're not her. But of course you are. The reflection looks away, embarrassed, trying to hide her eyes – which are yours – trying to suck in her gut before other people notice it and stagger back in horror. She looks away, trying to keep the heat from prickling across her cheeks, trying not to make eye contact with anyone.

"It was just a flash of the jawline. Breezing down the High Street. Walking away. Away from me. A young woman with high cheekbones and an oval face. And I knew. I knew it was her.

"I even knew I was wrong.

"She'd be thirty-two, now. It's hard to explain. It's not just that people stop asking. If there have been any sightings. If you've heard anything. It's that you stop spending time with those people. You don't need people. Even if you do need them, they're not the right people. You only need...

"And so, you start spending time with other people. People who don't know. People who won't ask. And if they do wonder if you have a family, you just say, 'no' and that's the end of that. You don't notice at the time, but after some years, you realise you looked sad when you were first asked. And perhaps they wondered, but would never ask, about low motility, spasmodic ovulation, the horror of lost chances. They'll never ask. It's not the done thing.

"And so you go on, in menial jobs, nothing important, no one close – you don't want anyone close. Even if there might have been, at one time or another, they'd never really get close. You can't allow them that. A couple of cats and the calendar, reminding you of how long it's been. A phone in the corner that doesn't ring. A letterbox that squeaks with lack of use.

"And then it happens. One day, you turn away from the cheeseburgers to feel bad about yourself – and there she is. And suddenly, you have something more exciting than the weather to tell the cats about. Something world-shifting, life-altering, like all of a sudden, gravity has come back. After so many years of floating, ghastly nothing, you still have hope. You might not have known it was there, but somewhere, right down in the depths, there was a tiny twinkle that couldn't be extinguished. Because, once the hope is gone, there's nothing left. Even though you wouldn't use the word, not even in conversation, the hope is etched into your bones, it creeps through the veins. It's always there. It tortures you but it's always there.

"And so, you dash out of the queue and I'm saying 'you' when I mean 'me' because – some things are just too painful to be mine. You know how it is. And you know it's not her. It can't be. There's no earthly way. But for that brief moment, when she might be, it means everything in the whole damn world. And you'd give anything to have that moment again.

"I. I would give anything in the world to have that moment again."

It's a different sort of silence that follows. I don't feel bad for not being able to chip in anything to the conversation. She's more fluent than she's ever been. At least, with me.

And so, we just sit here. She sits. I lie here. Both of us, thinking about what she's said. She seems to be thinking about it as much as I am. Maybe more.

"So, what do you do?" she asks. "You tell yourself it wasn't really her because it can't have been. Because that girl can't have been more than twenty-one. But then, maybe she looks younger because she hasn't had to live with you. And then you spend every Saturday for weeks on end, hanging around the Wimpy, hoping to see her again. Because whoever she is, she's someone important. And if she's brought these feelings back, and made you wonder if – she must be someone who's going to matter. Maybe it is her, after all.

"Well, I'll tell you right now, after three or four weeks of heavy snacking and spending several weekends on a bus stop bench, you realise – it's time to make some changes. Sometimes, you can't just force it. If you're supposed to get to know someone, if they're meant to be in your life, they just will be. And so, you step back. You re-assess. You think about what you can do to make yourself a useful person to the world. And then, you become a tea lady in a hospital. You polish your shoes. You get a name badge and a uniform.

"Okay, it might not be the first thing anyone else would think of and I don't pretend that I'm saving anybody's life, or making the world a better place, but somebody has to make the tea. And it's an important job. In its way. It's how we manage, in times of stress and sadness, if somebody panics or has an accident, if something, anything, is too much for a person to cope with, in the absence of brandy, we head for the tea. I am – important – in my life. It's a new feeling and I like it. For all kinds of people, there's something like loneliness that seeps through the pores, but, not when we have tea.

"And, of course, it gave me a chance to meet you, didn't it, eh?"

She goes quiet and I wonder if I'm frowning.

"Let's read some of these cards, shall we?" she rushes. I can hear the paper sliding. It's a slicing sound. The envelope hasn't been sealed.

It's the slash of paper on paper that tells me she's going to read something even my parents haven't opened.

"Lovely. It's a kitten with a sling on the front and inside... Let's see now. *'Hey there, Cam. I've tried to write this three times but I don't think there's any way I can tell you how worried we've all been without making you feel guilty. So. Enjoy the guilt. I would have got you flowers but guilt lasts longer. Anyway, I need my wing-woman back. It's harder to convince women I'm normal without you standing there, nodding. Please get better soon. Lots of whatnot, Simon.'* No kiss." There's a pause before she adds, "Shame."

"Who's next? A rose in the snow. Bit sombre. *'Dear Cam. I love you.* Oh, my. *I've always loved you. I can't bear the thought of anything in this world...'* Well, this is a laugh a minute, isn't it? Let's find a jolly one.

"Here's one. *'Cam. You're missing Tequila Tuesday and I can't write essays without you telling me what to put. Come back soon, sweet. We all miss you. George.'*

"They have an odd sense of humour, young men, don't they?

"*'Babe, I look forward to watching you go through these cards yourself, in a few years' time, shaking your head at how upset everyone has been, how deeply loved you are. I hope you know how much everyone wants you to be up and about, and for whoever did this to rot in...'* no, sorry. Can't read that. Terrible handwriting. Do you have a doctor in the family or...?

"I've done it again. Asked you a question. Dammit, Denise."

She sips her tea and I can't quite get past something she said.

"The worst thing about this job is the scrape of a comfy chair across a polished floor. Oh, it goes right through me. Maybe it's because of the absence of furniture. Normal furniture, you know: sideboard, chairs, bookcases, other things – to deaden the sound. But in a hospital – there's such an echo. And that scrape is the devil's music. Of course, they can't have an excess of furniture in here. Got to have room for all the equipment and, of course, the nurses have to be able to get through. Some of them are ginormous. And the sound howls its way right through the ward. An awful noise."

It is annoying.

"I suppose no one really considers that, do they? Someone slips into a coma, like you, because it's Saturday and that's what happens – and we all know we must talk to them. It's the most stubborn of the senses, apparently. Well, that and smell. But we all know we must be careful about what we say in front of someone who's in a coma. I was talking to one of the nurses and, do you know, there have been patients who remember things that were said during surgery? Doesn't bear thinking about, really.

"But that's what we do. I read every translation from the back of a packet of tissues when... It's so important that you know there's someone there.

"All things being equal, I don't suppose anyone really thinks about it though, do they? Maybe it's just me. Maybe everyone thinks about this sort of thing but it never occurred to me. You'll hear the chairs scraping on the floor, the woman down the corridor who won't stop crying, the squeak of the wheel that hasn't had a good coating of WD-40. You'll know there's someone here from their breathing, from the pouring of the tea, the spoon in the cup, the sounds of sipping. I don't suppose I've ever given that much thought to how loudly I sip. I very much doubt I've been dainty about it. I've probably been chugging it back, indelicate, unappealing. Quite revolting, when you think about it. I'm so sorry. We've all got enough going on without having to deal with heavy-tongued slurping.

"I suppose, if I were to have a clue about my possible-slurping, I would have expected to see spatter-stains on my uniform, but no... pristine. I mean, I say I'm clumsy but not usually with beverages. I'd never have lasted this long in the job if I couldn't manage a teacup.

"And I can make it round the wards because it's only the trolley keeping me upright. Like a walker. Lord knows, when I walk around town, I'm only one step away from a tumble or a totter. I once tripped over Percy and, from the bruise that came up, you'd think I'd broken my wrist. Poor little Perce. I must have frightened him something appalling.

"Anyway, that's just how it is, sometimes. We all have our little quirks. Maybe you don't notice it, not just yet, being so young, but as you get older, you'll notice how many of your friends should be studied. Not – removed from society – just, examined. For the sake of future generations, you know?"

She unfolds her newspaper and chuckles for a moment.

"I see she's in the papers again. I don't know why she puts herself through it. No way I could be an actress. It's my hands. I'd fidget. Make myself look like – I dread to think. I'd start pulling on my fingers or cracking my knuckles, jamming my thumbs into my pockets, something like that. Even if I could talk myself out of that type of thing, I can't do the big gestures. Not properly. I can only imagine, if I spent more than a minute in the high-kicking chorus, there'd be actual loss of life."

There's a pause and I wonder if she's attempting the crossword or checking out what's on TV tonight. She must have her own plans, her cats to get back to, her life to re-enter.

There's a screaming sound outside.

She said something. Something important. Hard to recognise it in the haze of everything else.

"D'you know, I might be here for a thousand years before I get used to the sirens. I know they do an important job – clearing the way, alerting people to the fact that something desperate has happened, that it's time to stop dawdling and get out of the way, but the sound of their approach is just – terrifying. Here's me banging on. If anyone would know..."

"When the ambulance came for you, I suppose you'd have heard it all then. Above all the panic. The tears. The screams. Above the feet circling you, the hissed out words, the fumbling for phones and the urgent instructions. You must have heard them then, telling each other who to call, what to say, what to check for. You must have heard them asking each other what happened, if anyone saw, if anyone knew. But things like – what happened to you – there's nothing you can do to avoid them. That's why they call it *an accident*. It's just – one of those things. Awful, but inevitable. Nothing to be done to prevent it. Nothing anyone could have done differently. Call it fate, if you like. It was always going to happen this way. Top of the steps one minute and then, all of a sudden, splashed across the concrete, a spatter of turquoise and red."

She sucks her lip for a good long while. Why aren't the family here yet?

"I know what you'll be thinking."

Well, I'm glad somebody does because I have no id...

Wake up!

"Did I plan this?" Denise stalls. "I can see how you might think that. Because we don't really know each other yet. That's the problem. But we will. I know we will. And, although this is terrible and I do feel really bad about it, at least we have this time to get to know each other. And I can explain, if you'll let me.

"All those months ago, I was so sure. You were her. I found myself thinking about you. Where you might live. If you were in student halls or at home with... I knew quite soon, of course, that you weren't her. But by that time it was too late and I was wondering about how you lived.

"It's a strange one, isn't it? When you're a student – it's the only time in your life when you live with people you didn't choose and who don't, instinctively, love you. You're assigned people. Perhaps alphabetically, or by subject, or however they decide these things. But they only become friends after a few months of beans and beer. In the interim, while they're strangers who live in your space, you're just stuck with them and their late nights and their boyfriends, their toenails and wet towels on the floor. You're stuck, for a time, with the empty toilet roll tube still hanging on the wall and the food in fridge, all clearly labelled yours: all nibbled, squeezed or missing. At any other time, you could have them removed or call the police but when you're a student, that's just your life.

"And then, I found myself wondering what you wanted for your future. If it was the sort of stuff *she* wanted. Or must have wanted. Not everyone's a talker. You can't blame people for not letting you in. Especially when you're that close. You might start out as the whole, great, shining world but, no matter how wonderful your intentions, a time comes when you become the enemy. Hopefully, that only lasts a few months, a year or two at worst. Sometimes, it never recovers. Sometimes, she just leaves and her father won't speak to you. Won't even look at you. Because he thinks it's your fault. And after a few months, you wonder if he's right. But he can't be right.

"And you find yourself, looking for her. Years later. In shops, in cafés, even passing the dentists'. You wonder if she might be in there. If she's working. If she's waiting. If there was anything you were supposed to know. By instinct. Because that's the bit that's always been missing. You can't know where she might have gone because – it's not as if she ever talked about it. You can't know because you never bothered to ask.

"And so, you spend the years, blaming yourself, hating him, distancing yourself from those who know, still searching, still wondering.

"I suppose you might wonder if some days are harder than others. Birthdays, Christmas, that sort of thing. Truth is, people don't talk about it: every day is its own disaster. Some days are horrific.

Others are far worse. It all takes a lot of effort. I don't think I can tell you how tiring it all is.

"But I was drawn to you. And in that moment, you were so desperately important to me. You made me feel something I hadn't had in years. The possibility. You became so necessary to me, I had to let you know.

"And you were heading for the steps. And it was so crowded, I didn't think I'd get to you in time. And my bloody hands, always in the way, always over-reaching, too close, too far, never where I expect them to be – I meant to tap you on the shoulder.

"I'm not sure what I'd planned to do if you'd turned or smiled or said something. I just wanted to..."

Wake up!

"It wasn't me. You lost your balance. And suddenly, you were just a look of horror, making way for a space. A gap in the crowd. Tumbling down, down, down, gone. A scream and then, a silence.

"They're such good doctors here. Mister Campbell, he's a wonder. I knew he'd take care of you. And I know you'll be better soon and then we can have a proper talk.

"When it happened, all I could think was: I've killed her. I have. I've killed her. Oh, I've never felt so sick in my life. I don't suppose anyone would have noticed my dry-heaving into the begonias that lined the walkway. Not with all the blood and the tears.

"I need you to understand: it's not as if I saw you, came up with a plan to take a job in the hospital and to injure you badly enough that you'd have to be admitted. Just because you look like her. That would be...

"You always love your children. Always. More than anyone else in your life: more than husbands and actors and smooth-voiced crooners. You never love anyone like you love your children. Certainly, I've never loved anyone like I love Natalie. But it's like the fella said: It's not the falling that does it, it's the landing that... Look who I'm talking to!

"I wish I could remember his name." She blows her nose. "Anyway, I should be getting this coffee through to the relatives' room. I'll see you tomorrow, love. Maybe you'll be feeling a bit perkier then, eh? We'll have another little chat. I'll let you get some rest now."

Wake up! Wake up! Wake up!

Desperately Seeking Spinach: A Short Story of Obsession

IT WASN'T AS IF I HADN'T heard of her before. Andrea Pinchbeck is a national treasure. She's been on TV for – well, if I told her that she'd been on TV for as long as I've been alive, I imagine she would make a noise in the back of her throat: a low grumble, like a sob without the ambition. On the other hand, if I told her that she'd been on TV since the beginning of time, she'd laugh it off and wave her hand to bat away the comment. Women are complicated.

The fact is: she's always been there. Through every triumph and frustration, every hope and devastation. It's always been her.

Every afternoon, the bus would pull in just opposite the end of my road, and I'd pick my way past little old ladies in rain bonnets, moaning about their varicose veins and husbands, and glaring at me, watching that I didn't kick their shopping on the way to the doors. I'd slide my way past the creepy guy who always stood, even when there were seats available, not looking him in the eye because – well, you wouldn't. It would be rude. Man can't help his face. Quick nod to the bus driver and I'd fly through the doors, patent leather pumps and satchel swinging back and forth behind me.

Sometimes, it would take a minute or two to find a gap in the traffic before I could cross. I hated days like those. I'd bob up and down like an overexcited toddler looking at an ice cream. Now I'm older, I can see it for what it was.

Whenever you're in a hurry, there's always traffic. It's just the universe, and tourists looking for Tudor buildings or trying to find the

Fort, conspiring to keep you in your thick eyeliner and ankle socks, to make you miss your favourite shows.

Being late for the dentist was irrelevant. He'd be there whether or not I turned up at all. Being late for *Afternoons With Andrea* was practically the end of the world. I can laugh about it now.

I don't laugh about it now.

She'd never know I'd missed it, and that thought made me feel so small, I could feel my shoulders drooping and my insides melting into a soup of guts and spleen.

I feel no shame at the memory of this. Sometimes, people think back to their first loves and they're cut to pieces by embarrassment, disappointment, scandal, horror and longing. I feel – fateful. Light. Not happy. Not unhappy. Like a dandelion puff on a warm breeze, but that's probably because I'm...

No. I'm getting ahead of myself.

So, I'd get off the school bus, growl at the traffic, curse the tourists and we're back where we were.

I'd dash through the front door, hurl my school bag to the floor, call a hello to my mother – this was back when she was still upstairs – and rush through to the front room. My dad would have already left for work but there'd be a tray on the coffee table: sandwich, bottle of Sunny D, and a note.

There was a theme to his notes. They were always different, but they all said the same kind of thing: that I was wonderful, that he was proud of me, and that Mum would need her pills at 6pm – three things that never changed. I don't suppose he knows, but there's an old shoebox on top of my wardrobe where I still have all his notes. I could never part with them.

Sorry, did it again.

So, I'd throw myself onto the sofa, pull at my school tie, slip it up over my nose and across my forehead like a headband, and flip on the

TV. Grabbing the sandwich and kicking off my shoes, I'd lean back into the cushions. And there she was – Andrea Pinchbeck.

Her eyes were – are – warm brown, impish, inquisitive. Sometimes, you can tell from the eyes of a person whether or not they have a sense of humour. Andrea Pinchbeck has a sense of everything. It's all there in her eyes.

Recently, she's started to let her hair go natural – champagne-blonde with just a hint of salt and pepper. Her skin is fresh, her make-up subtle. Her dress sense is what I would call *comfortably chic*; she looks like she's ready for a visit from her in-laws. Classy, without being standoffish.

Gorgeous figure, especially for someone who, presumably, spent the 1990s eating roast dinners and a huge amount of cake. That is, if she actually ate the food from her shows. Which she must have done, she's from Leeds.

They don't waste anything up north.

She's beautiful. Well, I don't need to tell you, you've seen her. But she really is.

There's a lilt in her voice, an echo of her hometown. I love that. Sometimes, people take the Mickey online. They say she's started to sound like a soft southern Nancy but they're not listening hard enough. The north is still in there. It's just – gentle, I suppose. They've been spoilt by too many regional dramas, with pickle-thumbed farmers, head to foot in manure, tugging a forelock for the lady of the manor, who was also never quite northern enough, but had a deeply dissatisfying love life to balance out her rounded vowels.

Anyway, Andrea's hair is cropped short these days. I know she bleached it for a while because it used to be dark, like mine. Thank God for YouTube. All of her old shows are on there. I must have watched them all at least forty-s... You know, it's enough to know I've seen them. No need for specifics.

Don't get me wrong, she was lovely when she was younger. She's just – there's no doubting, she's more attractive now. It's not just because of the absence of Richard. Although, he was an arse. Luckily, most people don't even remember Richard anymore.

I didn't get to watch *Eat The North* the first time round. I was at nursery. But looking at those old shows now, and the implied chemistry between them, she just seems – like she's trying to work out why he's there. I suppose nobody noticed back then; people didn't watch things the same way they do now. There was no freeze-frame, no instant replay. No one would notice that Richard was just standing around laughing at his own jokes. Really, he was there for decoration. He didn't even seem to understand what he was watching. The first time I saw Andrea using a pestle and mortar, I got chills. He just stood there like an idiot. I'll bet he was sleeping with the director.

See, it was a simpler time – the nineties. I suppose, even now, people will watch anything if they can believe that, when the screen fades to black, the co-hosts are going at it hammer and tongs and making the cameramen woozy. I can't believe anyone thought that of Andrea and Richard. Anyone could see she was too good for him. She'd have ruined him. And now he's on the shopping channel with a crease-free forehead and boot-polish hair.

I used to wonder what her perfume was called. It's a strange one – you see the photos in the magazines and the editors fall over themselves to credit the dress designer, the hair stylist, the makeup artist, the jeweller… but there's never a word about the perfume. Unless they have their own line of scents on the market, no one really knows what TV stars smell like. They might all smell of feet. Feet in a microwave. They don't, but you know what I mean.

There are some things we just can't know for definite until we're in the same room.

Of the things we know for certain, they're mostly disappointing.

Most of the time, we know which way is up. Although, sometimes, we don't care.

We know what it feels like to fall for someone who doesn't really see us.

We know that life was easier when we were small.

We know there are idiots no matter where you go.

These are the basics. These are the facts of life we don't need to be taught.

Sometimes, I shock myself with my own profundity.

Anyway, on *Afternoons With Andrea*, just after school, it was just her. In a kitchen. With a film crew. But it felt like it was just the two of us. The best episodes were from the pastry days. I could imagine the feel of the flour on her skin. I listened to the gentle tap of her hand on the side of the sieve, the eggs cracking on the side of the bowl before she lobbed the shells across the room. Her fingers feathering butter into the flour. The sandwich wilted in front of my open mouth. Eyes wide open, afraid to blink.

I'd come back to myself when she spoke. The return journey is always easier than the voyage out. She didn't just talk about the ingredients or the equipment or how to convert grams into ounces and back again. She would talk about the people she met in the queue. She'd talk about her grandmother's fat rascals and her uncle's missing thumb. It felt like I was sitting at the end of the counter, with my chin in an upturned hand, while she told her stories just for me.

And that would be my whole afternoon until the credits began to roll. Then, back into the real world. I'd make a cup of tea for Mum, get out her pills, make a vague attempt at homework until the whole page was one big doodle, and then fetch dinner from the slow cooker. But somewhere, somewhere quiet in the back of my head, I was still in Andrea's kitchen, watching her mop up melted chocolate with her index finger. Watching as the finger disappeared into her mouth.

Other girls my age had floppy-fringed boy bands plastered all over their walls, covering every inch except the doorknob and the windows. I had a *Radio Times* interview that Andrea gave. It was next to my bed, just to the right of me; I'd strain my eyes before disappearing into sleep. She was the first thing I saw when I woke up.

In my heart of hearts, I think the only reason I went to university was because *Andrea's Kitchen* turned into *Andrea's Pantry*, and moved to Sunday mornings. It gave me a lot more time to, you know, write essays on Chaucer and pick symphonies apart.

It's a gift: to be in my mid-twenties. Now, I realise that it wasn't always a given that I'd go to university. Please don't misunderstand me – I hate those people who start reminiscing when they're barely out of high school. Those people are evil. However, I'm on my way to thirty, so I'm allowed to see things for what they were. Of course, he never said a word about it, but my dad changed jobs so I could leave home. It would have been quite the pickle in the coffee jar if I moved and he was still on nights, and so, he took a lower paid but daytime job, and Jeanie from across the road came over in the afternoons to sit with my mum.

He's a good guy, my dad. He said he'd hated working nights; that he'd missed just breathing out at the end of a long day; how it wasn't quite the same when the *end* of a long day was around four in the morning. He said it all for me. He's such a liar. I love him.

It's hard not to compare, but my brother had it easy. As much as I didn't think about it at the time, he's my big brother and so he doesn't think at all. Andrew was the golden child, you see. He was born after thirty-four hours in the maternity wing, courtesy of a broken-down bus and a complicated delivery. He's always been waited on hand and foot. As my mother tells the story, it's as if all the nurses looked like film stars with fluffy white wings, and the doctor might as well have been Jesus.

I, on the other hand, was born behind a spiky blackthorn hedge just the other side of the A49. Like a rock star.

So, skip forward a few years and Andrew turned eighteen. I was on the sofa, with a sandwich losing its shape, and my big brother – fag tucked behind his ear – packed a bag and wandered off into the wild blue yonder. What none of us knew then was that the 'wild blue yonder' would include capped sleeves, a name badge and a girlfriend from the break room. Even though it all seems very – safe – he seems happy enough. He's not out to change, smash, fix the world, he just wants a simple life.

Whatever makes him happy, I suppose, but it's not for me.

I was covered in ink, almost head to foot, before I handed in my dissertation. It didn't seem the sort of thing to mention in the bi-weekly phone calls home, so I never mentioned it. We talked about the importance of spending money on memories rather than stuff, so I figured, deep down, they... didn't need to know.

Things to tell my parents about: impending financial doom, parties with new friends, the weekend I had a cat, the lecturer who walked like he was made of magic but who was actually made of moth balls and herpes, my last night in halls when I was burgled and decided never to leave Shropshire again – all good topics of conversation.

Things not to tell my parents about: my tattoos, my smoking, my various experiments with hangover cures. The morning of the egg-and-asparagus smoothie is something I'd sooner never mention to another human being. Except for you, of course.

I came back from uni for Christmas – because that's what you do. It's not like in kids' films; when everyone else leaves, you leave. Anyway, I was back. I didn't have a UTI so everyone was pleased to see me. I wore long sleeves, as befitted the season, and I would have got away with it, except that Andrew's dog did something slick and kind of green on the living room carpet. Not to act the saint, but I didn't even give it a thought. Grabbed the kitchen roll, slashed the itchy sweater sleeve up to my elbow before the smell could overpower Jeanie from across the road, and ran from the room with my hand further from my body than ever before.

On my way past, my mother made a noise. It was like she was struggling to say something in an unfamiliar language; trying to make her mouth the right shape while staring very hard. But instead of a phrasebook, she was looking at the sugar skull. In any case, once she'd recovered the power of speech and raised a glass to wash down the stuffing, she decided it was a form of artistic expression. She looked a little sad but a decision was made – we didn't need to talk about it.

The real shocker of university was that it was over within minutes. All the drinking, dancing, tattoo parlours, occasional lecture, bit of modelling, photography course, back to the dance floor, more drinking – and suddenly, it was finished. Three years of studious fun and laughs, punctuated by disaster. I had to get my roommates to pack for me. Couldn't go back in there afterwards. And soon, I was back in my old bedroom with the internet on and my socks off.

While my own drama seemed to be winding down, Andrea's was just starting to explode.

Like all the good things in life, it started with a cake.

Andrea got a whole new following because of that cake but there's no doubt in my mind, she did it mostly because she cared, and partly because she didn't think anyone would find out. You could see it in the stretch of her face, with the TV cameras bouncing on running shoulders, and the reporters, galloping across the pavement to get to her, saliva falling in strings across their chins, talking all at once, demanding her attention, pressing up against her.

She'd only read about it, online, like the rest of us. The happy couple couldn't get the caterer they wanted because the company didn't approve of... Long story short, some people are wankers. Of course, everyone's entitled to their own opinion but people were shocked in all directions. Some sided with the cooks and their right to serve only those whose bedroom antics were firmly heterosexual and could be fitted in to the ad break during *Countdown*. Others carried placards and rolled their eyes and explained themselves in small words, to people who weren't listening.

Nobody noticed when Andrea slipped silently into the fray. A couple of simple questions, allergies and numbers expected at the reception, and Andrea made them a four-tier wedding cake. She had someone bike it round. Nobody would have known.

Except they wanted to thank her. Invited her round. We wouldn't even know that much except it almost broke the internet. There she was – Andrea Pinchbeck – shaking hands with one of the grooms and turning round, startled as a camera flash caught her in mid-sentence.

Whether it was her agent or her stupid husband who told the press where to find her, I couldn't guess. But, suddenly, there was a new series. Even people who didn't approve of the wedding itself seemed to appreciate the gesture. Everyone wants to be in love and everyone likes cake. And in that single gesture, Andrea, although not deliberately, showed the world she had time for real people.

I mean, some of us already knew that. You get an instinct about people sometimes. And I'm one of the few – from the early days of her social media presence. I grew up on the shows, they were my night and day, but when she got to social media, I was all grown up. Delighted, naturally, that she didn't do that thing that so many of the others do – set up an account, tweet once and then – leave it alone for five years. No, no. Andrea posts every day, about herself, her life, her kitchen.

I was like everybody else – watching her timeline, reading her blog, kids' stuff really. I couldn't have known how close we would become.

It was never like a teenage crush. And now, it's a twenty-something-fifty-something kinship. It's quite a mouthful, I know. At least, it is when I imagine it.

There she was on social media. Just like that, in the quiet moments of the night, when the whole world falls to darkness and there might be nobody left alive, she'll post a picture of a salad or a fruit bowl, and it's like the first rays of the dawn.

She is built on waves of kindness; a friend we do not know. At least, not completely. But we get small glimpses into her life and ours become more bearable.

She hasn't mentioned the menopause yet, though she must be headed in that direction. I think she'd tell the truth about it. She wouldn't lie. It's not in her character.

Perhaps you'll think I'm overdramatizing but the fact is – she saved me from what might have been a terrible day with my mother's friends. I don't know whether the rest of her followers reply to her posts because they're excited to be talking to, even *at*, a celebrity, but I know she despises the word.

And I know that because when she finally replied to one of my messages, I was floating on a cloud for days afterwards. Weeks. Still, really. She is my famous friend.

And so, my life story starts here. In my bedroom. With my socks on the floor and my parents downstairs, and even blinking hurts. It's like my head is full of thumbtacks. The cat next-door is snoring. He knows when I'm hung-over. They're like that though, aren't they, cats? Attuned to the neighbours and determined to annoy them. But I'll know better than to dance with Grand Marnier again. Timber the cat has made me learn my lesson.

I can't really feel my face but it's probably for the best. It's too early. At this time of day, it would probably feel like someone else's regardless of the Schnapps. I mixed. Timber reminds me I shouldn't have mixed.

A roman blind shields me from the full assault of the egg-white sky. My coffee is too hot to drink. I don't care. I can't taste it but it'll do the job – wake me up, pull me through this head-fog. I blow the smoke under the blind, through my window and out into the morning. They can't smell it downstairs. Can't see the grey tendrils unfurling from my insides, out of my mouth and into the world.

I don't expect sympathy. I brought this on myself. See, parties in the student halls are messy affairs. Whether it's paint, cake, foam or god-knows, you're going to get something on you. There might be body-shots, brightly coloured, super-sour things, and it's all pretty wonderful... largely, because you're eighteen and have rarely been out of the house before.

Now, as an adult, in an adult world, there are parties that include mini quiches, wandering trays and cummerbunded waiters and, as much as it's all very sophisticated (there are often napkins), instead of new people whose names you struggle to remember, now there are famous people whose names are almost as familiar as my own. I expected the actors and the singers to be reasonably good at drinking. I didn't worry much about matching them shot for shot. What I hadn't bargained on was how quickly newsreaders could get through tequila.

I check for updates. Andrea hasn't posted anything for a while. It'd be – well, not *nice* but instructive, to see how much we had to drink. I suppose it's one thing to throw a party for nearly a hundred people. It's quite another to cater the thing and fold all the napkins into interesting shapes.

Maybe she's still in bed. I'm sure she made it to bed eventually. I'm in no position to know for certain. There's always next time...

Nothing to read, so I pick up a few select items that haven't made it into the laundry basket. It's an effort, leaning over and pretending that my stomach isn't swirling. I suppose I'd always wondered, not actively but somewhere in the back of my head, where all my nice bras had gone. For a time, I thought the washing machine had eaten them, or the neighbour-kid had stolen them from the washing line in a rush of pubescent kleptomania. But now I see, under the bed, I have a village of unloved lingerie, sitting, abandoned among the dust bunnies, waiting for a quiet spell when I can be bothered to find them and blow cobwebs off the lace.

God, when's she going to post the pictures?

It all started months ago. Before she knew my name. Before everything that really matters. Andrea baked some bread. A couple of thousand Likes. Several hundred comments. There were the usual half-dozen names right near the top. Their names come up so often, I almost feel like I know them. Most of the time, they don't really say anything at all. *'That looks nice,'* or *'Lunch at yours, eh?'* – that kind of thing. Empty comments, I call them. The same sentiment could be conveyed with a simple 'Like' but no, they insist on a clutter of pointless words because, I suppose, it tickles them to think they're basically friends of hers, that they have some sort of bond with her, but she doesn't know them. They must know that and yet – they just can't stop themselves.

Around noon that day, she posted a picture of her kitchen table with the bread on one side and a giant bowl of soup on the other. Ladle and everything. Fresh flowers, big shiny spoons, gorgeous. Meanwhile, I had a sausage roll that looked like it had already been eaten. And then, this guy came up – I hadn't seen his name before – and his comment made my blood run cold.

'I bet your place smells nice,' he wrote.

I don't know how people can walk around with the rest of us knowing they're that creepy. I suppose that comment is what turned me from a fan into a protector. I was ready to jump in, ready to call him out for the sad collection of biscuit crumbs he surely was, but my brain stopped. I had no words. I hate it when that happens. It's happened more frequently since I came home.

Equal parts, creeped out and irritated, I headed downstairs for a drink. Taking the bottled water out of the fridge, I had nothing. Reaching for a glass, I kept on thinking about what I could say to stick up for her, to make her smile, to make her wonder if, indeed, we could be friends – at least, to begin with. It was a lot to expect of a limited number of characters and a name nobody knew but I was frowning hard to force a thought.

In an instant, I knew what to say. The perfect phrase. Not too chummy, not too distant – wonderful.

It was only when I hit the button I realised what I'd done. It wasn't just the wrong thing. It was the worst thing. It was enough to make me feel itchy. Suddenly and irrefutably itchy.

Staring at the screen, my mouth going dry, my fingers flexing over the keys, wondering what to do. I bit my fist and tried to reassure myself: *she's famous. She's probably surrounded by sycophants. It might be refreshing to have someone be a bit bolshy and rude, and good God, she's northern! She probably likes that sort of thing.*

Maybe 'famous' is the wrong word. She's not doing worldwide stadium tours or marrying Nobel winners every other Saturday. She doesn't have to bear that kind of scrutiny. She just has weird blokes and middle-aged women filling up her comments with drudgery and creepiness, and me, with my fingers frozen over the keys.

She's small-scale famous. Passing her in the street, even in her dark glasses and her long grey coat, even employing a hurried, *where's-the-loo?*-pace, you'd know you knew her from somewhere. Because everybody does. She is watched by all the family as they eat dinner off their knees, staring at the screen. People invite her in and they spend their evenings together. And these are the moments they'll remember when it all goes wrong. When there's an empty cup beside the kettle, when there's a space in the bed and a hole in the world, they'll remember these evenings with Andrea. They'll remember and she'll become part of their history. Part of the backing track to their contentment. It's her and the *Antiques Roadshow*. She means more to people than she can guess.

I suppose, if people knew how awful it was to be famous, no one would aspire to anything even remotely noteworthy. To have every move analysed, every word captured, every expression picked apart, and it'll all live as long as the internet: why would anyone want that? I'm not really sure how I feel about social media. Maybe that sounds odd, given that most of my life is on it but I can't imagine what it is to be famous. The rest of us have our insecurities, maybe a whole room of them, but for famous people – they don't get to keep their demons to themselves. If the rest of us gain a little weight, say something hurtful, get a disastrous haircut, have a bad break-up – we can deal with it in relative privacy. Or ignore it, in relative privacy. But for famous people, whatever happens, they live their lives in a goldfish bowl. Every wrinkle examined, every indiscretion plastered across the front page. It must be terrible.

Anyway, I posted my reply, realised what I'd said and suddenly felt terribly itchy.

Even now, I know I'm not itchy. Not now. Not even then. And yet...

How is it that one word, even a word that you've brought into the conversation on your own, can make the mind generate a feeling? A real one. An itch. There is no sting beneath the skin. There are no bumps in the ink. But in that moment after I'd hit 'Send', I could have scratched off a limb before I felt anything other than embarrassment.

Of course, reading my reply, I might have brought that feeling to Andrea herself. And that thought haunted me. One stupid generalisation about Yorkshire-folk and I might have brought an itch to a television goddess.

A slight scratch at the back of her neck might not have been so bad, but what if it had appeared somewhere else? Somewhere unmentionable and dangerous? What if the thought echoed back at a later date, when she was answering the door to the postman? What if she started wildly scratching herself when she was supposed to be signing for a parcel?

Suddenly, I wondered if it was too early to crack open the brandy. 1 pm. Bit of a toss-up, really.

The screen lit up. *'Too true,'* she replied. *'You can take the girl out of Leeds but... you probably shouldn't. Ha.'*

See, it's that as well. 'Ha', not 'LOL'. Classy.

Some famous people, you just know they don't actually read their replies. Or maybe they have people to read things for them. Andrea isn't the sort to hire people to do her reading for her.

We all remember the woman who suggested Andrea go into panto. When I say 'suggested', it was more like a six-month daily plea. We all got to know Tina pretty well. She was always quite polite but, let's face it, she had her own problems.

In any case, Andrea did her stint as Madame Whisk-A-Lot in Shrewsbury and it's not as if I booked tickets for every performance. I've seen *All About Eve*, I know what happens. Once a week, though – not especially excessive. And, still in Shropshire – bonus. Mum and Dad thought I had a fella. I wasn't quite ready to burst that bubble and, besides, it meant I was free to go out every Friday night and we could all pretend I had a standing date. I had a sitting date with a little pot of ice cream, only blinking when I absolutely had to, but we were all quite happy.

Anyway, now I know, whatever I say, it's not the sort of stuff to make her scratch herself. I think she'd tell me. I hope she'd tell me.

I know what you're thinking. What makes me think I could get her, given that I couldn't be less like her husband? Well, for starters, I couldn't be less like her husband.

Nothing against him personally. He seems nice enough. But maybe he has to put that on for the camera. And now, having seen inside the house, I know there are too many spare rooms for people who actually sleep together so, I have that in my favour.

I know I have nothing to fear from the husband. People only ever want what they don't have. Lord knows that's why I'm so popular.

What I mean is – once a thing is yours, you can't really want it anymore. At least, not in the same way. You can appreciate it, arguably, but you can't have the same desire for something that's already yours. Anyway, everybody knows that a change is as good as a rest. That could be me. Given half a chance.

It's a strange thing – there are certain behaviours which, depending on the stage of the relationship, may or may not be frightening. For example, if you drive past her house, just to see the light in her window a) before it's officially a relationship, that's just giving kismet a bit of a nudge, b) once it's an established relationship, it's either wistful or controlling, depending on eyebrow-arch, c) once the relationship is over, terrifying. However, when it's at the very beginning, when the flirtation has begun and we all know where we're headed, that's endearing, isn't it?

Well, whatever, man, because I think it's endearing.

He might have been any of a dozen dark-haired actors, but Andrea was plugging his play. I swear she's a big part of the reason people still go to the theatre.

'You must go and see David's new play. Amazing cast, great story, I was on the edge of my seat from the off. Brava.'

Now, the me from a few months ago would wonder why in the hell I would go to a play when she's clearly already been. It's not as if she'd go back, we'd run into each other, strike up a conversation, realise we have too much in common not to go for a drink and run off into the sunset together, adopting chickens and kissing slow until the end of our days, because she'd already been, recommended, and put the programme in a drawer.

The new me knows better. She went to support a friend and now she's home. Old me would wonder if she would see the play again.

'Will you be going back, Andrea?' It's the creepy guy again. A little while ago, I would have resented his speedy typing and his quick mind. Now, I pity him.

No response. No 'Like'.

That's my girl.

See, when I was in halls, there was always someone else who could cook. Occasionally, I chopped things. For the most part, I washed up. The fact is, I watched all the programmes but I didn't learn to cook until I came home. And that's why I'll always be grateful to Andrea. No one else can teach like she can. No one else can move around a kitchen like she can. I learnt everything from her. I can poach and blanch, and julienne should the need arise.

It's all her.

Without my cooking, let's face it: I was only really contributing my sparkling conversation to the household. No need to sugar coat it (although I do know how), I'm deadweight, a drain on my parents' resources – but once I learnt to make a roux, I became useful.

I'd not long bought Andrea's cake book when I had a crack at crumpets. God, I love crumpets. Anyway, after the fire brigade left, we all decided that I would steer clear of baking for a while, so I bought her books on vegetables and soups. Soups are a lot more complicated that they look, I'll tell you that for nothing. And sweetcorn is a beast to strip from the cob. At least, it's not that easy with a bread knife. It was around that time that I clicked the button to be notified whenever she posted.

It's not creepy. It seemed the most effective way of asking whatever questions I might have had and get a heads-up on her new recipes. And personal appearances. And book signings.

For the longest time, I felt jealous when someone else's reply got a smiley face or, God forbid, a kiss. I'm so glad I'm over that now. Grown. I have grown as a person. I deserve a crumpet.

Somehow, being aware of her posts, as and when they happened, I felt I was training my brain to respond more quickly than – well, more quickly than me, really.

It's like – you know how you shouldn't go food shopping when you're hungry? It's that. You know, deep down in your soul, that you'll just come home with a pre-packed, overpriced sandwich, half a dozen ready meals (all with the same best-before date, which is probably the next day) and a packet of lettuce seeds on the off chance we have to self-isolate again.

In the same way, I never should have posted responses when I'd been staring at the screen all day long. Staring at my computer does strange things to my mind. Things that, in my twitch-finger state, had seemed funny were missing half the joke. Of course, I knew why it was funny, but then, I already knew the set-up. If I didn't stay on top of what I was saying, I'd type too fast and miss the story, so it was all punchline, no laugh.

Now I realise, you can't assume that anyone else in the world knows what you're getting at – if you don't tell them. And that's the thing. Before Andrea and I were friends, she couldn't guess what I was thinking. In some ways, that might have been a good thing, but it meant that she didn't get my jokes for ages.

It can be a bonding experience – a party with body shots. Certainly, it pushes acquaintances closer to friends. Maybe that's because of all the secrets that spill out across the floor.

It was a few months back, and I thought that Andrea would be more likely to see my replies than most other people's because I only went offline when I absolutely had to.

Like for Jeanie's funeral. It was pretty terrible. Mum was in bits. See, Jeanie had never been ill and Mum had never been anything else, so it started going round and round in her head – if Jeanie could be felled by a Christmas bug and questionable footwear, there were no guarantees for any of us. Mum was feeling pretty bleak as we crossed the road for the wake.

Of course, with all the sobbing and solemnity, I couldn't check my notifications for a couple of hours because – some things don't need explaining. As it happens, all I missed was a fruitcake. Several dozen comments, nothing I could usefully add. So frustrating.

Andrea used to post more of her schedule, then. For instance, if she was filming in some stately home somewhere for her upcoming series, or if she'd been to the cinema, or if she'd seen a pigeon in the park, she would post a picture and show us all something of her life. And then, I don't know what happened, but something changed. She stopped posting that stuff for a while. No disrespect to Jeanie, but that was like a death. And as my interest grew, and my days became hers, she began to withdraw and my heart tumbled down to the ground floor.

Luckily, whatever had made her close down passed, eventually, and she went back to showing us the herb tubs on her windowsill and the counter of her local butchers, with the shop name carefully, annoyingly, edited out. There was one picture of her butcher making sausages that got a lot of responses.

Andrea didn't rise to it.

Stunning.

Anyway, we all knew that Andrea was moving house. She'd posted the photos of all the boxes in her hallway and she looked – well, she looked shattered, but in a come-hither sort of way. She had the tousled hair, red-in-the-face look. She was working it. It was distracting, but in the best possible way. I burnt the soup I'd spent the afternoon making.

One of the first responses was: *'It's amazing how much crap you find when you move house.'*

No emoji. No reply.

Total silence.

And we all felt for him.

My voice was sore from laughing but once I'd got my breath back, I dabbed my eyes and went back to the screen.

He must have realised what he'd done and so, tried again. *'Not that you, personally, have loads of crap. I just mean generally. We all have it.'*

Nope. Still nothing.

'And sometimes,' he couldn't stop himself, *'it takes emptying out a house to find stuff. I once found a gas bill that I'd disputed because it had fallen behind the sideboard.'*

It was awkward. So awkward.

It's a thing I've noticed: something spoken, out loud, seems very different from the same thing written down. I think there's just more judgement in the written word. Or, at least, there seems to be when you don't really know the person you're trying to communicate with. Even when it's not in caps, the written word is shouting.

So, Andrea was moving house, some bloke had made a fool of himself by suggesting she lived in a hovel and, we're back. The other questions began. *Where are you going? When are you moving? What about the new series?* – that one comes up quite often, but not as much as – *Will you marry me?*

I mean – who's going to say 'yes' over social media, for goodness' sake? There's always one who doesn't think things through.

Crumpets notwithstanding, I'd already made every recipe in her baking book a couple of times. I was worried, to begin with, that my skin would be too hot. To make good pastry, they say you should have cool skin, but even the sight of Andrea's hands in the mixing bowl made my temperature rise. Still, once I managed to focus on the words, I followed the instructions and wound up with pretty good Chelsea buns. I took some across the road to Norman. It's difficult to know what to bring someone who's grieving. There are worse things than buns.

See, my parents have never been all that interested in red meat. Maybe there wasn't a lot of it about when they were young, I don't know, we don't really talk about it. Which does seem suspicious, now that I think about it. Anyway, I read *The Book of Beef* in the early hours of the morning and thought about what might have been.

The Chicken Book got a lot more use. I went round the world in eighty breasts, from Catalan chicken to Persian kebabs to stews of various nations. Chicken is everywhere. It's the standard soup for sickness or distress. It deserves its own book. If only in tribute. We kill a lot of them. Anyway, after four or five weeks of chicken dinners, the family got a bit fed up with it and we were, frankly, all looking forward to the new book, whatever it might be.

There was a lot of speculation online. Some people will speculate about anything. I'm one of them. We all wondered – would it be fish? Some sort of meat substitute? Perhaps she would go back to her first love, pastries? Those who asked directly were rewarded with a winking emoji. It took over a lot of lives there, for a while.

Like Christmas when you're eight. You're old enough to know where the presents are hidden because it's not as if your parents ever change the hiding place, but at eight, you've mastered the art of peeling back the sticky tape just far enough to see what the present is without tearing the paper. It's the perfect crime. And so, you see that it's a book. You can practise your grateful face but, unless you're really talented, all you know is: it's a book.

I kept myself busy. I made a few chutneys to pass the time. Had a crack at a mango and yogurt smoothie, with extra rum, that she'd made on breakfast TV one time. I tried not to obsess about it. Andrea, tipsy, in the morning – just pleasantly warm.

I told myself I could keep it as a surprise. I'd see it in the bookshop on the day it came out, just like everybody else. I didn't need to cross-reference interviews she'd given, looking for clues, seeking out spoilers. The paper was peeled. It was definitely a book – back in the bottom of the wardrobe – underneath the dressing gown that had never had a hanger.

So I waited. I ignored the idiots guessing at herbs and dribbling over exotic fruits. And I waited. And waited. Just when I thought I might actually explode, she posted.

Just one word – very early in the morning.

'Spinach'.

It probably sounds – well, I know how it sounds, but we know each other a bit now, don't we? I know I can tell you. All I could think was how incredible it would be to hear her whisper that one word.

Spinach.

I know. I know.

Anyway, after a little lie-down, I turned my head to the ping of the notification alarm.

'Get some iron in your diet, folks. Good for the blood. Stave off anaemia. Keep yourselves big and strong!' and there was a picture. Andrea, posing, clutching her own bicep and – bingo-bango, I have a new screensaver.

There was more. *'Stay tuned for a great little spinach recipe. One of my favourites and soooo healthy.'*

Well, I thought, it must be pretty good to cause an 'o' to snatch up three little friends, and off I went to the bookshop.

I don't know that I've ever seen anyone unlock a door so slowly. It was like the shopkeeper had never seen, much less operated a key before.

To be fair, he'd created a very pretty display on the large square table in the window, and I did get there twenty minutes before he opened, but still... it was exhausting watching him choose between his key and the keyring as he shuffled towards the door.

There must have been several dozen copies of *The Spinach Book* on the table but I only needed one. I snatched a bank note out of my wallet, thrust it across the counter, gathered up the book and dashed out into the world. It didn't occur to me that there should have been change until I was closer to home but it didn't matter. I got the book before anyone else in town.

The sky was heavy, the air thick, a threat of rain. It's strange how you can remember every detail from the important moments in life. It's like I'm still there. On the dank street with the damp air rushing against my face, running past the florists and their buckets of fresh flowers, past the bank with its stern-looking electric doors and chunky grey bricks, past the café with its outdoor seating and the chairs flopped, exhausted and wet, against the tables. Desperately flicking through the pages, underneath the awnings, looking up ingredients.

I had already decided, you see. I would spend my afternoon scrubbing and chopping, shredding and teasing. Watermelon, avocado, pumpkin seeds and spinach. I would be making things that had graced her kitchen. Things she had crafted. Things she had loved. That she had made for people she loved. That she had made for me. We would be closer.

Long story short, I went to the first greengrocers, polished floorboards, shelves from floor to ceiling, buckets dotted here and there, the scent of carrots – and not a spinach leaf to be found. He said something about a drought and honestly, I lost interest.

The second greengrocer was worse. The Saturday girl even suggested that broccoli would make a decent substitute. I jabbed my finger at the front cover, indicating the image of Andrea Pinchbeck, holding a bunch of spinach before her like a wedding bouquet.

"Does that look like broccoli to you?" I hissed.

Her mouth dropped open but no words came out. Rather than wait for her to think of something to say, I turned on my heel and headed to the edge of town and the supermarket.

I didn't want to be there. I felt a chill being away from the house for so long. There were so many other people. Too many. I didn't know what they might be up to, what they must be thinking, what they could want from me.

As I walked through the sudden blast of air conditioning and into the fruit and veg section, I got to thinking about Andrea.

There are times in life when something lousy happens and then, the news gets hold of it, and suddenly, you find yourself having to buy up every copy of the local newspaper to avoid a scandal. I remember when Andrea spoke about that. We can all laugh about it now but at the time, it was quite awkward. Everyone says something unguarded sometimes. She just – since then, she makes sure everyone else has had as much to drink as she has. At times like those, nobody much minds if someone says something truly thoughtless about... Well, anyway, everybody does stupid things sometimes, and she dealt with all that years ago. The lesson is: real heroes make mistakes.

And no drought was going to stop me cooking.

Even as I reached the large plastic box with its leafy fullness and its neighbour, kale, I wondered if I dared. I dashed back to the entrance, put my basket back into the stack and grabbed a trolley. It wasn't greed. Not really. It was enthusiasm. The two are often confused.

Anyway, once half the bags were in my trolley, I got the book out of my shoulder bag and thought about how great it was going to be. I'd cook everything from the first chapter and post pictures to Andrea over the next few days. I snatched up armfuls of nuts, fruits and microgreens.

It was only when I was heading for the checkout that I realised I might look a bit mad. I hesitated. Going ahead would mean making 1) a commitment to all this food, 2) an impression on strangers and shop assistants alike, 3) a huge number of tweets which, in turn, might make me look a bit... overly attached. To the spinach. At least, to the spinach.

I turned myself around. I put the first bag back gently, almost tenderly, like putting a teddy bear into a small child's toy box. By the seventh bag, I was hurling them back with abandon; the smack of plastic on plastic unnerving little old ladies for aisles around.

But sometimes, fate steps in to make the decision for you.

Boney M. *Daddy Cool.*

I answered my phone.

"Yeah Dad?" He doesn't like it when I don't wait for him to identify himself but he has to forgive me because I'm his child.

"Clea, it's Dad. Look, you know it's Mum's birthday..." he started.

I did. In the sense of – I knew it was coming up. Standing in the supermarket above a pile of recently discarded spinach bags, I was struck by that sinking feeling you get when you know you have to think of an excuse terribly quickly and the only thing you can think is – bollocks. Which are so hard to gift-wrap.

I made a noise in the back of my throat.

"Well, good," he said. "What it is, and they could have saved us all a lot of trouble if they'd just said something in the first place, but a bunch of Mum's old school chums have decided to come and see her. They'll be here later this afternoon. They wanted to make it a surprise and they're saying not to make a fuss but..." and then he just stopped.

"I know," I said, absently.

"It's just – I think we should do something. A lot of them haven't seen your mother since she got ill. I don't suppose you remember many of them."

"Not a one," I replied, biting my lip.

"You can understand it," he soothed. "They remember when she was young. She used to go hiking. They remember her then. Maybe they wouldn't cope with the change in her."

I nodded and thought them all a bunch of rancid bastards. "What shall we do?"

"I don't suppose you're anywhere near the shops at the mo, are you?"

I looked around myself. "Not far. What do you need?"

"Maybe a cake? They'll be here around half-one, two o'clock so…"

I jumped in. "Late lunch, then?"

"Darling," he soothed, "I wasn't really thinking of…"

I chased through the pages with my fingers. "No, it's fine. How about salads?"

Silence.

"You know," I went on, "you can put all kinds of things in salad these days. It's not just iceberg, cucumbers and tomatoes anymore."

"Really?" he asked. And he was serious. When he was younger, real men didn't eat salad. Back then, the closest real men came to salad was gravy.

"You can put prosciutto in salad if you want…"

"Probably better to avoid meat, darling. And dairy. Just in case. Don't want to poison any of them."

"Maybe you don't," I muttered as a woman pushed past me for a tray of cress.

Dad was unconvinced. "I was only thinking of rock cakes. Maybe some dips and breadsticks. Nothing too fancy."

"Rock cakes and breadsticks?"

"And dip," he added, hopefully.

I folded the book into my arms. "Rock cakes and breadsticks and dip?"

"Oh, my!" He laughed to himself for a good half-minute. "Oh, go on. That was funny. Like in *The Wizard Of Oz* when they're walking through the… in the forest. 'Lions and tigers and…' okay, then."

"Leave it with me, Dad." I had him promise me that he'd take a break when he needed and then got to work. Forget tweeting Andrea pictures over the next few days. The time signature had changed. I was going to make basically everything in the book for my mother's former friends – they'd feel bad about themselves for not visiting, Dad would be allowed three minutes' shaving, uninterrupted, I'd have a load of pictures to send to Andrea, and Mum would have a good day.

What I wanted my mother's friends to feel was, not so much sated as – shamed.

I've never actually admitted that before. It's true but that doesn't make it sound any better, does it?

Anyway, after a good few hours in the kitchen, chopping, frying, sautéing, laying the table and taking pictures every few minutes, the first of the women appeared.

She looked like she was auditioning for the role of disgraced MP's wife. All she needed was a gravel driveway and an awkward side hug to complete the look.

Within minutes, a load more of them arrived. By that point, I was just pleased to have made so much food. By the time I stopped counting, Mum was in her element. I was passing round the canapés while the rest of them sipped Prosecco and asked each other how long it had been since they'd all been in a room together. Mum was holding court, telling stories, pointing to her favourite azalea through the window. She didn't notice their embarrassment. She was just happy to have her friends back.

And all through the day, I posted pictures, tagging Andrea with every dish. Not giving away her recipes, obviously, but making everything look as good as possible. I'm better at portraits than food photography – telling a plate it looks beautiful doesn't make it smile – but I did my best and it looked impressive. Because of course it did. I didn't post anything that came out wrong.

All in all, it was a near-as-dammit perfect afternoon. Mum had a lovely birthday. Her friends almost certainly felt bad about themselves but didn't make a fuss about it. Andrea replied to me, and in that moment, the world began to turn.

'*That looks great,*' she wrote. '*Thank you for making my recipes part of your mam's special day. Hugs, A.*'

Hugs.

All those months, waiting for a '*Ha*' or a '*Cheers*'. The others must have been weeping into their vodka, cursing my name, wishing me a future of failure and blisters, but instead, what I got was – '*Hugs*'.

I know what you're thinking, and maybe I should feel guilty. Hugs, even typed ones, should be for people who aren't actively trying to make other people feel bad. However, it's something that's come about relatively recently. I've decided to stop making myself feel bad about the beginnings of things.

I came home – not because my mother was ill but because my life fell apart. I cooked for my mother's birthday, not because I'd remembered, but to destroy a large group of middle-aged women, while impressing another one.

Anyway, there we were – I'd posted a bunch of pictures, Andrea had responded with kindness and I knew I'd have to be very clever with my next move. If I'd gone straight into a whole long speech about how much I thought of her, how much I'd like to meet her, how important we could be to each other, that would have been an error. I imagine I would have sounded like a telemarketer. I can imagine little worse.

And so, I played it cool. Liked her comment and moved on. There were two solid days when I didn't post anything at all.

It was torture.

I kept up with her posts, obviously, and I was very excited to hear more about her house-move, but I didn't respond to any of it. Not a word.

I had an ache in my chest for hours. There was a tightness. I couldn't tell you where it came from or how to stop it, but it seemed to be in every room. Following me around. A tightness of being. I could breathe, I ate, I slept, but there was something constricted about every minute.

And so, we come to Andrea's change of address. She didn't say where she was going. It wouldn't have been safe for her to do that, but there were pictures. Nothing too specific. No town names or famous skylines. Just pictures of fields – yellow, purple and green – the same fields you get all over the country. And in my silence and tightness, I let myself believe that she might just come to Shropshire.

There was a lot of talk about whether she would be promoting local produce in her new series. It would make sense. She's always been a champion of local produce. My picking the supermarket clean for my mother's birthday aside, I thought a lot about local spinach.

Quick bit of internet searching and I discovered that spinach grows best in Lincolnshire. Maybe the others checked, or even knew that sort of thing. I had to put in the effort. And so, we waited. Patience went from thin to skeletal to pile of ash and then, quite suddenly:

'Will definitely be getting my spinach locally.'

Oh, the hope. I rechecked. Lincolnshire was about three hours away if I drove like the wind. It would mean leaving Shropshire but there was time. I could talk myself into it. Given time.

Really, travel time would depend on which bit of Lincolnshire she was moving to. I was sure I'd be able to borrow Mum's car. She didn't use it, but it had been her pride and joy; she didn't want to part with it. Naturally, I didn't know whether there was enough petrol in the tank to get to France or the end of the road, but I could check that later. Part of me wondered if it wouldn't just be easier to get the train and find a taxi at the station, but that might have been difficult, given that I'd have spent my retirement fund on the train ticket. I'd need to be pretty sure of whereabouts in Lincolnshire I'd be aiming for and then just work out whether it would be an idea to walk the rest of the way. Because I didn't want to look... One *'Hugs'* comment wasn't really enough to justify searching a whole county for one house and then kipping on her porch.

And then, I saw it. Lincolnshire was 2,687 square miles, all told, which is pretty massive, I think you'd agree.

'There's a big garden,' she went on, *'with space for a vegetable patch worthy of self-sufficiency in the 70s, an orangery for the more exotic plants, and already a few bee hives in situ. Will only need shops for newspapers and cheese. Bliss.'*

Brilliant, I thought. If the spinach can come from her new garden, she could be going anywhere. I wouldn't be looking for a needle in a haystack, so much as looking for a needle in the world. Presumably, she'd be staying on land, so that narrowed it down a bit.

Under other circumstances, it might have been enough to know I was in the same hemisphere as her. Better, the same century, the same country. Practically neighbours, then.

But all the time I was wondering about yellow, purple and green fields and the possibilities of an orangery, someone blew the world apart. Forgive the hyperbole – someone started getting stroppy with Andrea.

It was the bread-sniffer. He needed her postal address to send her a happy housewarming card. It was important, he said. She stayed silent, and the angrier he got, the more frightening he sounded.

She didn't need to respond. Her mega fans came to her aid and I stayed on the sidelines. Like an idiot. It wasn't as if I didn't want to defend her. I just – didn't know what to say.

'*Why won't you just narrow it down to a region?*' he asked. '*It's not as if it won't be up online inside an afternoon anyway, and you're bound to have security people. You're hardly defenceless. Just tell us where you're going!!!*'

Three exclamation marks.

Well, she's bound to tell him now!

What a douche.

It's not as if I can't sympathise. Getting a bit soft about a famous person isn't that unusual. Any number of us might look up to someone who's talented because – maybe we're talented, too, or we've been told we're talented, or maybe we've even wondered what would happen if we were told such a thing. We all seek to identify with others. It's the human condition.

'*Leave her alone,*' a deeply imaginative defender says.

'*Yeah, back off, you oddball,*' another one chips in.

They have all the clever arguments, you see.

After about twenty minutes of dithering, he comes back with, '*I'm surprised the #SpinachGirl hasn't spoken up. I suppose you realise she was using you for the publicity, Andrea? The whole 'mother's birthday' was probably designed to pluck the heartstrings and you went ahead and fell for it. At least I'm honest. I just want to send a card.*'

Well, there was only one thing that could happen. My heart freaking stopped. The blood stood still in my veins. My throat closed. It could have been a blackout, I suppose, but it wasn't as if I passed out. It was a step beyond clarity. I could see my fingers on the keyboard. I heard myself typing. I couldn't really see the words. All I knew was darkness and a now familiar need to destroy a fellow human being.

'*Just realised who you remind me of. There was a girl I knew at school. A horrible bully who picked on everyone because she had no self-esteem. She married a man who looked like her Mum & now she doesn't get invited anywhere. Good luck with that. #SpinachMeUp #MicDropMoment* '

Well, the world went totally insane. Within the hour, all things spinach were trending, including me. There were thousands of Likes, hundreds of retweets and Andrea sent me a private message. To begin with, I assumed it was someone from her team, but by that point, I was hyperventilating. The second message was much shorter and there was no question in my mind – it was from her.

In no time at all, there were articles and interviews. Hardly any of it about me, not really. Most of it was about the rise of antisocial behaviour on social media and why people act like other people's feelings don't count when they're looking at a computer screen with only a bag of crisps and their farts for company.

Like everybody else, I thought it would fizzle out quickly. Mum and Dad were just flabbergasted by the whole thing. Every time I wandered into the kitchen, apparently, I was on the phone. I don't think it was quite that bad. Seemingly, it was. Quite soon after the #SpinachMeUp moment, I started the blog. It would be silly not to. I was like Batman with a Wordpress account, fighting injustice with stories of old school friends and people who hated everyone.

Messages filled my inbox. I struggled to keep up. Comments came flying left and right. People agreed, people argued. I went from 56 followers to nearly twelve thousand and, more importantly, a conversation had begun.

I don't mean in the general sense, although there was that, too. I mean Andrea was speaking to me.

There were a few weeks between my hashtag moment and the housewarming. I didn't dare hope for an invitation. I calmed myself down, like a hero. But from what she'd said, she was going to cook. Her husband was going to be away somewhere, filming for some series no one really cared about. She wasn't prepared to wait for him to be back in the country. Andrea Pinchbeck had a house to warm.

She'd already had a lot of RSVPs before she sent the last of the invites.

The posts came thick and fast. She was pleased that the bathroom had been fixed before the masses would descend. There had been a knocking in the pipework, like a bunch of rich boys rattling their empty pint glasses.

She was expecting so many. She knew everyone. Daytime, primetime, late night, breakfast TV, all of them. They would all be there, sucking up the nibbles and updating their own accounts with pictures of drinks and extreme close-ups – an earring, a selfie that was mostly nostril, the pinkish corner of an eye.

And here I am, the morning after, hung-over, exhausted. Might as well have a little look – see if she's posted…

Oh, my God. There they are. Of course, the pictures Andrea posted during the party were a little blurry. I wouldn't have thought of it before but now I know – it's better not to be too precise about where everyone is – you never know when the house-sniffer might be reading.

I don't need to double-check who was at the party. Apart from Andrea, I couldn't begin to care. The thing I'm really looking for is how many shots we did. From the fur on my tongue, I'd guess about a hundred.

That's not right.

Seven?

No. She just hasn't put up all the pictures yet. Maybe it just hit me harder because I could only find Grand Marnier at the back of the drinks' cabinet. The back of the drinks' cabinet is, naturally, reserved for the drinks we don't go near, except in cases of desperation.

Words will be had. Grand Marnier might seem like a decent enough substitute for Cointreau but it doesn't sit the same way. I don't think it goes off. Although that would explain the smell.

I recognised the soap star straight away. Forget the blurriness, even with a drink in one hand and a mushroom frittata in the other, those lip fillers have been part of my Monday, Wednesday and Friday nights for the last six months. We're practically family now.

The woman with her, I think, was a producer. I don't really know what a producer does. She might have been doing it even as she reached for – what looks like onion dip. In the photo, she looks like she's been caught dipping a breadstick into someone else's husband. Whatever she is, she's not an actress, I'm sure of that.

At least, I hope not. That would be embarrassing.

Andrea's not in every picture but when she does appear, she's breathtaking. Her smile is easy and relaxed, impossibly white. Paper white. I can't help but wonder if her teeth are capped. Certainly, the afternoon I lost looking for her high school photos online left me no closer to knowing whether or not her current toothy-pegs are actually made of bone. Always gorgeous, but it doesn't look like she smiled, even in passing, before 1992.

It's harder to explain myself. I am the Spinach Girl: watching, reading, liking the better pictures of the night; a night I missed, sitting on the end of my bed with a bottle of Grand Marnier, picturing myself there. She didn't come to Shropshire.

On reflection, I think I would have enjoyed it more if I were there. I could have got a whole heap of selfies with stars who have whole teams of people to maintain their makeup for them, instead of sitting in a room that used to house my beanie babies.

Some of the actors haven't posted their thanks yet. Some may be feeling a little worse for wear. Some might not be awake yet. Maybe they're in bed. Maybe they're in hospital.

I only notice Dad's head, popped around the doorframe, when he speaks. "Darling, I need to nip out for a few. There's some problem at the Shrewsbury office. Could take a while. Are you – are you going anywhere this afternoon?"

I just smile. He knows I don't go out unless I have to. The world is big and invitations are meaningless; most people have learnt not to ask me out.

"I was just hoping you'd keep an eye on your mum for me. She's had her pills and she's got everything she needs but – she had a bit of a difficult night."

"Was I singing too loudly?" I ask.

He just smiles. "Just keep an ear out for her, eh? For your old dad?"

"Sure."

There is no pen nearby, so he says it: "You are made of magic and you are the most important thing in the world to your mother and me. Her pills are due again at six."

"Yes, Dad."

And away he goes with a classic boy-scout salute. I listen to his engine argue with him in the driveway before he sets off. I don't know why he doesn't take Mum's car. It's both old and sporty – therefore, a classic. Smooth lines, low-slung, growls at every traffic light. It makes an impression. He spends hours polishing it on the off-chance Mum fancies a little blast across the countryside but she rarely does.

I spend a few hours, looking at the swirls in the ceiling, drinking coffee and counting my blinks per minute.

Around two o'clock, Andrea posts again.

'Great night, everyone. I think that's the house warmed up now. Very good luck to Seb and his book signing this afternoon. Couldn't be more proud if we were related x.'

And there's a photo of the two of them. I don't recognise anything in the background. I see what might be the edge of a church, but that could be anywhere.

Lots of suck-up messages from simpletons wishing Seb all the best and ignoring the fact that he forgot to thank Andrea in his first book.

Seb is a former student. You probably remember the story: he cooked something for her and she saved him from dole-queue obscurity. It's a long story and it's not really important. Except that he has a book signing, and she's clearly with him.

Sometimes, we get a second chance.

I need something practical to give me a direction to head in. This is so thoughtless. She makes a detective of me. I wonder if anyone else would go to all this trouble...

I check Seb's profile. He's wearing one of Andrea's spinach shirts. Damn leech.

'Good afternoon, Stafford!' he bellows from the page. *'Looking forward to seeing you all later on when I'll be taking over the Wandering Bishop Bookshop with books, t-shirts, general merch and appetisers! Plus, some special guests!'*

Quick Google. Nothing serious. It's not as if I can't control myself.

How far away is Stafford?

Fifty-two miles.

Dear God, fifty-two miles. Fifty-two miles away from the house. I can't. I won't.

All the way to the kitchen, I know I can't do it.

I won't do it. I'm not invited. It's weird.

Even as I upend the bottle and chug milk down the drain, I can't. I won't.

"Mum?"

Silence.

"Mum, we're out of milk!" I call. "I need to pop out and get some. Will you be all right for a little while?"

She sounds pretty positive but it's really just a humming sound. She's probably got a pen between her teeth. She's doing the crossword.

"I won't be long," I say, snatching up the keys. "Don't mind if I borrow your car, do you?"

"What's that, love?"

"Thanks, Mum."

She won't even know I'm gone.

I can do this.

If This Were A Swedish Film, We'd Already Be In Love: A Brief History of Fiona

1975

JANUARY

Let's face it. You shouldn't be reading this.

No, wait! Please, don't go.

Although this may look like a diary, with days and months and a place for addresses (which I'll leave blank to maintain the privacy of the seven people whose addresses I have; I don't like to brag but yeah, seven), and as much as it came with a strap from back to front that closes in a lock which is secured with a very thin gold key that looks like it might melt if I left it too long on my windowsill – this is not a diary.

This is an art project.

Having talked it over with Mr. O'Brien, and been told in no uncertain terms that I should not make it too personal, I intend to complete this only slightly diary-like book with the events of my life from now until the end of 1979.

Over the months and years, I suspect I'll change pens, switch the ink from black to red, there may be an occasional pencil, my handwriting might change (there are bound to be nights when I'm too tired to focus and my handwriting will spill and shift from cloudlike to spidery), and once it's all over, I'll reopen this book, yank out its pages, tear them apart, and reassemble them to make a self-portrait.

I fully expect more than one pen to leak. There may be an occasional tea stain or a spray of perfume, depending on mood. Both tea and perfume fade with time and so, this piece will keep evolving as it ages. Which is only fair. I plan to do the same.

I cannot be afraid of what would happen if anyone found and read this book because that is the point of it. Of course, it will be more viewed than read. At least, I hope so.

If it's not actually good enough for a place on the wall, this piece will represent an incredible waste of time and, in all probability, a desperate search for something to write about. It's not like *The Riordans*. In real life, there can be weeks, even months, when nothing much happens at all, at least in my experience.

Enough of that. I'm going to try to keep this light and bouncy. Not too personal, not too fraught. Should be easy enough. I have no major neuroses, if you don't count my mother, and am not expecting any.

Further proof that this is not a real diary: I'm going to introduce myself. I very much doubt anyone does that in a proper diary. And besides, this thing will want signing anyway.

My name is Fiona Weaver. I'm sixteen and live, surprisingly enough, at home with my parents. My whole life has been spent in this house. We don't go away, as a family. Daddy keeps odd hours, he has to, it's his job. Mammy always lays the table as if we're expecting company. Not sure who she thinks might come for dinner, but if they ever show up, they'll have to bring their own oregano. My mother doesn't much go in for herbs. I don't think that's too personal. It's not a judgement. It's an observation.

I plan for the diary-portrait to be complete when I finish university. It feels like a long way off but my mother assures me I was a toddler last week so, perhaps not.

I assume there'll be a final show at the end of university. Not sure how many pieces I'll need for it; I'll find that out closer to the time.

Fact is, this portrait will take the longest to create. I don't suppose any of the exhibition pieces are supposed to take longer than the degree itself but this one will.

I must go to university or risk hearing about it for the rest of my life. Mammy didn't go and I'm going to have to remember to tear through this bit.

I'm from a long line of doctors and sensible people. I think an artist is a fine change of pace. Maybe even an evolutionary step. After all, it used to be the poets who held the top spot in Irish society. So why not a painter?

Of course, this can't be helped. I'm bound to tell you a fair bit about myself but whatever happens, I'll flick back to this page and remind myself that this is art.

This is not about me.

Not directly. Not intentionally. Maybe a little bit. I'm working on the theory that people are composed of their words and thoughts, and, in practical terms, this made more sense than recording my voice and sticking strips of cassette tape to a canvas.

I suppose it would be tempting to believe that, when I rip this book up, I'll be tearing apart the person I used to be. It might be like a rebirth. For those who might believe that's what I'm doing, I've got to remind you – this is a self-portrait. This is the opposite of getting rid of me.

God, I hope I still think this way in five years' time.

FEBRUARY

The Leaving Cert won't be for ages but I feel like I'm drowning already. Wondering if I'll be able to worry, non-stop, for another two years. Leaning towards a great big shiny 'yes' on that one. I have a talent for worrying myself silly. Mammy says it's my age but lord knows how she worked that out. There's no way she could remember. They didn't have teenagers when she was young.

I'm not too concerned about English or Irish, and Art should be fine (at least, I hope so, otherwise, I don't know what I'm going to do with my life and I'll probably wind up drinking too much and despairing of the broken veins where my face used to be, so yeah, art had better work out). My Geography is limited to the areas I've actually visited: school, Papa's house, the city centre, and bingo that one time. And Maths is an evil beast-monster.

Nina says she doesn't want to be a millionaire largely because she can't count that high. For years, apparently, she'd count up to nineteen and go straight back to ten. She had to concentrate really hard to get to the number twenty. Nina says numbers should come in two categories: lots and not-a-lot. We had to write out pretend cheques in After School Skills at the library, and I stayed back late while she experimented with decimal points in place of her usual commas. She held the cheque up to the light and frowned at it. The librarian came over to help her.

'Why do we have to learn this?' Nina huffed.

'Sometimes, a cheque is easier than cash. This is a worthwhile life skill,' the librarian offered, although she didn't sound convinced.

'Jesus,' she said, *'I'm just going to become a jewel thief and be done with it.'*

She's so funny. It's good to have a funny best friend.

I've had this feeling – that's the word, it's a feeling – for Nina since we were eleven. It's not a crush. I can't bear the idea of a crush. It's cutesy and simpering and eugh. No. What I feel for Nina is – it's not-the-life-and-death-of-everything, but it's not a sissy crush-thing either. It's not candles and flowers and all that stuff.

All it is... I consider her more important and special, than anyone else. It's not romantic. It's just – something. Something different. I don't harbour much in terms of emotions. I'm not fraught with feelings that might be demons, and thoughts I can't control. I don't have that part of myself. Maybe it's because I draw. My feelings don't have time to fester because I scratch them into pages, into paper, out of me.

It's not a crush. I just really like her.

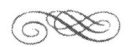

MARCH

Mammy's written a letter of complaint about the chickens next door. She's told Mr. Flaherty that she doesn't mind them waking her up on Sundays – they save her setting her alarm clock – but she doesn't care to be woken that early for the rest of the week. *Could he, perhaps, train his rooster to crow only after 8 o'clock, Monday-Saturday?* Wondering what sort of letter she'll get back.

Enda Flaherty, for the sake of posterity, has been making my life a misery since before school. He used to pull my pigtails. He used to trip me over in the playground. He used to call me names and then get me to do his homework for him. I'm going to take some consolation in the fact that now, posterity knows: Enda Flaherty is a gowl, a terrible bully and I hope to snip him out of my life as soon as possible.

One of my old teachers, whose name I've chosen to forget (Miss Twomey. Dammit), once said that Enda only picked on me because he liked me. Mammy said it was little wonder Miss Twomey wasn't married.

No, Enda Flaherty has made it very clear, since we were babies, he doesn't like me in the slightest. Lord knows, I can't imagine anyone liking him. Maybe that's been the problem all along. Maybe he's so un-liked that he has to pass the pain along. To me.

Anyway, he lives and works at the chicken farm next door and I have to see him over the fence every day. Mammy says he needs a haircut and a damn good wash. She also says I'm not to repeat that to another living soul.

It's okay. I'm not breaking a promise. You're a piece of paper.

⁂

APRIL

Daddy's been working nights. If I didn't know he was still asleep, I could tell by the consistency of the porridge these days. Mammy doesn't like porridge. She's never liked porridge. She'd rather have a fried egg sandwich but Daddy likes porridge, so she makes it every day. But, with him still asleep, I think she forgets about it on the stove, so it just sits there and bubbles, getting thicker and thicker, until you could stand a spoon up in it. By the time she scrapes the pan and pitches it out, it's like wallpaper paste, sliding down the inside of the bin liner, not reaching the bottom until the evening news.

It wouldn't really bother me except that, since my last birthday, the washing up duty is mine. Mammy will soak the porridge pan to save me the effort (such an effort), but it gets this papery crust that hangs in towards the middle of the pan by the time I get to it. Meanwhile, the bottom of the pan gets all gloopy and revolting in the soak of water. Seems pointless, clogging up sponge after sponge, and stuffing the pipes under the sink, for a breakfast that nobody wants.

Spring has sprung. The air smells lighter, with only a hint of chicken. The cherry blossom is out. Daddy says he'll give it three days to stay on the tree and then it'll start covering his car every night.

Last year, all the blossoms fell during a storm, and covered the whole driveway. For the first few days, it looked like we'd been to a wedding, but once the sunshine came back and the petals started to toast, it looked like we'd been attacked by a flock of incontinent seagulls. I'm sure he'd park it next door, except it's a bit of a toss-up as to which is worse: old cherry blossoms or splatters of farmyard.

MAY

Mammy has started visiting people who can't get out much. She says it's in preparation for when I leave home and she doesn't have so much to do. It's a church scheme, I think. People who are sickly, elderly or don't have family nearby now get weekly visits from my mother.

I'm saying nothing.

All I can think is: armed with her Jackie Kennedy handbag with the angry snap, her powder pink turban and her smile slashing her face in half, they must be a pretty desperate bunch. And if they weren't before, they must be by now.

JUNE

Have started working on Saturdays. Nothing special. Record store in town. No staff discount, but at least with my own money now, I'm not stuck with Mammy's taste in music. Listening to Captain and Tennille. I don't dare turn the volume all the way up until she goes to bingo.

Enda came skulking in on my second shift. He had his shirt open to halfway down his chest. When he saw me, he spun round and when he turned back, he'd re-buttoned. I might have allowed myself to think he was being considerate but Nina says he probably didn't want to show me his chest hairs, given that there are only three of them. She's so funny.

My supervisor decided that, since she's nearly twenty-four, I should be the one to go over and assist Enda with his browsing. I thought about feigning a severe bout of lady-problems but, by the time I reached for my stomach, she was already pushing me out across the floor.

She deposited me beside him and I just stood there, like a standard lamp with elbows, while she nodded for me to talk to him.

'Can I...?' I cleared my throat. '*Can I help you with anything?*'

He mumbled. I had to strain to listen. I might have pulled a muscle. '*Need something for... mother's birthday... yesterday.*'

'Oh, well,' but I got no further. He considered the ABBA album for a moment, then he went for Made In The Shade instead. Don't understand how his mother can be so cool when Enda's so... Oh, God. The album's his, isn't it? Not sure how I'm supposed to feel about the Rolling Stones anymore.

⁂

JULY

Finding myself getting angry for no reason. Everything annoys me lately. Gave a customer the wrong change and I kind of bit his head off.

Tore up the start of a self-portrait.

Jabbed myself in the mouth with my fork from dinner. I'm eating in a huff. That can't be right.

Mammy folds her arms and shakes her head at me. Sometimes, she mutters, '*Puberty*'. She says it louder when I roll my eyes.

Only person who seems to understand is the cat that isn't really ours. She comes in from time to time. Daddy and I have been feeding her sardines, so maybe she's adopted us. Neither of us has bothered to name her. She jumps onto my bed sometimes, forcing me to get my head out of the pillow and dry my face. It shouldn't be like this.

Nina has started going out with Enda Flaherty.

⁂

AUGUST

The days are not just stretching out, it's like they're rolling around in something. Fed up with seeing Nina over the fence. She seems to be there all the time and, frankly, I have no idea why she has Enda walk her past the chickens so often. It's clearly not his idea; she basically drags him along behind her. Even if she has a soft spot for poultry, how much can really change in a single day? Every day, like clockwork, there they are again.

Anyway, I think I'm going to have to ask around for another job, if only to get me out of the house and away from them and all their chicken-staring.

Mammy hates the idea. She said, having gone to all the trouble of marrying a doctor, learning to make porridge and building me in her lady-cavern, the least I could do was to not bring shame upon the family by working two jobs. Too exhausted to argue. Think I'll just look for a single job, with more hours.

See, we all have that one person in our lives who talks as if there's going to be a pop quiz at the end. Just to check you've been paying attention. They usually arch their eyebrows quite a lot. It's as if they don't even know they're mimicking every cartoon villain ever.

For myself, that person has always been Maeve. Apparently, she was a very reasonable person before she became my mother. I imagine that's quite true.

SEPTEMBER

Well, it only took eight and a half months for her to notice –
Mammy: So, it's a diary...
Me: Yes.
Mammy: But people are allowed to read it?
Me: Well, not exactly read...
Mammy: Even strangers?
Me: Well, it won't really be legible.
Mammy: How can it not be?
Me: I'm going to tear it up.

Mammy: Then what's the point of doing it?

Me: (blinking too much) It's art.

Mammy: Oh, I see! It's a-art. (She stretches this last word out to annoy me. I insist on it not working even as a muscle twitches underneath my eye.)

New school term. Going to force myself to concentrate more in Maths. Really falling behind in it and working at the record shop, using the till and making change, hasn't helped at all. I can't think when I'll ever need algebra but I'm going to master it on the off chance that people replace all numbers with letters, which I really think would be a good idea. Still not a hundred percent on the seven times table so anything that reduces how many numbers I genuinely have to know about is fine by me.

Got a haircut on the day before the new term. Must remember not to do that again. I need a few weeks to get my hair into some sort of order before I inflict it on the general public.

Enda Flaherty all over Nina. He might as well have her stand still so he can piss in a circle around her. Wouldn't be so bad if she was anyone else. Don't know why she doesn't think enough of herself to find someone better. Which, given who she's going out with, is honestly anybody else. The cat that isn't really ours would make a better choice.

OCTOBER

Halloween. Best time of year. The leaves are turning rusty. We haven't got too far into the party season so my hair is less of an issue than it might have been otherwise. With the nights starting earlier, there's somehow more time to read. Maths is improving. I've finished all my reading homework weeks before I needed to, so have got myself into some Saul Bellow. Sure, he must have been in a bit of a huff when he wrote *Herzog*.

People seem to need more records to pass the time so the shop is busy. Even Mammy has found space in her life for Glen Campbell. She says he looks like Daddy. He doesn't, but it helps her to think so, so I leave it. Daddy just looks over his glasses at her. I don't think he knows who Glen Campbell is so he doesn't say anything.

NOVEMBER

And my mother's started planning what we call my birthday party but what is, in fact, a party for my parents – to celebrate the day they had a baby. It's a bit like Christmas, just a week early.

It'll start very early in the morning. Mammy will wake me with breakfast in bed and tell me whether I've started looking my age. We'll get the presents out of the way because *'they clutter up the place'* and then Mammy will spend at least two hours hoovering the living room and polishing the doilies before Papa and Aunt Pat and Uncle Byron come over.

There'll be jellied vegetables and a mutton and mash igloo and, at some point, she'll have Daddy carve a melon into the shape of a swan.

It all sounds like a lot of work and Papa will roll his eyes a bit to make me laugh but it'll be great, really. Nina will be there. She's promised not to bring Enda.

DECEMBER

My birthday. Mammy didn't bother telling me how old I look. She woke me with, *'Happy Birthday, you're so odd,'* and putting a tray over my bed with a cake on it.

I'd the fairest head of hair that anyone had ever seen at Mallow General Hospital. Almost silver, I know this because my mother has told everyone she's met in the last seventeen years this story, including, very often, me. *Her silver beauty*, she called me. I was the first girl in my father's family for forty years, but around the age of four and a quarter, I turned dark and broke her heart, and that's where the story ends.

My parents' friends keep asking how old I am. It's as if they think I have no other conversation. All that happens is – I tell them I'm seventeen and they ask me how school is and which subjects I like best. When I say, *'Art,'* they look like they don't know what to say and my mother shakes her head from across the room. Papa smiles. It's good to have an ally.

'How old are you?' – It's right up there with, *'How much do you weigh?'* and *'What's your bra size?'* – there are things you don't ask so much as guess.

1976

JANUARY

New Year's Party at the church. They'd saved over the tinsel from Christmas and put up a homemade banner so it was all very festive in a tragic sort of way.

Nina is still in Drogheda, visiting her cousins, but Enda Flaherty was there. He opened his jacket to show off his new shirt, and then poured himself over this frankly flabbergasted girl, leaned in and whispered something to her. Whatever it was, she turned bright red and, before long, he spilt his drink all over his shoes and glared at her like it was her fault.

Didn't get to hear too much about it on the night because her boyfriend came over to them – all smiles and snake hips – and gave him a good thump.

Everybody laughed. I tried to keep myself quiet by sipping my punch. Several of the others had said they were going to add vodka, schnapps, whiskey, or whatever they could borrow from home, to the aforementioned punch but I don't think they did. I didn't even hum, much less sing.

On his way out into the night, Enda shoved me, and hissed that I was to keep my mouth shut if I saw Nina before he did.

I wish the other fella had knocked out a couple of teeth, just to make it worthwhile. Checked with Daddy, and it sounds like Enda will have healed up by the time Nina comes home. It's a pretty vicious looking black eye and people will be talking about it for months to come – there's not a lot of news round this way lately – but I reckon he'll play it down. Sure, he'll probably make himself out the hero. What an awful thought.

See, the important thing about this five-year-diary-that's-not-a-diary is I have to remind myself that it's an art piece. It's not really about giving myself an outlet, until I tear it up and turn it into me.

The other marvel is that I don't have to make a New Year's Resolution. I don't think I believe in them. Just a lot of fuss that forces everyone to spy on each other to see who's slipped and gone back to smoking, drinking and mad acts of carnality before we've even got through the second week of January.

No. My New Year's Resolution is a five-year resolution. I will be busy and fabulous enough to keep this thing full until the end.

FEBRUARY

Mr. O'Brien asked me to stay after class. He wondered if he'd seen me working at the record shop in town. Well, I couldn't begin to know what he'd seen but I decided, rather than be a pedant about it, I'd just nod.

'Well,' he said, *'are you happy there?'*

I didn't know what to say. I'm not unhappy there. It gets me out of the house. I don't have to watch Enda and Nina as they walk among the chickens. I just shrugged.

And then he told me: a friend of his runs an art gallery a few streets away from the record shop. She's been looking for someone responsible and clean who can package up paintings, get them ready for delivery, and talk to customers, if necessary. Mr. O'Brien wondered if I'd like him to put my name forward. My mouth fell open. He blathered a bit – I'd gone very quiet. He said he'd be happy to give me a reference – as a responsible, clean, occasionally talking person. I hadn't said anything at this point.

'If you'd like the job, that is...?' he stumbled.

'Yes,' I managed. *'I – I can talk.'*

Can't really escape the image of myself, putting little red stickers on the walls and making hats out of bubble wrap.

Think I'd need to be better dressed for a gallery job. It's not the sort of thing that comes with a uniform. I'll need sleek lines. Maybe a long black skirt and white blouse, to set off the bubble wrap hat.

Mammy says if I'm going to work in a *'better class of shop'* – there's no talking to her – then I'm going to have to stop biting my nails. She's trying again with the clear nail varnish. Didn't work when I was little, can't think it'll do the trick now. Still, with a solid goal in mind, I might be able to get control of myself and move on to nail clippers.

Caught Enda Flaherty staring at me from over the chicken fence. He looked around for a moment and, truth be told, I thought he was going to say something cruel, like he normally does. Instead, he threw an egg. He missed me, but managed to get Dad's car. Daddy came storming out of the house and ran down the drive, shaking his crossword puzzle at him and shouting. I've never seen Enda move so fast. I didn't know he *could* move so fast. He's not really the right shape for speed. He's a bit square about the shoulder for running.

We found out later that the egg wasn't fresh.

Daddy's livid. Mammy says we'll still be smelling it in the summer and that I shouldn't antagonise the local lads.

MARCH

Handed in my notice at the record shop. Got myself quite worried beforehand. Thought I might be letting them down if I offered any less than a months' notice.

Annie said that, ordinarily, they'd want me to carry on for two weeks or – *'...however long it takes to find a replacement. We don't usually have to wait that long.'*

I must have done that thing with my face because, quite quickly, she came back with, *'Actually, if you could give us the full two-weeks, that would be... great, you know.'*

Don't know whether she meant it or not, but now I have two weeks to find the perfect, sophisticated but understated outfit, and convince Mr. O'Brien's friend to hire me at the art gallery.

He let slip that the gallery owner, Mallory (love it), only stocks local artists. If she has any interest in young painters who mostly work in biro, this could be the start of something serious. Trying not to think too much about that. I know if I think too hard about it and don't get the job, I'll lose all my weekends to hidden snacks and 10cc records.

Mammy says I should go for the interview after three days in the same clothes and very little sleep. Her thinking is: I should get the job because I know my stuff, not because I look right. She didn't quite say it that way.

'You know, sweetheart, I think you've a lovely face, but if you wear a lot of makeup and dress yourself up smartly, you'll just be making a rod for your own back in the long run. If she doesn't want you with your own face, she doesn't deserve you covered in glitter.'

On the other hand, Nina's been really supportive. She suggested we go out for a bite to eat in town, afterwards – to give me something on the other side of the interview to focus on. It's strange how she knows me so well. It's lovely, actually.

APRIL

Nina spent an hour on my hair before the interview. I was just about to head downstairs when she grabbed my arm, dug into her pocket for her lipstick and put it on me. She had this intense look in her eyes while she did it. All I could think about was how quickly I'd have to get past Mammy in the kitchen to avoid getting a talking-to.

Had a drink with Nina at the Sin é in the evening, music banging through my brain, and got some chips on the way to the bus. Nina got off before me – obviously, because she had to go home – but she gave me a peck on the cheek before she even stood up.

I decided not to take the short cut and walked the long lane down to the house, to think about my day. Enda Flaherty leaned over the fence and asked me why I was all dressed up. Didn't much want to tell him and I like the idea of being a figure of intrigue, at least for a few days, so I just smiled.

He asked if there was some sort of 'dyke convention' in town. He had a good chuckle to himself and told me I must be completed deluded if I thought Nina would ever go out with someone like me.

I lack the parts she really loves. He didn't say it in those words exactly.

I'm ashamed of myself.

I couldn't speak.

I tried to keep my head down and walk faster, but it's not the easiest thing to do in long grass when you're wearing pleats.

He followed me along the fence for a while. Told me I shouldn't wear skirts. It wasn't fair, he said, for me to try to be pretty when it was clear I wasn't interested in boys.

He's such a shit. I suppose it's a bit of luck I won't have to see him on weekends anymore. I start at the Mallory Gallery on Saturday morning. I know I should be excited about it but, if I'm honest, I'm feeling pretty dismal at the moment.

MAY

Well, you know what? The hell with Enda Flaherty. Mammy always says only the chronically insecure try to bring other people down, and they only do it so they'll have some company.

When I told her the story, I left out the 'd' word. No need to confuse the issue.

Didn't speak to Nina for a few days after what Enda said. It would be different if I knew for sure that she hadn't asked him to say something. But the more it went round in my head, the more convinced I became that she might actually despise me, but be too polite to say so. Maybe she needed Enda to say it for her because, blunt as he is, he'd get it said.

Staring at my wallpaper in the moonlight, I realised it's just the way of things: some people are always more liking than liked. I mean, I've seen it. It's the lover and the loved. The carer and the cared-for. They're always the same people. Maybe that makes sense. Still thinking about it.

But there must be some people who are destined to love more than they can be loved in return. We're not talking about love here, of course. It's just a friendship. A close friendship but no, actually – not *just* a friendship. Definitely a friendship. Why should friends be regarded as a lower form of relationship? Nina is certainly my friend and, if I like her more than she likes me, what does it matter?

No. Enda Flaherty can go and clean out his chickens.

Just as Mammy seemed to soften, she went and said the worst thing possible.

Mammy: You know, if this art thing doesn't work out, you can always stay home and take care of your father.

Me: Why? What's wrong with him?

Mammy: Well, nothing. Not yet. But we'll all need looking after one of these days, and you're like me – you're a giver. You need someone to take care of. And it'd give you some purpose.

She knows I can't bear it when she calls it 'this art thing'. She waves her hand dismissively. She might as well carry a balled-up handkerchief and sniffle for dramatic purposes.

JUNE

It is so hot. Just impossibly hot. It must be awful in the record shop right now. If it turns out all the vinyl has melted and made sticky black puddles in the carpet, I plan to exhibit no surprise. Largely, because it's too hot to go around moving my face on purpose.

The air is thick. Irish air isn't supposed to be thick. It's meant to be damp. Not misty, as such, but something close. Cool and spitty.

This is different. Every breath is thick. It's like soup. Chewable air – if anyone had the will to chew anymore, but it's too much effort. It shouldn't be possible to sweat through a t-shirt just through the effort of sitting and yet, here we are.

I don't know how Mallory manages in her poncho. She says she holds her face up with a very expensive cream from Paris. I suspect some surgery but she's such great company, I don't plan to bring it up. She says the cream is useful because, when selling art, it's good not to look too keen. A big toothy grin and lots of nodding might be the natural reaction but, even to the novice art buyer, it looks like you can't believe they'll pay the asking price.

We have a lot of electric fans going in the gallery. They're not for Mallory or me, or even the clients. They're for the art. The more delicate pieces are in the back but we've got to protect the floor works as best we can.

Mammy isn't sure she approves of my new perfume. She thinks it's too peppery. Perhaps it fits better with the gallery than it does at home but I like it. She says it wouldn't go over well at bingo. It would distract people.

In positive news: I am now excused from bingo.

JULY

Not sure what Enda said to Nina but whatever it was, she wound up coming over after lunch and staying 'til it was dark out. We mostly just listened to music. At one point, I think I was changing the LP from ABBA to Chicago, she went all serious.

'Enda wants to stay here,' she said. 'He doesn't want to go away to study, or to travel or anything else. It's like he's got no ambition. He just wants to drink beer with his friends and laugh at the people he used to pick on.'

Used to. I left it alone.

'You're going away after the exams, aren't you?' she asked.

'Well, not right away,' I managed. She has the bluest eyes. 'I'll need to stay and earn some money first.'

'See, but that's it,' she said. 'You have plans. You know what you're going to do.'

'I know what I want to do,' I hedged.

She looked me square in the eye. 'You know you make it really hard for people to like you when you've such a poor opinion of yourself.'

And it wasn't like a telling-off. It was really beautiful. I swear, I didn't blink for a whole minute. I just looked at her.

And then Mammy appeared at the door. 'What are you girls up to in here? Lordy, how is it still so hot? Anyway, I thought you'd want some squash.'

She had a tray. There were sandwiches cut into triangles and pre-bent plastic straws in the thinnest orange squash imaginable. Like, as pale as you picture it, and then cut it in half.

Nina made her excuses and left. I didn't get off the floor for a few hours after that.

AUGUST

Sometimes I wonder, if I concentrate really hard, empty my mind completely, no distractions and just focus, I wonder if I could make Enda Flaherty's brain explode inside his head.

I think the problem would be distance. I wouldn't want to be nearby when it happened. The splat factor would be enough to ruin any number of cardigans.

At least, it is when I picture it.

I think I'd need to be close by though, if it were to work. But I don't want to get anything on me and I'll need an alibi.

Enda called Nina by the wrong name. Didn't need details. Thankfully, she didn't supply them.

SEPTEMBER

Last year of school starts here.

Occurs to me now that I should have spent some of my time on the till actually adding up, rather than letting the till work it all out for me. But the fact that Mallory is still in business is the proof I didn't do that.

She says she looks forward to my first exhibition.

Have talked her through this project, which, as it turns out, takes a lot more explanation than I would have thought (should probably apologise to Mammy), and Mallory wants to see the finished piece. I think the thing that threw her was that it won't be complete until the end of '79.

Keep going back and forth on whether I'll include the first day of 1980. Seems like it might be a good thing to span two decades but maybe it's long enough already.

Mallory said to show her what I've got in stages. She seemed really excited but there's no way I can show her this before it's shredded. Don't remember what I might have said about her eyeliner, but I know it wasn't kind.

Okay. Had a flick through. I hadn't said anything about it. Of course, now I have.

OCTOBER

Cannot wait to drive. I can just see myself, driving off into the sunset, watching the house get smaller and smaller in my rear-view mirror until I round the corner and move into my life. My real life.

Mammy asked where I'm going to get the money for a car. Or petrol. Well, practicality is nice to visit, but I don't plan on living there. Didn't want to turn it into an argument so I just sloped off to my room. She called up that Papa was coming later in the afternoon.

I sighed, but I think she took that as reluctance to see him. Nothing could be further from the truth. Papa is the only one who really understands me. Mammy says it's easier for him because he doesn't live with us.

Had a good talk with Papa. He says travel broadens the horizons. Mammy started tutting at him, so he must be right. Told Papa I plan to go to Dublin for university. He smiled and nodded. Mammy muttered something about hayfever and had to leave the room.

No one gets hayfever in October. I'm sure she didn't really believe I was just going to stay home forever. Not really.

NOVEMBER

So, it's all decided. When I go Dublin for my degree, I'll stay with Aunt Pat and Uncle Byron until Nina and I can find a flat somewhere.

Enda may or may not visit, depending on whether they're speaking at that point – more on that later. And then, once we've finished our degrees (she's doing History), we'll stay on and work until we've earned enough to get to Paris. Or Barcelona. It's not certain yet, but it doesn't need to be for a while. I only really want to go to Paris for the skin cream. Nina doesn't care where we go, so long as we go.

Now, Nina and Enda: well, it all fell apart because he couldn't stop himself from saying that history was a waste of time because it's *'all been done'*. She hit the roof and asked him what the point of chickens was. And it all sort of spiralled from that point.

Anyway, we're off to Dublin next summer and then, we'll take over the world. That's the plan anyway. Got some filthy looks from Enda on the bus. So, no change there then.

DECEMBER

Mallory is running a local photography competition for the next few weeks. We've had a good number of professional-looking shots come in, but mostly they're the ordinary type – in colour, square, with rounded corners. Mallory started by saying that there would be an overall winner, but she's struggling to choose between the couple of hundred that have already come through. She's decided to have an exhibition of the lot of them some time early next year.

And I'm eighteen. Doesn't feel like very much has changed. All my life, eighteen has been this huge milestone. I'd turn eighteen and everything would just slot into place. I'd be an adult and that would be that.

Mammy came in just after six in the morning, with a tray and a word about how strange I looked. She said sorry for the time, but she had some church visits to do before the party in the afternoon.

Anyway, eighteen. Until recently, Mammy was happy to agree that eighteen was the start of adulthood, but in the last few months, she's started suggesting, pretty loudly, that eighteen is still late childhood. Adult life starts at twenty-one, apparently.

I can guarantee, when I hit twenty-one, she'll decide the true landmark age is twenty-five and we'll just keep going until one or both of us is dead.

Not sure what she's going to do when I move out. I can't picture her taking a job. Not a job-job. She'll carry on, I expect, with her visits to the afflicted, and bingo, but otherwise, I don't really know what she wants from life.

Is it terrible that I've always thought she already has what she wants in life? Maybe I'm dead wrong. Maybe I couldn't be more wrong. I don't think I'm going to ask her about it and I don't think she'll tell me but, sometimes, I wish we were those people.

It seems I was watching her over dinner. She said she didn't like it one little bit and she'll have words with my father about it because I didn't get that look from her.

Happy birthday, Fiona.

1977

JANUARY

And the third year begins. Wondering if I've actually failed and gone a little too personal in this diary. Too late to do anything about what I've already written but perhaps I can be a little more circumspect in future. It seems doubtful, but you never know. I might learn to stop trusting these non-judgemental pages and keep parts of myself hidden completely in shadowy half-truths. Am slightly concerned, should a day come when I sell the finished portrait, wonder how much of myself I'll actually be selling?

That's a worry for another day. Right now, I have History coursework to finish.

Would normally ask Nina for help but don't want to crowd her. She's just getting used to her time away from Enda, and I went and made some stupid but apparently profound thing about how she should be all right as herself without needing validation from someone else. Don't know what I was thinking. I suspect it's good advice but there's a time and a place.

Enda's still giving me weird looks on the bus. Heard a whisper that he thinks I've got into Nina's head, and something about how I've made her single for myself. Don't know what to think about that. He must think I have a very high opinion of myself. Like I could charm her or something. Don't know where to begin on what's wrong with that.

Still, sick of seeing him on the bus, with his eyebrows and his face. Really need to start driving soon. Aunt Pat and Uncle Byron only live round the corner from the university but still, it would be good to have a little car. Think Mammy's softening to the idea. Told her, if I could drive, I could come home at weekends.

Mammy's got into Wings. *Silly Love Songs* has been playing non-stop for a couple of weeks now. She told me not to read too much into it and went back to Johnny Mathis. No idea why, but she's decided she won't have Glen Campbell's name spoken in the house. Poor old Glen.

FEBRUARY

There's something very calm about Mallory's place. It's not just that the main gallery is large and bright, high ceilings, it has a great sense of air. It's that people's voices never go above a whisper when confronted with art in real life.

A lot has happened since the local photography competition. Mallory has had to hire a new guy to work in the gift shop. He's there through the week and on Saturday afternoons. I have seen him but for some reason, when Mallory introduced us, she didn't tell me his name. I suppose it's a bit of luck that we don't take our breaks at the same times. I've just been calling him 'new guy' in my head but that probably wouldn't go over so well in person. When I've offered to bring him a cup of coffee, I've got away with just saying, *'Coffee?'*

Enda sat behind me on the bus home. He leaned forward and muttered that I'd got more than I'd bargained on with Nina. He was well rid of her, he said, and, as much as he'd like to be the bigger man and wish me luck – he couldn't bring himself to do it.

His breath was sour, like he'd not brushed his teeth for a week or two. A few snoots of that and I became wistful for the chicken farm in the height of the summer.

MARCH

Nina came over and brought a present. She had to sneak it past the kitchen door. Mammy won't have coffee in the house. Doesn't believe in it. Thinks it's a terrible American invention and that everyone would be happier if they stuck to tea.

Nina was hiding the jar under her jacket. When we went up to my room, she had me bring up two cups of boiling water and called down to Mammy that she was on a health kick.

With no spoon in my room (because it's not as if I'm a psychic or a deviant), she just tipped the jar into the top of the mugs and we stirred with one of my newer paintbrushes. It was bitter but I loved it.

And now, I have a secret. I love coffee. Thankfully, I won't have to keep it quiet for too much longer. Don't know where I'll hide it when Mammy and Daddy come to visit us in Dublin but they never go anywhere without ringing ahead. I'll have time to find a hiding place.

As it got later, Nina didn't seem to be going anywhere. She said Enda's been hanging around on the corner opposite her house. Just looking up at her window. Sometimes, he calls from the phone box and tries to put on a voice so her mother will pass her the telephone, but he has no talent for accents and she always knows it's him.

He must have her scared if she doesn't want to go home. Asked Mammy and she's said she can stay for a few days. Nina doesn't seem to want to sleep. At least we have coffee.

APRIL

There's something about the heat of Enda's breath on my neck that makes me want to wretch. It's unfortunate that I know when it's him, just from the quake in my veins. He started by asking me if I knew what I wanted. Although it didn't sound so social-worker-cardigan when he said it.

'You know what you want, don't you?' he asked.

I don't know where it came from but heard myself telling him that if he was struggling with their breakup, he should talk to someone. Not Nina. I told him he couldn't go on hanging around near her house, crank-calling her.

He went quiet.

I went on, because some people just can't help themselves and it turns out, I'm one of them. I suggested he should just take a few weeks and try to recover himself. I told him, deep down, he wouldn't really want Nina if she only came back because he begged her.

He frowned and gulped really hard. His Adam's Apple bobbed up and down in his throat.

'What are you talking about?' he asked.

He said he hasn't been hanging around outside Nina's and if he catches me lying about him like that again, I'm dead meat.

Think I looked like I was doing really hard maths in my head all the way home.

MAY

Busy times at the gallery. Setting up for the summer season. Went to Pat and Byron's to check out their spare room. Vinyl wallpaper, thick plum-coloured carpet, paintings of ships on the walls. Just the one bed. It's big. Nina and I will have to share. Going to have to be careful how I word it. Don't want her getting the – not exactly the *wrong* impression, so much as – an impression I'm not sure I can live up to, even if she wanted me to, which she clearly doesn't.

Came home and Papa was sitting at the kitchen table. He asked how this project was going. Thinks I'm probably the first in the family to carry on with a diary for longer than the first few weeks of January. Felt quite chipper. Mammy said she can't imagine what I find to write about. She hopes it's not all about her.

'Only the worst bits, I'm sure,' Papa said. Once she was out of the room, he held my hand and suggested I do a series of self-portraits, all in different styles. Told him, straight hair is hard to do in pencil. He didn't miss a beat. *'Curl it,'* he said. *'Gram-Gram's hair was curly.'*

And so, that's how I'm spending my weekend. Mammy ragged my hair. I think she tied the knots too tight. My head started banging, like something was trying to get out, so I took the rags out. My hair had got as far as a soft curl, but I fancied that was enough.

Started drawing. I kept going 'til it got light out. I think I've got my lips wrong but otherwise... not too shabby. Will carry on with it until it's finished. Think I'm getting better at knowing when that time has come. It's just after I think I've got it right, and just before I think I hate it.

JUNE

I don't really know where to start.

Sometimes, you might imagine how something will be, not really expecting it ever to happen, and then it does – and the whole world changes. The problem is it never changes in the way you think it will.

I should start at the beginning, really.

Nina came over for some last minute History cramming. She brought a bottle of brandy from the back of her parents' drinks' cabinet. History goes better with booze. She said she liked what I've done with my hair. Pretty sure I blushed, although that might have been the drink.

All through our chatter, which had very little to do with History and lots to do with my hair and my plans to move abroad, she kept touching my arm and looking into my eyes. Like, really deeply. As if she saw a breadcrumb in there.

For a moment, I thought she was going to kiss me. She didn't. Of course, she didn't. Because I pulled away pretty sharpish, asked if she wanted some tea, and yelled out, *'Mammy!'*

On reflection, that might have been an error.

I know I should have just waited to see what might happen. Leave it to her, let her make the decision. If she'd wanted to, she could have kissed me, but all I could think was – later, when she's had a chance to think about this, she'll regret it, she'll be ashamed, she'll never speak to me again. And as much as I've thought about what it might be like, I don't want to lose my friend.

And for God's sake, my Mammy was just in the next room. She might have burst in at any moment. With or without teapot.

I'm an idiot.

JULY

It's strange how, in the passage of just a couple of weeks, everything moves away.

School is almost over. When that's done with, I can't imagine I'll see Enda again, except over the fence. Something tells me he'll be a nicer person when he doesn't have to see me on the bus all the time. Maybe I'm kidding myself.

But, when school finishes, any excuse to see Nina will disappear as well. And I won't be working at the gallery for much longer. I'll stay on until the middle of August, but then I'm off to Dublin and I'll want some time to settle in.

I've had this thought. It was only small, when it first popped into my head; so small, I barely noticed it. A freckle of thought, I would have shrugged it off if I'd known what it was.

It's true: I've basically done all I can do here. I've done art shows for school. I work in the gallery. My room is covered in drawings. I have more sketchbooks than a single person could possibly find a use for. They're all full to the brim with ideas and portrait pieces in extreme close up. I've learnt that hands are a nightmare: they've filled a few books on their own. And I've outgrown this place. It's obvious, I need to move. And then the thought came. Small, almost insignificant. But growing. Always growing.

What if I'm only talented because I'm here? What if, when I get to Dublin, I find out I'm just average? Or less than average? What if I'm just plain ordinary? I suppose I'll be back by Christmas. Back to my mother, and Enda over the fence, sneering in his wellies, pulling Nina to his side while the chickens squawk approval.

I must be good. I have to be good. I can't come back here.

Just a couple more weeks and I'll be – you know what it's like? It's like how I think the world must be for babies. If you think about it – baby is in their carrycot. Baby falls asleep in the living room. Baby wakes up in a different house entirely. Something has happened, a whole journey, they've missed the time in the car, they've missed the introductions and the nibbles, they're just in someone else's living room, with someone else's smells and wallpaper, with someone else's artefacts decorating the walls and surfaces and they just – accept it. It's not as if they have the linguistic skills to argue about it too much but the sudden change must be confusing.

And that's what I'm headed towards. Being transported to different rooms, different cooking, different times to do different things, and all I can think is: I hope I accept it with the equanimity of a baby. Great word, equanimity. A new one for me, I think I'm going to use it once a day until it's part of my standard vocabulary.

But I'll need that sort of calm. Especially given that I'll be doing it on my own. Nina isn't coming with me. She wouldn't specify, and I didn't want to labour the point but – did she not get in? Did Enda insist she stay home and have a bunch of babies, blessed with equanimity? Did she just not want to go with me? I can see how it would have been awkward, staying with my family, with me just the other side of the bed but I think she could have said something.

I know she couldn't.

AUGUST

Pat and Byron's place is a riot of colour. I hadn't noticed how brown and orange my life used to be but Pat and Byron have redecorated their front room and there are dashes of green and blue everywhere.

The college is pale grey. Almost entirely. The columns are Roman-looking. Beautiful scrollwork and heavy blocks. Gorgeous. The air is different. It's going to sound clumsy, at least it must do coming from me, but even though the air is sharper, grittier, I feel like I can really breathe here. Maybe we were all too close at home. I was starting to suffocate.

A brief chat over the first extended family dinner, and it was decided. I'll go home at weekends to see my mother and check on Daddy. And it'll give me a chance to try and patch things up with Nina.

Although, that wasn't decided over dinner. That came later. In the dark. On my own.

SEPTEMBER

Well, we're two weeks in and I've already found five things to march about. I've made a few new friends. The course structure makes a lot of sense. There's room for all kinds of expression and interpretation. Doing lots of practical work; trying different styles already. There's a lot on the syllabus: paint, ink, pencil, watercolour, clay, glass, and all kinds of styles: classicist, impressionist, realist, abstract, surrealist, pop.

We haven't made much progress yet but we're all sort of learning how to be adults, as well as everything else. I don't really want to live in digs but I know I will. Not wishing to outstay my welcome with Pat and Byron, I'll be staying with some of the journalism students. Think it'll keep me on my toes more than living with other artists would.

Wish Nina was here.

It's been lovely with Pat and Byron but it started getting awkward early on (my fault) because I kept asking permission to use the phone. They insisted it was fine, and I was only calling Mammy, but I didn't want to run up their bill. Besides, Mammy prefers letters to phone calls anyway. *You can keep a letter*, she says. *A phone call is almost instantly forgotten.*

There'll be all kinds of shows during the course. Some of the guys are talking about street art. Not sure about that one. Sounds like my mother would have an opinion on it.

Have decided to start calling Mammy 'Maeve'. She doesn't much care for it but she prefers it to Mother. She says there's too much potential for venom in the word 'Mother'.

OCTOBER

Visiting Maeve and Daddy.

Felt a bit bad because I haven't come home every weekend. To be fair, I had Dublin to explore and new friends who I rather wanted to spend time with.

Also, the first time I came back for the weekend, Maeve acted like dinner was the last thing I'd ever eat. It was insane. If the plate had had even one more carrot on it, it would have cracked in two.

Was good to see Nina again. She's back with Enda so, yeah, I've missed my chance.

I thought I'd feel better seeing that written down.

I was wrong.

It's a dreadful feeling, like a stirring in my stomach or a stabbing in my throat. There's no point mentioning this to anyone else. They either wouldn't understand or worse, they would, but they wouldn't approve.

I'm going to make a concerted effort when I get back to Dublin. I don't need to forget her. I just need to not think about her all the time.

I really like her. A lot. I always have.

It's started messing with my sleep.

NOVEMBER

Focussing on my coursework. Really enjoying it. It's good to be absorbed by something outside my head.

Weekly kitchen parties on Thursdays and Fridays, with cheap beer and cheese on toast. One of the guys from next door was telling a story the other night. When he was back home in Sligo, he went to night school to do a course in Women's Studies. He said he'd been certain that everyone else on the course would be a woman and he'd look like such an evolved man that he'd be completely irresistible to them. When he got to the first class, it was populated entirely by men who'd had the same idea. I don't care if it was a joke. I laughed for the whole night. It was great.

When I got back to my room, there was a message by my bed that Nina had called. Went to the payphone outside my door, it must have been close to midnight, and called her back. She answered on the first ring.

'I don't want to talk about it anymore, Enda,' she sighed. *'We both said some pretty lousy things. All right, I said my things first but I can't be doing with having this conversation again.'*

I cleared my throat but couldn't think of any actual words.

'It's far too late to go through it all again. Obviously, I didn't mean to call you Fiona, especially not when I did, but I don't appreciate being called a... well, you know what you called me. I think it's clear neither of us is really in the same relationship. So...'

Especially not when I did. Oh, my God. Especially when I did?

'Enda. Enda? Fine, be like that.' And she hung up.

Oh, my God, she likes me.

Oh, my God, she likes me.

Oh, my God and I'm not supposed to know.

DECEMBER

Nineteen years old. Nina likes me. She hasn't told me, as far as she knows. Wonder if she said my name in any kind of bedroom-context. A very distracting thought which made for a really uncomfortable birthday party. Nina spent much of it looking at her shoes.

Enda sent a card. Hadn't seen his handwriting in so long that I'd forgotten that he puts capital 'N's in the middle of words. Really annoyed not to have remembered in time, rather than opening the card in front of the family. It was just the sort of message I might have expected. Managed to slip it into the fire before anyone noticed.

Papa asked if I was getting thin. Maeve whipped up a shepherd's pie in seconds flat, which I've been instructed to take home and eat in the middle of the night so I won't be able to burn it off with my father's metabolism.

I'm to set my alarm to go off at three in the morning, have a spoonful of pie, and she'll send another one along with Pat and Byron until I'm a shape that doesn't elicit comments. This should be fun.

1978

JANUARY

Decided to spend New Year's in Dublin. Didn't go out. I could hear the music from my bedroom window and I didn't fancy getting sucked in to the throng of people.

Stayed in, with my hair in rags, drawing. Made myself think of Nina and got my hair to fall over one eye. Made a lot of sketches. Once I've got this picture into some sort of shape, I'll experiment with some makeup. Get something more like the grown-up version of me.

Didn't go to bed until it was, without doubt, 1978. Spent the rest of the day in bed, taking occasional bites of Maeve's barmbrack.

I don't do New Year's resolutions. We already know this. But if I were to make a resolution it would be: Don't have another New Year's like this.

FEBRUARY

Getting a little bit tired of Maeve's cooking. Luckily, it seems I'm gaining weight. When it was time for me to leave, she didn't thrust a pie dish into my hands. Not sure if that's a compliment.

As I was heading for the door, Papa felt in his pocket and pulled out a twenty-pound note.

'I think you dropped this, sweetheart,' he smiled.

Of course, I hadn't.

He pushed it into my hand and whispered, *'You must remember your mother's at a difficult age. She can't help the way she is. It's just her...'*

Maeve was suddenly at my side. *'What are you two mumbling about?'*

'Hormones,' Papa said.

'It's like you have your own language,' Maeve marvelled.

MARCH

Rather than have a sketchbook full of myself, I've been painting Ciaran in the next room. It's true, a self-portrait is easier. I'm always with me so I don't have to arrange times or locations, anything like that. I don't have to worry whether my model is getting tired because I already know. Still, I couldn't bear for anyone to think of me as arrogant. It can't all be me. And Ciaran's usually leaning over a workbook anyway so, once he's got his coffee, he doesn't move for a couple of hours in any case.

Maeve thinks she'd make the perfect model herself. I already know it's a trap. Even if I captured her perfectly, so perfectly that people who haven't seen her in twenty years would know who she was, she still wouldn't be happy.

See, and this is something I've learnt from my time with Ciaran: everyone has an image of themselves – it's not who they are – it's who they want to be. When they sit for an artist, hours are spent, chatter is had, tea or coffee is drunk and a relationship is formed. It's a special sort of trust that's built. And so, when the model is finally allowed to see the finished piece, it's quite normal for them to make a face. Because, no matter what the artist has captured – it's never what the model expects you to have seen.

Ciaran frowned for twelve solid minutes before saying he liked it. As he walked away from the easel, he turned round really fast to catch another glimpse of it.

'*Yeah,*' he said. '*Nice one. That'll do.*'

Maeve would never say that. She'd start out wondering why I'd made her look like her mother when she was dying. Then, she'd catch a glimpse of Papa and ask why I was trying to turn her into an old man. And she'd sum it all up by asking why Daddy was spending so much money on my education when I still couldn't draw women who looked human.

To avoid all of that, I've said we're focussing on still life. Until the end of time.

APRIL

Papa has been teaching me to drive on Saturdays. He offered and, as much as I've heard horror stories about relatives teaching their young people and screaming at them, Papa wasn't worried and that put me at ease.

After our first lesson, he took me out for a rum and coke and handed me a pair of fluffy dice. He says *that's* how confident he is.

During our second lesson, I nearly killed us at a roundabout, so he's going to help me find a driving instructor.

MAY

Have decided to stop lying to myself. This diary is only partly an art project. This has become my confessional, and I'm all right with that. Largely because I know I'm going to destroy it. If my luck holds, I'll be able to patch it back together in such a way that no one knows what I was talking about anyway. Slightly concerned about how many times certain names have popped up but am relying on the fact that you'd really have to stare to notice how much I wonder about, and concern myself with, specific people.

Anyway, we're having a student exhibition over the summer. We've been working on our pieces for some time. I've been attempting a still life in a small café nearby but, and I really don't know why, as soon as I set up my easel, someone stops to talk to me and I don't get anything done until the light changes and I lose the impetus. Dithering a bit over whether to carry on or just do my best from memory. Will have a few portraits to choose from. Luckily, it's not me doing the choosing. Not sure whether I'd want to put all of them in or none. It changes from day to day.

Pat and Byron dropped by for a surprise visit and took me shopping. Maeve worries that I'm living in a filthy flat, wearing a beret and nothing else, because that's what she thinks artists do. Have tried assuring her that the cords and blouses she's used to seeing me in are basically my battle dress. She doesn't believe me.

Not sure how any artist could function in just a beret. The bar heater would be on all the time and no one makes that kind of money. Actually, you'd need two bar heaters and you'd probably set the flat on fire. You'd have to stand outside with a fireman and a blanket, and your beret smouldering in the damp Dublin air. Somehow, don't think that idea would give her any comfort so won't mention it.

JUNE

Passed my driving test. Didn't tell anyone I was going to take it so no one noticed when I failed the first one but honestly, that bus came out of nowhere. Anyway, I doubt it'll ever come up in conversation but if it does, I'll just say I passed first time. It's what people expect.

Actually, I think it probably makes you a better driver if you don't pass straight away. I suppose I'm less likely to think of myself as infallible. I'm pretty fallible. Really, this diary could be seen as an exercise in my fallibility. The point is, I'll say I passed first time. But only if someone asks. Can't imagine why they would. But if they do, I'm very capable and I passed first time.

I'll just hope it doesn't come up.

JULY

Something strange has started happening. When I first started coming home at the weekends, it felt like a little holiday. A little holiday where I could see my parents. After a while, it was more like walking into their home, not mine. But now, it's more like stepping back in time. Not just the house, even seeing Maeve and Daddy feels like poring through a photo album. It's a different time. A good time. A happy memory to visit. Just, not quite real. I'm walking in sepia.

Made a decision. I'm just going to have this thing with Nina going round and round my head if I don't do something about it, so I'm going to ask her to dinner.

Oh, but I need to take a breath.

Okay. A restaurant, a small one, no candles, nothing especially romantic. If there's something there, any added atmosphere will be too much. Like those plastic covered greetings cards, with the very thick plastic that looks like jelly. I don't know how anyone manages to read them. They'd be so bendy. And do they stretch in the sunshine? I'm a winter baby, I can't know.

Yeah, I don't want any jelly-plastic-coating distracting from the message. I just don't want to look like I'm trying. In case I'm wrong. Those cards are wildly overpriced and they only say the same as any scrap of paper would.

Addendum: I'd been rehearsing how to ask Nina out for a few days. I did both sides of the conversation, which I thought was for the best. Didn't want to include anyone else in this thing, whatever it is.

Anyway, I was sure that when I asked her to dinner, she'd ask if I meant like a date. I was going to say, *'Not* like *a date, an actual date. Just, if you wanted to.'* To the point but totally cool, laid back.

And then, she didn't ask. She just said yes.

So, we're going to have dinner next week. I don't know if it's a date, or if she wants it to be a date, or, when she said my name at an inopportune moment, if it's the moment I hope it was. And, naturally enough, I don't even know that that happened.

Exhausted.

※

AUGUST

Dinner with Nina.

Now, this could have been awkward. I realised in the morning that I had no idea what to wear. What do people wear on dates that might not be dates? This isn't really my area. I stared at all the clothes lying on my bed and couldn't imagine what I was thinking when I bought them.

A dress would be flat-out wrong. A dress carries certain expectations. No matter what you say out loud, a dress tells her *it's a date*. Cords and a t-shirt are too everyday, like it doesn't matter what it is.

Settled on caramel suede flares, cream blouse, flat shoes. Had to go with flats, just in case. Nina is barely 5' tall and – how would that even work? Either I'd have to lean down a hell of a long way, possibly showing my hand too early, making myself look a fool – or she'd have to point her face up (basically to the ceiling) and I can't picture her looking that needy. Wondering how people date with height differences.

Anyway, dinner – I picked the restaurant largely because it didn't offer oysters or anything vaguely seductive. The problem, of course, with not being too obvious about it is that I had no clue what we were actually doing there and it was my idea.

Thought she might order steak. After a fair few years with Enda, she's surely used to manly, meaty, bleeding-food. She ordered fondue. So we both had fondue. She kept twirling the cheese around the toast point and...

It was torture. Melted cheese isn't supposed to be alluring. We drank some wine. Not a huge amount. It was red. I don't think she liked it either.

When we got back to her place, she asked me in for coffee. Couldn't tell if it was a euphemistic coffee or not. I must have looked as confused as I felt because she said, *'I know your mother wouldn't allow it in the house, not if she knew, but there's nothing frightening about coffee, you know?'*

'I'm not sure I can,' I stumbled.

'Are you okay? You look a bit flustered.'

And she looked so worried that I rather hated myself for what I said next.

'This... this wasn't a date, was it? I mean, it wasn't, was it?'

She looked at the carpet in the corridor.

'Only,' I went on (only became proud of myself for this bit later), *'I don't think I could quite bear the sight of you, in your kitchen, making coffee. Because I'd want it to be normal but it would be amazing.'*

She looked like she'd swallowed a fly. *'Oh, I see.'*

'I should go.'

'You know...'

And there was a silence. A horrible, hateful silence and I thought I'd better apologise or blame the wine, or something.

'You know, I suppose, that it's only good manners, when you've had dinner with someone, to offer them a peck on the cheek?'

'Right.' I nodded. *'Yes. I see.'*

And when I leaned down to kiss her cheek, she turned her head at the last second and we were on her doorstep.

Nineteen years old. Her hands in my hair, the shock of her tongue in my mouth: a heady mix of cheese and cheap red wine, and I thought I might pass out. All I could think was: *If this were a Swedish film, we'd already be in love.*

She giggled. It was sweet and breathless, ragged. And then, it just kept going.

I didn't know what to say to her. It was hardly a mighty guffaw but I couldn't tell: was it a joke? Was it a prank? Did it mean anything at all? No words would come. I turned and walked away. Scrubbing my first kiss from my mouth and memory.

We'll have to speak eventually, probably, maybe not. Maybe I'll just leave the country. Might be easier than trying to pick it all apart from a distance. And now I feel rather silly because I could have lost my heart and underwear to a girl like that.

Whatever I might say, it's going to take some rehearsing.

SEPTEMBER

Thinking a lot about Nina. Planning out our conversations for the next few weeks. I wonder how she'll respond if I mention the kiss. Maybe I shouldn't say a word about it. Maybe I should just play it cool, like this kind of thing happens to me all the time. I think that might make me a bit of a dickhead.

Yes, I know I was supposed to forget all about it but it's only been a month and it was quite breathtaking. Dammit.

In other news, the second year has begun in earnest. Trying to learn how to put lentils into everything. Apparently they're no good unless you put them in everything. Trouble is, they're taking all night to soak and by the time I get round to them, all I can think is how long I've wasted soaking the damn things. Went back to sketching Nina.

OCTOBER

One of the guys down the hallway is in his first year of Psychology. He says I have a saviour complex; that my wanting to save Nina while simultaneously being unable to save myself is a classic feature of the condition.

He smiles and tuts at me as if he's seen it all before. He's eighteen and I think I might hate him. I'm just grateful he's nothing like qualified. He could really worry people, if they were of a mind to listen.

NOVEMBER

Visiting home and I stopped by Mallory's Gallery. Had promised I'd come over for a coffee one afternoon and I've been very slack about it. She says she understands how much time my degree is eating up. She's been there herself, of course. I'd love to carry myself like her when I'm older. Mallory has this way of sweeping through a room, taking it all in, not noticing the people and their staring. She just has this air of... I don't know what it is but she has oodles of it.

Opened the door, a small bell dinged overhead – a new addition, not sure I like it – and then, I saw her.

Nina has taken my old job. She dashed over, hooked a hand around my elbow, and dragged me through to the back room.

When she let go, she said, 'Why won't you talk to me? I've been staring at the phone, day and night. You haven't called. You haven't answered any of my letters. What happened?'

'I...' I managed.

'All right. I know what happened, but we could have talked, surely? It's all right for you. You get to go back to your fashionable life in Dublin, while the rest of us just wait for you to bother to visit but – not even a phone call?'

Asked Mammy when I got back to the house. She didn't care for the way Nina had addressed the envelopes – she put 'Fiona W.' rather than 'Miss F. Weaver' – so she put them on the fire. She's always thought Nina was a bad influence. I could swear and stamp my foot but it wouldn't bring the letters back.

Will call Nina later. I think the phone will be easier than anything in person.

The only thing Maeve hadn't burned was a card from Mallory. An invitation to her birthday party. From her walk, I'd have put her at forty, maybe forty-two. She's turning thirty. Ten years older than me, don't know how I managed to mistake her for a grown-up.

DECEMBER

My birthday. I am now twenty, so asked if we could end the enforced fun of parties with hats and games. Think Daddy and Papa were secretly delighted. Neither of them really cares for dragging out the crackers a week early. Maeve took some persuading. Papa took care of it.

'Do you really want people to know you have a twenty-year-old daughter? Twenty, though. She's practically retired.'

Maeve nodded solemnly and I was allowed to go out with my friends instead. Went to Spike Island with Nina. Too cold to be outside. Can't say I noticed. Only realised how cold I was when we got back to the house.

1979

JANUARY

And we're into the final stretch. Once this year is over, the diary will be finished. After all the years spent with this thing, I'll be sorry to see it go. Maybe it'll be different when I come to read it back. Not sure I'd really recognise the person I was before. Pretty certain I've written things that could be socially uncomfortable.

No. I'm risking a touch of the maudlin and I don't think that's who I am anymore.

It's been quite a wrench coming back to university after Christmas. It was the turning point, I think. Spending time with Nina, getting comfortable with feelings and such, it's been an eye-opener. Not sure I like her taking my old job, though. If I'm honest, I don't know what she's trying to do. The gallery is not a place of history. It's not going to get her to university. It's not about anything, except me. Is that self-centred? Maybe. Don't care. I will learn to be all right with myself.

But not today. Right now, all I can think about is what Mallory might say about me. Maybe it's assuming too much to think they talk about me. Let's face it – they have other things to talk about.

Nina doesn't know a thing about art. That must be the main topic of conversation. And I expect Mallory, being older, will have been a help to Nina, getting her away from Enda. Not sure what their relationship really was. I mean, yes – boyfriend/girlfriend, but I don't know whether I believe it was more than just for show.

Lord knows, he couldn't do any better if he had a crack at every woman from here to Tralee, but I think he was more interested in how Nina made him look than anything else.

FEBRUARY

Payphone outside my door is broken.

I suppose it was a little silly for me to imagine that Nina had asked for my address because she wanted to visit. That said, it has forced me to keep my bedroom tidy. Not that I expected... Or even imagined...

To bed early, wondering what I thought I was keeping my bedroom tidy for.

Valentine's card from Nina. Really sweet. It was a collage of sweaters cut out of clothing catalogues that she'd stuck in the shape of a heart. I think Mallory probably guided her on how to make it. It's not as if it's the most complicated discipline but Nina's more about history than anything else. She doesn't have much need for golden gum glue. She included a poem. It was Yeats. She didn't credit it to him but, it was Yeats.

I probably should have sent her a card. Too late now. Can't really blame the post and it's not as if I forgot, I just – what it is, I don't see the point in sending a card and not signing it. There's something about that kind of behaviour that feels like maybe there should be a criminal record at the end of it. Like, that sort of thing is not normal.

Like, if you watch the films at Halloween and you see all those American children, begging for sweeties from strangers, it's just – any other time of the year, they'd be risking death in the basement for the sake of sugar. Yet, somehow, in October, it's so normal, it's a national pastime. Same thing with Valentine's. If you sent someone a card, telling them how much they meant to you, in pretty pink writing, and then didn't sign it, you could really frighten them. Which would, surely, be flying in the face of the very thing you're trying to achieve.

I didn't want to have the card arrive a couple of days late. Which it would have. By the time I'd have thought of something worth writing down, it would be at least the 17th, and then, it falls into the creepy category.

Pain in the arse that I can't even call her.

<hr />

MARCH

Having missed Valentine's because, well, it's just the one day – as opposed to Easter, which moves about a bit, and Christmas, which lasts for a few weeks – I decided to write a letter.

There's something timeless and romantic about a love letter. It's not something that can be rushed. It has to be sincere, without being vomit-worthy: that's a challenge in itself, but more – it has to be so well worded as to make the person reading it go a little gooey round the middle.

I know this because I've seen it in films. There are some things you can only know from films.

I sketched ideas into the back of my workbook during lectures, I wrote extra lines on park benches, I wandered round the city, looked in bookshops, I sought inspiration everywhere. I revisited her portrait. It took me ten days to write the letter.

I don't know that I would have used the word 'love' if she hadn't sent the card, but now I know I'm not crazy.

Popped the letter into a postbox near the library.

It was three days later that I found out: she's left town. The only positive is that she didn't go with Enda, who still may or may not be fuming but certainly hasn't followed her.

<hr />

APRIL

No word from Nina. Have forced myself into work. It's time to focus. Coming to the end of the second year of university so there's only so much time for parties and drinking.

I know, because of books and such, that there are people who drink wine with dinner every night. I can't imagine being that drunk all the time. Maybe it's just something that happens when you get to your forties. Will have to watch out for that. Must be more fun that it sounds.

Maeve and Daddy never much bothered with wine at dinner. They've always been more tea-driven people.

Can only imagine that wherever Nina went, it must have taken some planning. I know a Valentine's card, even a Valentine's card with a heaping helping of Yeats in it, doesn't really lend itself to the whole – *by the way, I'm leaving home* thing, but I'm surprised she didn't tell me.

No other correspondence at home. Checked with Daddy. He's been looking after the post since Maeve went and set fire to the last lot.

Might need to check with Papa. If this is part of the age she's getting to, I should probably take notes for when I'm older. A checklist of sorts. I'm not relying on someone else being there to watch me go mad. But whether there's somebody there, or I'm on my own, I'll be okay. I think. So long as I have a list of things to watch out for.

MAY

Will, across the hall, has been playing chess alone. I think it's a correspondence thing. He has a large stamp album on his bookshelf. I'm surprised the shelf hasn't collapsed. Anyway, Will says he can only concentrate when he's got me on the other sofa, talking about my problems. *They're not problems*, I keep telling him. *They're eccentricities at worst.*

Anyway, he tells me that the fact that I came to Dublin without Nina – even though she was supposed to come with me – and that I've managed to see her when visiting my parents without going to pieces, is the proof that I can live without her.

I don't doubt that. I can live without all manner of people. I know I can live without her. I just don't want to.

I suppose, if I make myself think about it, what I really want is for someone to love me, who isn't biologically obliged to do so. I want someone who sees me, really sees me, and loves me anyway. Don't want to say that to Will but I have a feeling it'll slip out if I don't write it down and out of me.

Everyone else seems to find girlfriends so easily. I mean, I am talking about the boys here, but it seems the preferred method is this: they try their luck with every woman they encounter, and even if it takes a while, they have a success. Like, if they ask out a hundred women, chances are six or seven will say yes, but if they only ask one or two, they're pretty certain they'll fail. I just don't know how they get through the first couple of rejections without feeling like they're going to pickle in self-loathing.

Have decided that the best way to deal with not knowing if Nina's okay is to fix my lips in my self-portrait with the raggy hair. I went too far with the Cupid's bow and it's not accurate. I've never had a mouth like that. Mine is a mouth for wine not whiskey. Is it me? I think the Cupid's bow sits better over the rim of a whiskey glass.

JUNE

I should have learnt French.

I think I always knew that, but it's time I faced it. Paris, after university, is going to be a bit difficult when I can't speak the language. True, I'll need a couple of years between Dublin and the world, to earn the money to live on my own. But, if we're going to be practical about this, I'll have to live at home while I earn enough to travel and/or study. Not sure whether I'm really wanting more study after all of this. I suppose that's because I'm in the thick of it. Once I've had a month or two of the life outside, I'm sure I'll long for another quadrangle.

Papa says student life is the best and the real world is overrated, and if anyone would know, I reckon it would be him.

Ultimately, I could do French at night school while I'm working but, if I've got my calculations right, I'm going to need to spend every waking moment out of university at work. It would be different if I just had to plan for my travel arrangements, but I'll have to pay for food and rent. And skin cream.

JULY

Good news. Nina is safe. She's gone to stay with family in Waterford. She wouldn't go into detail. Things were tricky at home. Not sure how Enda fits in to any of this but he surely does. Some difficult conversations were had and she decided it was time to get going. The phone started beeping, her money was running out, so I couldn't press her on the topic. Whatever happened, I don't think it could have had anything to do with me. She only called because her mother forwarded my letter. Nina said thank you, but very little else.

I don't think I could say I've been spurned. But let's face it: I've been spurned.

She did say she'll be coming home in the summer, so maybe I could see her then.

Two rings, and then I'm to hang up. That's how she'll know it's me. Maybe her brother's gone back to listening in on her phone calls. I suppose it must have been awkward, her brother being so pally with Enda. Enda likes a drink and no one needs to know that much detail about their own sister. I assume that was a problem. I can't see how it wouldn't be.

Not holding out a great deal of hope for whatever Nina and I might have had. I don't think she means to flip-flop but she changed her mind about university, she's been going back and forth between me and Enda for much of our lives actually, and she ran off to Waterford without a word. Not sure I can really trust her. It's going to take more strength than I believe I really have but I need to make my peace with it. It's over. It never really began. A chronic flip-flopper has no business getting involved with an uncertain artist with self-esteem issues.

Have heard about an art school in London, the Stonebrook Institute – it has an excellent reputation and doesn't involve learning a new language with accents and hats on. Wondering if my destiny might not be in London after all.

AUGUST

Did the thing. Let the phone ring twice.

Nina came over. We stayed in the garden so we could talk without Maeve offering tea every few minutes. Daddy was out at work. Nina didn't say much until Maeve was on her way out of the driveway on her way to visiting.

'I can't be without you again,' she said. 'I don't care what they say, I'm not going back to Waterford. Let me come with you, to Dublin.'

I took a breath.

'I can pitch in. I'm a great cook and I'll get a job, help with the bills and... God, I've missed you so much.'

She threw an arm around my neck, kissed me so hard I nearly fell down. Suddenly, her hand was up my blouse.

A few minutes passed that way and then, she must have sensed something because I surely didn't. She pulled back a little and, as

I opened my eyes, I saw her turn her head. She went very pale. A tremor reached into her hands which, although still on me, withdrew pretty damn quickly.

I tried to follow what she was looking at. And then I saw him. Enda was watching over the fence.

Nina jumped back.

'Oh, my God, Fiona! What are you up to?' she yelled. 'Enda, thank God you're here! I thought we were just having a chat and she – launched herself at me. For God's sake, Fiona!'

Enda paused, like he knew what he'd seen but didn't know what to believe.

'That's hilarious,' he hissed. 'You're a freaking lunatic, Weaver.'

She straightened out her dress and made to leave. 'For God's sake, Fiona.'

WHEN I REALLY SIT DOWN with myself and explain the story that is me, I realise that my most fervent desire is to be wanted. And sadly, to the people I truly want, my longing is – unfortunately – completely repulsive.

Don't know that there's any way to fix that. Don't think I'll bother to tell Will about that. In fact, since I'm analysing myself, I don't really need Will for free and troubling therapy any more. I'll just learn to play chess. We'll be two friends who've sworn off relationships, playing chess and not talking about things. Good to have a friend for these things.

SEPTEMBER

Into the last year of university. Have decided to cut back on my visits to my parents. I'll spend more time on the phone to them because, of course, they're my parents and the payphone is fixed. But I don't want to run into Nina. I don't need to see Enda. Have decided I'll get my head down, finish my work and get myself over to London as fast as I possibly can.

It's not the embarrassment. Or the shame. Or that she rejected me so completely when she realised someone had seen. It's that she loved me. I really believe she did. She loved me. And she ran, all horrified looks and pointed fingers, away from me.

So I'm drawing a line. It's over.

OCTOBER

Now, the problem with leaving my demons behind me is that they keep bloody phoning. It's getting easier to hang up though.

The first time she called, Will got to the phone before me, asked who was calling and looked over the receiver, mouthing her name to me. I shook my head and – he's a saint, he really is – he told her I was out with my girlfriend and that he didn't know when we'd be back because she was a bikini model and it would probably be a late one. He might have gone a bit too far with his explanation though, because she kept calling back.

For the first few weeks, I apologised before putting the phone down. Now, I just wait to hear her voice and hang up. There's no way that she'd believe there was a model, bikini or otherwise, but I don't want to entertain her excuses.

NOVEMBER

Maeve is planning my birthday party. She insists it has to be resurrected. Last year, with me out at Spike Island, was no fun for her at all. She likes an audience, a crowd of people to appreciate how old her daughter is and to be astonished by how she's kept her figure and teeth.

She did mention that she hasn't seen anyone over the fence.

I feigned disinterest. Had a moment when I wondered if Nina wasn't so much flip-flopping between Enda and me, as in love with both of us.

I'm just making excuses for her. Got to stop doing that. I don't really believe that anyone can be in love with two people at once. At least from time to time, they'd have to come up for air. I'll accept, you can love elements of two different people at the same time – maybe more than two people, maybe seven or eight – but really having true, deep feelings for more than one person seems a little far-fetched. Plus, Enda and I are hardly the same type.

I've spent too long thinking about this. If Enda's the more suitable choice then that says more about her than it does about me. At least, I hope so.

Maeve insisted that Nina must be invited to the birthday party, unless I had some reason why she couldn't be.

Even if I could explain it to myself, I don't think I'm ready to explain it all to Maeve.

So, I'm going to spend much of my birthday afternoon with Papa, avoiding eye contact (he always knows when something's wrong) and talking about Stonebrook's. It sounds great, but I wish I knew some fun facts about London. I wonder if anyone would notice if I just made them up.

꧁꧂

DECEMBER

'Happy Birthday, you're so odd,' and the day begins again. I waited for the tray to pin me into the bed linen and was shocked to find I could still feel my limbs.

'What's going on?' I asked.

'I just wanted say...' She stopped for about a minute and closed her eyes. *'I know things have been difficult. I wish you felt you could*

have talked to me about it, but we're neither of us those sorts of people. But, if you're going to lose your heart to someone, make sure they're worth it. You only get one heart, my love. Don't worry. It will heal.'

I was shocked. Wondered, briefly, if she'd been tempted to have a read of this diary because there are only so many places I can hide it and it's not as if she'd blanch at the very idea of invading my privacy.

'Enda Flaherty isn't worth your time, you know.'

I breathed. Relieved. She doesn't know me that well after all.

'And neither is that Nina.'

It's time to tear this up. With regard to the bits I'd rather forget, because I know I've got some of those, I'm going to mix up some paste and bring in some relief work. Those moments with Nina will disappear below a paper pile of Maeve's barmbrack and Papa's advice. I know I won't be able to scrub her from my mind, but I don't need to see her in my face.

Going to bed, I watched myself in the mirror. I'm twenty-one now so it's official: I'm an adult.

And from this moment, my life will be what I decide.

I hope.

Love Letters To The General Public: A Little, Widespread Romance

I MET OTISINA HENRY in the spring of 1972.

It was my first day of primary school and all I wanted was to turn right round and go home. Of course my parents had told me what school was, but through the filter of their devastation and a heavy dose of brave face, it sounded more like a party than the beige walls and poster-painted coat racks could begin to suggest.

Leaning back at the sort of angle that, ordinarily, could only be achieved by Liza with a chair, I strained to catch the last fleeting glimpse of my mother's fast-disappearing Mini Cooper. (*'Like Liza with a chair'* was a favourite phrase of my mum's. It would be fourteen stockingless years before I knew what it meant.)

Miss Tompkins smiled a little too widely for her face, causing it to pucker in a rather perplexing way, and led me out across the playground. This was, after all, not her first rodeo. She held my moist, podgy little hand with the practised skill of a lifelong educator. Little did I know, she had spent the last thirty years with the label sticking out of her blouse.

Otisina Henry was a pile of dark curls, sitting in a sandpit, presiding over the wedding of two of Jeremy's plastic army men under the pink arch of her discarded Alice band.

"Girls and boys," the teacher began, brightly, "I have a new friend for you. This is Joni McPherson and I want you all to be very nice to her because..." Her nose crinkled. "Otisina, what are you doing?"

"Nothing."

"Are you *marrying* those army men?" she twittered.

Otisina shrugged. "They're in love," she said, quickly returning her attention to the service.

"Army men don't marry each other, my dear," Miss Tompkins managed, an awkward giggle creeping into her voice.

Otisina looked back to the small green men and frowned. "Are you sure about that, Miss?" She pouted. "All right, then. They'll have to kill each other."

And with that, she made the noises for pretty impressive artillery fire, had the army men fall down, and buried them in the sand with a sweep of her fingers. "Right then, Joni," she said, lumbering to her feet. "Have you already had your milk? No? Let's get you a drink and you can tell me all about yourself."

I doubt such a mature five year old has ever existed as Otisina Henry. Of course, at that age, you think the friends you have will be the friends you keep, but Otisina really was.

***

TWENTY-FOUR YEARS LATER...

Whether it came to changing the results of magazine quizzes, cancelling my accidental membership to a monthly CD delivery service, or tackling over-interested newspaper boys, Otisina has always been there to save me.

It's not as if my parents weren't involved in my life. Far from it. She saved me from that, too. See, they're very positive people, my mum and dad, and they raised me to be the same way.

I'm old enough now to know that it's vital to look on the bright side as much as possible, but constant optimism can make it hard to see things for what they really are. I know. It's not as if I suffered. It's just – it can be hard having a family who throw a party for the neighbourhood when you start your period.

I used to struggle to see what other people saw when they looked at me. I got distracted, tongue-tied, while I tried to picture what impression I was making. It can be difficult, trying to see yourself from the other side of the room. I suspect I should have tried something wildly elaborate with a load of mirrors and some gaffer tape. I'm just not very good at communicating with people out loud. Unless I've had a lot to drink. And then, I just wind up repeating myself more and more loudly until I'm politely encouraged to leave. Anyway, I'd had some experience in making a fool of myself. But it only happened only once or twice, because Otisina did what she was born to do and saved me from myself.

I just shouldn't talk to people. It's a simple rule. I wonder if I'll stick to it this time.

"Come on, Joni," she breathes. "Let's get you a drink."

Her hair is incredible. It's long but doesn't come past her shoulders. Gravity-defying hair, it makes her seem taller. Her skin is beautiful; warm and rich, like antique wood. Everything she wears looks as if it was made just for her. And when she speaks to people on my behalf, their eyes grow wide, as if they can't quite believe she's really there. More than that, I've seen the blink of relief when they realise it's not her they need to impress. But even as the conversation starts to flow, I feel the bubble burst as their eyes wander back to my friend.

While I spoke in short bursts and said the wrong thing, Otisina gathered a crowd around herself, like a clutch of diamonds against her skin. They clung to every word, every move. It didn't begin to touch her.

Whether they were on or off again, there was always the possibility that Annie was waiting for her at home. Their arguments were almost as frequent as their candlelit reunions (the candles repurposed from half-remembered birthday cakes), but I could never tell if they were still a couple or if I'd romanticised the whole thing in my head. In the end, I gave up asking.

Whether coupled-up and blissful or heartbroken and on the hunt, Otisina would come to bars, if only to save me from myself.

Everything changed when I met Eliza. Suddenly, my Fridays were busy and my weekends were full. I was happy and blissful and achy, in a rapturous sort of way, but I didn't see Otisina for quite a while. Eliza said she didn't like to think what we got up to on Friday nights without her. To be fair, I should have heard warning bells at that point but then she kissed me and I forgot what I was thinking about.

Eliza wore blouses with short sleeves to show off her knock-off Rolex. When she was nervous, which was quite often, she ruffled her hair and her cheeks bloomed. Poor thing looked like she'd been pelted with strawberries. Falling for her was like falling off a cliff: exhilarating, but with the sure and certain knowledge that the ending would probably kill me.

Somehow, I always knew it would end. I suppose I must have thought we had more than thirteen months in us, but I was wrong. And it ended not with a bang, which might have been nice, but with the silence of an empty apartment. And when I called Otisina needing her assistance with my bashed and broken heart, she acted as if no time had passed since we last spoke.

Luckily, on that Friday in the summer of 1996, Otisina needed the warmth of other people's eyes every bit as much as I did.

By that time, songs from primary school had their own night of the week. Singles and possibles came in their droves to boogie on down to Bay City Rollers and early Aerosmith. In grease-and-leafy south London, where the blocks were breezy and the air was thick with the atmospheric screeching of car alarms and police sirens, we made our way to the mirrored bar of the Purple Pumpkin.

Having had more breakups than relationships, I should have known exactly what to say to guide her through her heartache. Unfortunately, I managed to say something troublingly philosophical that threatened to kill the whole evening.

She frowned at me as we passed through the doors. "As much as I appreciate the distraction, bunny, that makes – absolutely no sense."

"Well, I can see you've given it a lot of thought..."

She ignored me.

It was the right thing to do.

"Hey there, cutie," she called to a barmaid with fraying blonde dreadlocks and khaki trousers. "Can I get two Dirty Martinis over here?" Otisina looked at me from the corner of her eye. "What do you want, bunny?"

"Just a lime and soda," I shuffled.

"And a Bacardi Breezer for my friend, please," she purred.

The barmaid turned, her eyebrow glinting as the bar lights caught the twin silver baubles that intruded upon her face. Otisina saw me watching and clicked her tongue at me. "Really? Already?"

I shook my head. "Oh, God no. I'm not – I'm not looking for anything. I just want to have a little drink and spend some time with you."

"That's why you're watching the barmaid, huh?" She smiled.

"No!" I hissed. "You know how I feel about piercings. I'm just a bit..."

"Snobby?"

"Of course not."

She was joking but I couldn't leave that word hanging in the air.

"I was just thinking about how much something like that would pinch, and just above the eye like that... am I welling up?" I tried to blink the thought away but it was making my eyeballs sting.

"What are you doing with your face?" Otisina asked.

"I... no, it's nothing." I felt a breeze across my cheeks. "Am I blinking too much? I don't want her to think I'm flirting."

Otisina laughed. "She's more likely to think her perfume's too strong."

"No!" I moaned, "That's not... oh God."

The server walked slowly, gingerly, with our drinks on a tray. Otisina smiled and muttered under her breath, "I'm going to ask her. Thank me later."

"What? No!"

"Not that. I'll ask her what she thinks of your..."

"Anything else for you?" the barmaid asked.

All I knew was that I had to stop Otisina from saying anything that sounded like I wanted her number. It wasn't as if I'd be able to talk to her anyway.

I handed over a bank note and smiled. "Your perfume isn't too strong."

Otisina giggled. I pulled the bottle to my mouth, trapping any more ridiculous words inside.

"My friend here has a theory," Otisina jumped in. "Tell her your idea, bunny. You'll love this." And with that, she dived, head first, in to her Martini.

"Really, it's nothing," I rushed.

The barmaid raised her eyebrows briefly, hopefully. "I don't mind," she said, draping a bar towel over her shoulder. "Until the DJ digs out the *Best of Leo Sayer*, I've got nothing else to do."

"This," Otisina threw an arm over my shoulders, which quickly fell to my waist. Righting herself in her chair, she took a glug of her second drink and went back to her train of thought. "This is my best friend. My best, best friend."

"She means the Martini," I mumbled.

"Hear her out. It's a fun theory," she teased. "You'll enjoy it."

I think if I could have gone any redder, I'd have popped. "All I said was..."

"*'Love – doesn't exist,*'" Otisina boomed.

I stumbled, "No, I... O, you know that's not what I said. I was trying to be comforting." I turned back to the barmaid. "I told her I don't believe in The One, that's all."

"Time for another round," she slurred, fishing through her wallet.

I'd seen Otisina like this before. It wouldn't be long before the string of drool and the recitation of disasters past. She could name all her exes in order, and would find reasons why each and every one should have worked out.

"Maybe we should slow down, eh?"

She lowered her eyebrows and pointed at my bottle. "You're barely at the label. If you go any slower, you'll need dusting."

"So, this idea of yours...?" the barmaid prompted.

I glugged my drink and thought for a while. "All right, fine. The One: the idea that there's one perfect person out there for all of us."

"She must be a busy girl," Otisina muttered.

"As a concept, The One is absurd," I told my friend, "and thinking about that made me feel better. I just thought it might do the same for you. Not that you need it, of course, but you look like," I didn't want to say it.

"Like she took her toothbrush back," Otisina wobbled.

There was a silence. Without either of us noticing, the barmaid had started crab-walking her way back down the bar, until she was just a thin string of woman with white-blonde dreadlocks, talking to some guy down the other end; probably the boyfriend.

It made sense. No one wants to spend time with the brokenhearted. We're a depressing bunch but we need each other more than anyone else.

Otisina plucked an olive from her cocktail stick. "Go on, then. Explain it again."

"Well, if you insist." I've never needed much encouragement. "Say you were living in thirteenth century rural Scotland..."

"Like in *Braveheart*?"

"Like in *Braveheart* and..."

"Can I manage the accent, or am I doing the full Gibson?"

"You've got the accent. Very broad, and..."

"Excellent." Looking rather proud of herself, she popped another olive into her mouth.

"And your perfect other was living somewhere south of Tokyo. Before budget airlines or any real knowledge of the shape of the world, you'd never even *meet* them. Do you really think you'd be destined to live alone?"

Her face drooped.

"Of course not," I attempted a note of cheery satisfaction. It came out a bit mangled because of a Bacardi Breezer burp. "Because there can't just be *One*."

"That's not very romantic, you know," she arched.

"Okay, but before romance, before people got together for love – what if your perfect other lived just down the road, in another village, with no money, and you had to marry an earl or a duke or something, to keep your forty-seven brothers and sisters out of the workhouse?"

She looked up suddenly. "People did used to have massive families, didn't they?"

"Yeah, well. They had no telly."

"So, wait, are you saying you don't think Annie's my perfect match?"

"No," I replied, rather more brightly than I should have. "I don't think anyone is."

"What?" she choked.

"No, I mean, I don't think there's just One. There are bound to be loads of people who'd be perfect for you. Tonnes. Too many, maybe. You'd never get through them all. Look at you. You've got nothing to worry about."

She sighed and picked the exact wrong moment to watch herself in the mirror above the bar. "I look drunk." She sipped her Martini.

"But not drunk enough. I'm going to wander over to the dance floor and find a mistake to make.

"Hello there!" Otisina beckoned the fast-approaching barmaid. "Here's my card. Top her up, listen to her stories, smile if you must, and I'll collect her later on, okay?"

As she sashayed out among the dancing lights, I already knew I wouldn't see her again until we were thrown out.

"So, this theory of yours," the barmaid began, passing me a fresh bottle.

"It's nothing, really."

See, barmaids are paid. Whether pouring or listening, they're paid. And all I could think was, if I got talking about something rather personal to me, she wouldn't have to actually hear a word, she could just make the noises and get paid regardless. I would have liked a little more respect for something I put literally minutes of thought into.

"Embarrassing, huh?" she deduced. "Okay. My name is Shawna. I'm twenty-six, Sagittarian, originally from Cardiff and I've been working here for three weeks. So, now you know me, there's nothing to be embarrassed about, is there?"

I pondered this for a moment before completely surrendering. "All right, fine. Just going by the maths, The One can't exist. On a planet of, however many billion people..."

"Five," she replied.

I frowned. "Really?"

"Five point something. Five point seven? It was on *Going For Gold*."

Suddenly, I felt better. "Okay, call it five billion. Just think about that as a number. If I gave you 'til next Tuesday to think of everyone you know, you'd probably come up with, what a couple of hundred? Working in a pub, even for a few weeks, you've probably met loads of people. So, if we say you know three hundred or so...?"

"Could be," she nods.

"So, does it seem especially fair that there's only One out of five billion, and you only know about three hundred of them?"

She didn't say anything for what felt like hours. Then, "Why does it have to be fair?"

"Are you seeing anyone at the moment?" I asked.

She looked at me as if I'd said something brazen. I still don't think I had.

"Okay," I blathered, emboldened, I suspect, by the drink in my hand. "I'll just work it out for myself. So, if we take it that half the population is male, that's two and a half billion men to choose from."

It was a very small smile, but I saw it.

"Of course, that's not the end of it," I cautioned. "If we take it that half the men are married or near as dammit, and a quarter are children, you're down by seventy-five percent without trying."

"Is that right?"

"And don't forget the gay men," I urged. "That could be another ten percent, easily. So that leaves you with...?"

Shawna took a short breath. "As much as I'm enjoying this, I'm not great with numbers, so..."

I watched her for a moment.

"Okay, fine," she said. "I don't know, four?"

"Three hundred and seventy-five million," I nodded.

Her eyes went wide; she looked lost. I reassured myself that big numbers can do that to people and went back to what I was thinking.

"Even if we add in the x factor: the ones with creepy ex-girlfriends, those in prison, submariners, oil rigs workers, fellas with a fear of commitment, those with clingy mothers, the psychologically dangerous, those who have absolutely no interest in you physically, and you've still got thirty-seven million and change."

I tried not to watch too closely but she took a deep breath. "Well, that's pretty good," Shawna beamed. "I mean, you saved it in the en... hang on. That's only ten percent. Really? Of all the men who could fancy me, only ten percent would?"

I half-closed one eye. "Ideally, we'd correct for the men you won't meet at the right time."

"I don't think my self-esteem can take it."

"But that's the thing: if we call it thirty-seven million, for the sake of simplicity, you'd need about four hundred and... sixty lifetimes to meet them all."

"Are you serious?"

I nodded.

She smiled.

Otisina shimmied to a near-dangerous degree to *Gonna Make You A Star* by David Essex.

"But don't you see? Thirty-seven million men, and only One of them is perfect for you? How can that make sense?"

"Bad break-up, huh?" Shawna asked.

"Eh," I waved the bottle around, "they'll work it out. They never stay broken up for long."

"I didn't mean her."

I drained my bottle and handed it back across the bar. "Okay, so the maths thing isn't working for you. So, from a poetic perspective – we're all made of clay, right? Well, clay doesn't just sit as two little lumps in the middle of a field. There are whole counties that are basically clay. So, is it just the strip of clay that was next to you who's your soul mate, or is it every clod of clay in the field? And everything on the surface of the earth is connected, because of gravity, so why shouldn't you be more drawn to a piece of clay from another hemisphere?"

She pursed her lips. "I'm not attracted to clay."

"I'm not talking about actual clay," I struggled.

"I think I'll have a drink with you," she smiled.

"But that's just it. If there's only One person for you, there might as well only be one drink."

She arched an eyebrow. "Ah, but drinks can be topped up, can't they?"

"Thank God." There was a long pause before I said anything else. "My partner left me this afternoon. I'd just written her a love letter. It's pathetic, right? I didn't get to send it. God, I worked on it for weeks. Got home and her key was on the side. She'd taken all her clothes and her ficus was gone. That was the proof. Without the ficus, there's no reason for her to come back."

"What happened?" she asked.

I shrugged, real words proving too difficult to find.

"Do you really want someone who could do that to you?" Shawna asked.

I couldn't answer so went back to what I knew. "That's the other reason, you see, why The One doesn't work. If she was The One then, okay, I'll never know this kind of pain again but I'll never be as happy as I was with her, ever again. But if she was The One, she couldn't put me through this, right? God, it's like my insides have been scooped out. Sorry, you don't want to hear about this. And I don't want to talk about it.

"But it makes you think. How many other people are in this kind of pain, right now, like me, but they're completely alone? At least I've got…"

Shawna passed me a drink and raised her own. "Here's to the Several. May we live long enough to find them all."

Looking out to the dance floor, I became aware that I couldn't see Otisina anywhere. "Did you see where my friend went?"

"Last I saw, she was heading to the Ladies'. Now you mention it, that was quite a while ago. I wonder where she got to…"

No sooner had she drawn breath to call out to the security guy, I got an image in my mind – Otisina, kneeling in a cubicle over someone else's girlfriend. It was too early to go home to an empty apartment and I couldn't bear to be thrown out to the strains of David Soul.

"So, yeah," I hurried, "has anyone ever sent you a love letter, Shawna?"

She sank back to the balls of her feet. "Not that I can remember."

"I hadn't actually put it in the envelope. It wasn't at that stage. And I know I can't send it to her. A woman who won't bother to say goodbye is not a woman to send anything to, unless it's ripped up or burnt, but what am I supposed to do with the letter now? I can't keep it. There's something truly tragic about keeping it, and I can't send it, so what am I supposed to do?"

"Burn it," she suggested. "Are you going to look for your mate, then? Or should I get security on it?"

"I'm sure she won't be much longer." I sounded shifty.

"You think she's still in the bathroom?" Shawna asked, her eyes narrowing.

"She doesn't eat a lot of fibre."

Quickly, Otisina was back on the dance floor, straightening her straps and giggling at the flannel-clad lovely just behind her. Before I could say anything else, they headed straight over.

"Hey, bunny," my friend said, more for her companion's benefit than mine. She could be under no illusions. Whatever they had done, it didn't make them a couple. "You still on the same Breezer? Hell, get her another one, will you, cutie?"

Shawna dipped below the counter and emerged with another bottle.

"This is Hazel, by the way," Otisina added as an afterthought. "We met in the queue for the Ladies'. Are we, are we interrupting anything?"

"I was just asking Shawna's advice about something," I said.

Hazel looked uncomfortable. I don't think she had been expecting to meet the best friend and a barmaid when her breathing hadn't quite settled down. For the sake of making it less awkward, I made it more awkward by telling them what we'd been talking about.

"So, now I don't know what to do with it." I didn't think I was wailing but from the looks I was getting, I suppose I must have been.

"Why don't you send it to someone else?" Hazel asked. And just like that, I knew exactly what to do.

I NO LONGER UNDERSTAND the clock. The time is fickle and plays with my heart, tangling the beat, putting lead into the meat, making it sink and fly with alternate clicks across the face.

It's not just the hours that seem to multiply, distort, since you left my bed, my door, my street. It's the days and the weeks and the endless stretch of time since I realised I couldn't bear another minute without you.

From that first dizzying moment when I saw you and the world stood still, across a crowded room, a crowded day, a crowded life – I saw you and I knew you were my perfect other; the answer to a question I had no words to ask.

It was almost as if I recognised you, from a memory or dream, I could not say, but I knew you and every thought from then to now, has been filled with glimmers of you.

And in those awful days and nights, when fate and the world kept us apart, I thought of nothing but that perfect, crystal-lit moment when I first saw you.

There's a small, sweet smile, like the one you're trying to hide right now, that has spoken to me, since before the two of us had speech, before we knew each other, before I knew anything.

There's a chill to your skin when your shoulder escapes the duvet, and in that smooth and tender coolness is a universe of beauty.

And until I have no voice, no words, I'll speak your name as the truth of my heart...

I couldn't bring myself to read the rest of it.

She'd never read these words. She'd never know. I could have said it, a dozen times a day, but instead, I forced the words into pages of scribbles and rewriting and frantic crossing out; hours of my life, and Eliza would never read a word.

Some people have no idea. That is their blessing and their curse. They can breeze through all of life, leaving lovers tremble-lipped in their wake. I wonder how many of us are broken, not by accidents and trauma, but by love. I don't know why I thought she was so special, with her buffed nails and her herpes. She walked in sunlight, chest out, shoulders back, and just like that – I didn't just lose my heart. I lost myself.

Recovering from a broken heart is a lot of work. It's not just a case of mending the torn parts, the shattered thoughts, it's necessary to replace the missing parts as well. And Eliza took so much of me with her when she left, I felt I'd have to learn how to rebuild internal organs as well as everything else. It might have seemed hopeless if it weren't for an idea. A small idea, but enough to keep me going for a while.

If I wasn't supposed to do it, there would have been a knock on the door, a ring on the telephone, the universe would have stepped in before I put the stamp on the envelope, before I found the book, before I made my way across the road to the blood-red letterbox.

WE ONLY HAD A FEW MINUTES left of Otisina's lunch break and I still hadn't told her. I was actively stalling. I could feel myself doing it. One of her best qualities was and always has been her total unshockability, but time was running out and I couldn't make the words come.

She popped a breath mint into her mouth to chase away the tang of midday gin. I don't know when cocktails during office hours became socially unacceptable, but that was the world we were living in. It could have been a lot worse, I'm sure, but the bus pulled up directly outside her grey trouser-suit of a building. She'd have been fine.

"Okay, bunny. I'm going to have to make a move if I'm going to get in before my next meeting," she announced.

"No, wait!" It practically fell out of me. "I sent the letter."

Otisina took a deep breath and narrowed her eyes. "Fuck it, they can have the meeting without me. So, what did she say?"

"Well, that's the thing," I stumbled. "I didn't send it to her."

She frowned.

I hadn't noticed the little line between her eyes before but, with it staring at me, it was as if she was daring me to mention it.

"I thought you said it was a love letter?"

"That's right, it was. Well, it is."

She made a face at me. It was as if she was using her tongue to work something out from between her teeth. "So... no, I'm not following. Did you change the wording, then?"

I hesitated. "Not as such."

She signalled to the barman for another round. I'll say this, it wasn't as if I could hear the cogs turning as she thought it through, but my hearing has never been the same since Metallica in '92.

Haltingly, "You – sent it – to someone else."

I nodded.

"Hold on, you took Heather's advice over mine?"

I cleared my throat. "Hazel."

"Yeah, that's what I meant. Hazel, of course. But, no, you're not getting out of it that easily. You took a stranger's advice over mine?"

"Your advice," I reminded her, "was to drink myself silly and I did that."

The barman, who had a nametag – which not only smacked of desperation, it made me want to call him 'garçon' and nothing else for the rest of time – lurked as if he had a vested interest in the outcome of our drunken lunchtime. Quietly, I suspected that sobriety was a burden to any bartender, always observing, serving, always invited to the party but never asked to enjoy it, only to work.

"Hold on, what did she suggest?" Otisina asked, dragging me back to the point.

"Incidentally, you took a lot more than her *advice*," I pointed out.

She rolled her eyes at me. "That was it! She said to... You sent it to someone else? Who? An ex, or...?"

I shrugged. "I don't know."

Both Otisina and the barman looked at me.

"You know how, years ago, when people got together, they just stayed that way despite how unhappy they were? Maybe it would have been an idea if you'd stayed with Sharon, back at college. At least you wouldn't have had all this time in your head."

And just like that, Otisina had morphed into my mother. The barman must have realised he had nothing useful to add because he walked away. Perhaps he was confused or disgusted. Luckily, I've never needed the approval of a lunchtime barman. Except I was so focussed on his sudden departure, I lost track of what I was saying and admitted entirely too much.

"I picked a name out of the phone book." I slurped my drink a little louder than I meant to. I think it was the embarrassment. I sounded like an angry horse.

She shook her head. "So, how's this supposed to play out? What, you tell her that you've already moved on with someone else, some nameless someone else? And not just moved on, but moved on to the point of love letters and then she'll, what, kick herself for a few years?"

"I'm not going to tell her!" I turned back to my drink. "And who said love lett*ers*, anyway? It was just one."

"Do you even know whether you sent it to a woman?" she asked.

I made a few mouth shapes but nothing I could fix a consonant to.

"Tell me you didn't include a return address!" she shrieked.

"Of course I didn't." I finished my drink quickly. "Besides, she'll never know."

"Of course not," Otisina smiled.

"What? I have some self-control."

She didn't believe me.

Neither did I.

SUMMER SEARED HOT LITTLE lines through the blinds across the windows. It was early evening, but it might as well have been noon. The sunshine had blasted me for days. My skin was burnt bright red right down to the bone.

I knew what I should have done. It came crashing in on me like the most complete realisation I'd ever had. I should have taken a copy of what I'd written. Not for the reason you're thinking.

Well, probably not.

I wouldn't have wanted to keep it as a reminder of when I had had love, like some terrible epistolary approximation to Miss Havisham, but in Streatham, with a box of words to reread on the gloomy days to make myself feel worse, and better. A stash of letters to fall into between trips to the fridge-freezer for ice cream laced with cider.

No, I should have kept a copy because later, all I could think of were the things I should have said. Except, I didn't remember. Maybe I did get it right the first time. See, the trouble with going through a massive number of edits and different pens is that – I didn't remember what made it through to the final cut.

I think I said I'd loved her for hours, days, weeks, but did I say that I'd been in love with her for thousands of years? Before I knew her, before I knew who I was, before I knew what love and its associated parts were for?

The thing is: it only sounds stalkery and weird because she left. If she was still in the picture, it would be sickly-sweet and probably lead to all manner of bathroom activities, but it would be real. And without any actual knowledge of what I wrote in that first letter, it became a sham. Worse than a sham. It was a half-remembered sham.

Thank God, I'd thought to fold the page in, pointing to the stranger's name. It wasn't as if I could contact them and ask what I'd written but it was good to have options.

The trouble was the more I thought about the letter, the more I realised what I should have said. If I had sent it to her, I should have spoken of the dream we kept and nurtured for the last six months – of a home in Umbria, with the sun setting scarlet across the golden hills, stretching out the days with watercolour certainty. I should have written about the summers we'd imagined (it was always summer in my mind), the hot months spent on beaches, in parks, walking along sun and cliff. If I'd sent it to her, she could have traced the truth in the ink and the scent of the hands that had written those sweet words.

Except she never would have read it, of course. A minor detail. An annoyance, more than anything else.

The letter wasn't perfect.

There. I said it.

Poorly remembered phrases teased me in the night when sleep was elusive and the dreams tumbled across my unblinking, ceiling-staring eyes. I should have written something better. It crossed my mind: perhaps that was why she couldn't stay. My unwieldy, lazy tongue was not sufficiently piquant to hold her dwindling interest. *Maybe, if I'd had the words,* I thought, *I could have kept her.*

It was only when the first strands of light poked through the paper-thin curtains, that I gave myself my regular, Otisina-style talking-to.

Would I really have wanted a woman who I had to manipulate into staying with me?

Would I actually respect her if I knew she'd been weak enough to fall for a bit of well-worded blather?

Yup. Double yup.

I could have told myself that, whether she'd stayed out of guilt or desperation, it wouldn't have mattered. As long as she'd stayed.

Otisina wouldn't stand for all my moping. I got over Sharon. Pat on back. I was okay after Tina left, and she wanted us to start a centre for diseased rabbits in the Cotswolds. She had plans for our future. As I recall, I partied like a maniac after she left. I doubt anyone is grown up enough for Tina.

I knew, as well as I know myself, that Otisina would tell me that there's no need to settle – down or otherwise; that young love is so named because it doesn't last; that I should stop worrying about why nobody wants to stay with me because it's people repellent.

Absolutely true.

There's no doubting it.

But the words sat unused within me and they needed to be written down. I couldn't stop myself. And soon the words were laid out neatly, the paper made its way, almost without my permission, into an envelope. I watched as my hand skimmed the phone book and once again, a stranger would become the recipient of a cursive delight. It crossed my mind they might spend days, weeks, years, wondering who among the people they saw on any given street had been harbouring this wash of emotion and perhaps it would give them the lift, the boost, the inflated sense of feeling that was so lacking in my life.

I wondered, as I traced the name – A. E. Reynolds of Lime Way – if they already knew they were loved, but with so much emptiness in the world and the absence of The One, I doubted it.

I decided, regardless of my own life, it might be enough to do something kind for someone else. As I pushed the envelope into the letterbox, I prayed that Otisina would run into Hazel again. It would be nice to get some confirmation that I was doing a good thing. Otisina would suck her teeth and think I was crazy. Unchecked, she'd give me a look that would make my eyelid twitch, but it's good to have a friend who can tell you these things.

It's also important to ignore a friend like this at every opportunity.

***

THE PHONE WAS RINGING as I entered my apartment. It had been a long day and I really didn't want to extend it any further with yet another work call. But it was automatic. I was compelled to answer.

"Hello?" I said.

"Babe." Of course, it was Eliza. Why wouldn't it be her? I couldn't begin to guess how she had found out about the letters so fast – yes, lett*ers* – definitely plural now, there was no point in lying to myself anymore.

"So," I breathed, "how are you?"

I don't know why I asked her this. I didn't really want to know. When someone ups and leaves, their general health is frankly irrelevant until they get to their deathbed and ask the unplanned family to look you up so they can beg your forgiveness before it's too late.

She wasn't at that point. She sounded positively perky. I mean, it's not as if I wished her death by falling piano but she could have sounded a little less bouncy. Frankly, it was unkind.

But while I ignored her response, all I could think was that somehow, having put my feelings out into the ether, she must have sensed it. *Deep down,* I thought, *she knows that I loved her enough to spill a pint or two of ink on writing, rewriting, best handwriting, love to other people.*

"So, when would be best, do you think?" she asked.

I had no idea what she was talking about.

"What, Wednesday?" she suggested.

I wondered if Eliza had asked me out to dinner, to explain.

"I can find a space for you on Friday," she hedged, "but there'll be no time for coffee."

I frowned, unable to process the idea that she was suggesting cutting short our reconciliation dinner.

"I suppose we don't really need to do this in public," she added, cheerily. "We're neither of us dangerous, are we? How's about I just pop over one evening?"

She had never been this presumptuous when we were a couple. *Just popping by for a quick coffeeless dinner, a small segue into bed and then... what, are we calling that a goodbye now?*

"I'm sorry, what?" I attempted a haughty tone. I sounded ill.

"To pick up my DVDs." She sounded exasperated. "I think I got everything else but I plumb forgot about the films under the TV."

I said nothing for a little while. Eventually, "You want your films?"

"Well, yeah," she breezed. "Marlene Dietrich was never really your girl, was she? So, I thought I might just collect her up and make sure I didn't leave anything else. I don't think I did but... Anyway, Wednesday or Friday?"

I didn't even realise I'd said anything until she replied with a smile in her voice. "I suppose you'll be going out with Otisina on Friday night. Should have thought of that. Wednesday it is. See you then, babe."

I blinked at the sound of the dial tone. I replaced the receiver and wondered how likely it was I could get my MP to propose a bill in parliament to have overly cheerful people hunted for sport.

I reached over to the writing paper and made a start.

FRIDAY CAME AND I FELT my shoulders relax. Heading over to the crowded bar, I saw Otisina with three Martinis in front of her and Hazel standing beside her. If Hazel lasted one more week, she would officially be Otisina's longest relationship.

"Hey bunny," she smiled. "If you can't manage yours, I'll drink it for you. I'm all heart, you know that."

"So kind," I said, grasping the thin stem and slugging back half the drink in one fierce, chilly swallow. "Hazel, right? How nice to see you again."

Otisina flashed me a look and asked, "Who wants to dance? Nobody? Okay, I suggest you take turns watching my drink and watching me. I'll be back before closing."

And off she went, flirting her way across the room; a blur of bright blue straps and a diamanté smile.

"She's making a night of it, eh?" I said.

Hazel frowned. Her whole face drooped. Of course, she'd never known Otisina any other way. As her eyes tracked my friend across the floor and into the arms of an astonished bridesmaid, it felt like a good time for a change of subject.

"Hey, I wondered if I could bend your ear about something?" To be frank, I'd hoped to be a little further into the drink before saying anything at all but it wasn't as if she was bombarding me with chatter.

"Yes?" Hazel sounded hopeful. It was so sudden, instant switch-on, it took me a moment to process it.

"You remember..." I mean, I didn't want to ruin her night and I had a horrible feeling I would, but she did ask. "...I wrote a love letter to my, umm, *ex*," the title pained me, "right before she left?"

She nodded. "What did you do with it?"

Hazel didn't look up from her drink. I couldn't tell if she putting up with me and my conversation out of politeness, or if it was simply distracting her from the sight of Otisina, having a good time, without her.

"I sent it to a stranger," I announced.

"Okay," she said.

I know. I expected more, too.

"Well, yeah," I went on, unable to stop myself. "But I got kind of caught up and then, one thing and another, you know how it goes, I wrote another one."

"Another love letter?" she asked.

I lifted my eyebrows in what I hoped was an expression of only-slightly-sullied innocence.

"So, what did you do with the second one? Did you send it to your ex?"

"Not exactly."

"Who then?"

I shrugged and almost spilt my drink. Tragedy averted, I took another swig.

"Wow." Hazel looked genuinely impressed. Really. If I had a fan club, she'd be the president. I'd get a restraining order but she'd be president regardless. "Your ex must have been quite something," she added. "Even sending them to other people, for you to keep writing to her this way, she must have been amazing."

I shrugged and nodded. Both. Catching a glimpse of myself in the mirror over the bar, I gulped. I looked like De Niro.

"Thing is..." I leaned in and lowered my voice. "I – I didn't just leave it at those two."

It was the strangest thing. As much as I felt rather naughty and I was blushing up a storm, I couldn't help but wonder what the point of a secret was if it didn't come out eventually. Even those few hours when only I knew felt like an ocean of time.

"How many have you sent?" Hazel asked, her voice bright and gentle.

"Well, it's not like it's an addiction," I replied. I suppose it might have sounded a little defensive because...

"I mean, if you don't want to talk about it..."

I puffed out breaths, one on top of another. "I just did like you said. It felt like I was putting something good into the world and then I just – didn't stop. Totally could have. Obviously."

"How many have you sent?" she repeated.

"Five or six."

Her eyes grew wide. "Are you serious?"

"No," I chuckled. "No, of course not."

Eleven. I sent eleven of them.

Okay, twelve.

"It's not bad, is it?" I asked.

Otisina shimmied her way over to her waiting drink. "What's going on over here? You two getting along all right?"

"I wish someone would send me a love letter," Hazel moped.

Otisina clicked her tongue. "Just tell Joni your surname. If she can find you in the book, she'll send you one."

<hr />

OKAY, SO I WASN'T EXACTLY honest with Hazel but I hardly knew her. There was nothing to feel bad about there. Regardless of how many love letters I'd sent, or how much the residential listings were swelling from the folded over pages, none of it really mattered. What mattered was that I was sending out positive vibes to people who didn't know who I was and therefore couldn't reject me.

Maybe it was just – you know how everyone gets a bit soppy about the Queen at Christmas? It was like that. In allowing myself to feel something almost real – in the sense that I hadn't met any of the people I professed to love, or the Queen for that matter – maybe it was as good as feeling something authentic?

Not quite feeling something for someone who's just a name in a book – was it really so different from going a bit soft over the Queen's speech? I knew I'd never have breakfast with my strangers but, in its way, that distance kept them perfect.

RIGHT AROUND THE TWENTIETH letter, I realised I'd been drinking more since the break-up than at any time in my life. The thought was only fleeting because either Otisina or Hazel would order a round of shots and I'd forget what I was worried about. I was at least tiddly most nights, but none of us had drunk enough to drown so it felt more like a hobby than a habit.

"You'll get through this, bunny," Otisina said. "They say you can't put a size twelve body into a size eight dress. I say, bring me the body. It's just anatomical origami. If you can fold with precision and keep your creases tight, you can make it work. Your situation is exactly the same. Emotional origami. Just turn it into a crane and launch it across the room."

"Are you sure you want these?" Shawna the barmaid asked, setting down a tray. Her jaw was set at a strange angle, like she'd broken a tooth on her favourite flavour of Dorito.

Otisina waved her off. "We're chasing away the pain. It only looks like we're pissed because it's a delicate process."

Hazel clinked glasses with Otisina and led her out to the dance floor. I'd barely licked the salt when I heard Shawna's voice in my ear.

"I hope you feel better soon," she said. "I know we don't know each other and I swear I'm not trying it on, but it's hard to see you so broken up."

My glass was poised mid-air. Time slowed. The salt was like a crust on my lower lip. It was sharp and made me want to bite down on something – a cricket ball, an elbow, a hamster, I didn't care. But as she moved down the bar away from me, my head started to swim. All I could think was how it might not be so awful to make a connection with someone I'd actually met.

The problem was so obvious, I should have thought about it before. A new feeling stewed in the pit of my stomach; something close to regret. It was annoying. I suspected, in that moment, that it would be easier to deal with if I had someone with me.

FOR ALL OF THE DAY and night before, I reminded myself of one thing: It was not a date. It was a bag of chips on a park bench. Nothing romantic to be construed here, move along, please.

Shawna was worried because she only ever saw me spinning on a bar stool, on the slurry side of sober, and insisted that carbs were fast becoming a necessity.

And so, she bought me chips.

I suspected she already knew something of the love letters. She must have heard something, half-heard something, through my drunken blather. And I was never sure how Otisina explained me when I wasn't around. I decided it would be better if I described it all from my perspective. And so I did.

The streetlights had come on. The clocks had changed. It was still a surprise. It was barely autumn but there was a terrible nip of Christmas in the air. As if the sun had been expunged from the sky and we had absolutely no business sitting outside as the sky dimmed, eating takeaway from newspaper scandals, in the drizzle.

"Have you actually thought this thing through?" Shawna asked, skewering a fat, greasy chip. It was practically leaking as she took the first bite of it.

I sighed.

"I have got this right, haven't I?" she asked. "You're sending letters to random strangers, is that it?"

"Yes," I huffed, sticking out my lower lip. I dared her to find a problem with what was, in effect, a charitable endeavour.

"Random people from the phone book..." she chewed another chip. "So, you're just cherry-picking names from something that was printed and popped through the door, what, last year?"

"Yeah."

It was nice to feel understood.

"What makes you think these people are still alive?" Shawna asked. "Anything can happen in a year. Can you imagine what a letter like yours would do to their families? Even if they *are* alive..."

"Of course, they are," I protested, although admittedly on shaky ground.

"If they are alive, you can't pretend to know their set-up. They might be widowed. I can see you didn't mean to, but did you even think about the pain you might have been inflicting on these people?"

My mouth dropped open. I knew because I could feel a chill reaching into my teeth.

"Or, or..." It was like she'd been hooked up to the mains. "What if the people you've sent the letters to are in fragile relationships? Or worse, abusive relationships? Letters like this could do serious damage. Like hospital, worse, why would you do this?"

"Oh my God," I whispered. "I didn't think." It was quite possibly the truest thing I'd ever said. I didn't have time to feel proud of myself because Shawna went on.

"Please tell me you know who you sent them to."

I shuffled. The bench was starting to feel damp. "Pretty much."

She threw the last chip into her mouth and rolled up the paper packaging before slinging it into the black bin to her side.

"I marked the pages," I told her, my voice rising.

She rolled her eyes at me.

"Well, I made sure the corners pointed at the right names." I was whining. I could hear myself doing it.

"Okay." She licked her lips. "What you need to do is write back to them and apologise. Say it was a prank or something, and hope for the best."

"Write back to them?" I asked. "*All* of them?"

"How many are we talking about?"

"A couple," I muttered.

"How many is a couple?" she asked. Very calm, very sensible. Very annoying.

"Thirty-two." Well, there was no point playing it down.

From the look on her face, I should have tried to play it down.

"God," I wailed, "it's going to take me weeks to get the wording right and send them all out."

She was frowning again. "Hold on. Where d'you find the money for that many stamps?"

I rolled up the paper packaging, ignoring the cold chips I hadn't touched. "I don't have a lot of hobbies. My free cash is my own."

"And you spend it on stamps? You're so random."

I threw the balled up chip packet. Aiming for the bin, it rebounded off Shawna's shoulder and bounced along the pavement. Quickly, she scrambled to her feet, snatched up the rubbish and popped it into the tall black can.

"Sorry but I couldn't leave it there," she sighed. "We've only got one planet."

I was flustered. "Yeah, no. I know. That's what I was aiming for but…"

"My ex was an environmentalist."

"Oh, I see." I went quiet and decided to feign interest. "What was he like?"

"She had a good heart," Shawna said. "But she never told me how she felt. About me, I mean. The world, definitely. But not me. Wasn't her style."

"Well," I was spiralling. "I should probably get back and start work, I suppose."

"I'm going to regret this," she said, "but… do you want some help with it? I won't write letters but I can seal envelopes like a maniac."

※

AND AS WE SAT AT MY kitchen table – me, writing letters of apology, her, affixing stamps and smiling – all I could think was: if things had worked out like they were supposed to, I might still be playing second fiddle to a ficus.

"Shawna?" I began.

"Hmm," she replied.

"You're not in a relationship, are you?"

"No," she said. "Not right now."

"And you're not, by any chance, bereaved, are you?"

"No," she chuckled. "Thanks for asking."

"I'm going to put the kettle on," I announced. "Would you like a coffee?"

"That sounds good," she replied. "I'm just going to stretch my legs a minute."

When Shawna nipped off to the bathroom, I took the opportunity and slipped the best love letter of all into her jacket. I might not be comfortable talking out loud to people who can see me, but I think she'll like the letter.

But only when she gets home.

You can't rush these things.

The Good In Goodbye: A Short Story of Revenge

I'VE ALWAYS TAKEN PRIDE in the fact that when I know something is none of my business, my aversion to it is near total. For instance, other people's love lives: nothing to do with me – *avoid*. Other people's feelings about their lady-business: even less to do with me – *run for the hills*.

Similarly, my stuff is my own. Such as – oh, I don't know – my personal correspondence from when I was thirteen years old, with braces and a double-A cup: totally mine, and I will take down anybody who tries to make it theirs.

Which is how we came to the phone call in the first place.

"Charlotte," she sighed, her voice a sixty-year-old example of withered exhaustion. "Why are you bothering me with all this?"

I could practically hear her rolling her eyes.

"I'm just saying..."

"Oh, please. It was twenty years ago! How, *how* have you been holding onto this for so long? Surely you have other things to occupy your mind..."

"I'm just saying, when you read my letters to Pierre before I sent them, that really wasn't... Mum, that wasn't cool."

"You know, I do, I blame myself."

I settled in for the coming rant.

"I knew I should have made you go to Sunday school," she said. "Your sister never brings up this sort of thing. You know why? She went to Sunday school. *Honour thy father and thy...*

"You know, I think I'd relaxed as a mother by the time you were born. But with the first child, you worry all the time. You send them on every play-date and nudge them into every extra curricular activity. Because you've never done this before. You need to make it a success. And so, you give them an extra event, call it 'school', and they create far fewer problems than the hellion who comes in second.

"I don't care who you ask. With your first child, you give up dinner, sleep, quiet nights in. Frankly, Charlotte, it's a wonder you were born at all."

"I don't think that's quite…"

"Really, why are you calling me about this now?"

In truth, it had only just popped into my head. A little bit like the cat who was sent to work on a soap opera. It didn't occur to me that they'd put him down until I was every day of twenty-six.

"Forget I said anything."

She took a long breath. "Pierre *was* only a pen pal, wasn't he?"

I responded the only way I knew how: I groaned.

"Only it would be something of a surprise to your lovely girlfriend. How is she, by the way?"

"Fine." As a word, I rather shrugged it out.

"Still doing the party planning, is she?"

At that point, I hoped quite fervently that the audible eye roll was hereditary. It would have been a shame if she hadn't been painfully aware of it, too. "It's her business, Mum. And she's doing well. People always have things to celebrate and they never want the work of it. She's going to be busy 'til she's dead."

"You sound awfully confident about that, Charlotte." She almost sounded impressed.

"Well, I've been watching her work for almost eighteen months."

"And you're," she lowered her voice to a whisper, "you're sure she's not taking up too much space in your apartment, are you? You can tell me. It's a terribly small flat, darling, and if she's taking advantage, I want to know you have someone you can tell."

I took a deep breath and started counting. "We're fine, thanks, Mum."

"You can understand why I'd worry. She did move in remarkably quickly and it's not as if you really had a chance to get to know each other before you started sharing a bathroom. Intimacy like that can break a couple, you know."

"Great, yeah," I managed as Marisa squeezed past me.

"Before you know it, there are yellowish toenail clippings on the edge of the bath. Or a knot of thick black hair, clogging up the shower drain, that you can only get out by using a knitting needle like a swizzle stick.

"Sometimes, there's a bottle of something that's missing a label and reeks to high heaven, but as much as you'll never know them well enough to ask what it is, all you can think about, while you're watching the telly or filling in the crossword, is where they might apply it. Things like that take all the magic out of a relationship."

I plastered a big smile to my face that my voice couldn't match. "Got it. Please change the subject."

"Okay so, you're fine," she affirmed. "Put her on, will you?"

"What now?" I spluttered. It wasn't attractive. I did it anyway.

"I'm not going to embarrass you. I just want to say 'hello'. You don't mind if I say 'hello' to my near-as-dammit daughter-in-law, surely?"

Marisa held out a Bloody Mary to me that could have been an awful lot bloodier. Rather than say any more, I swapped her the glass for the phone.

"Hello?" she said, her voice as light as sunshine. "Oh, hi Carole."

I couldn't begin to guess why, but she kept smiling. It was remarkable.

"How are you?"

I had no interest in their conversation so I plucked the green stalk from my drink and knocked in back in one. With a skilful flick of my wrist, the celery flew in to the food waste bin – the only place for it – and I went over to the counter to make myself another.

It was true, as much as my mother used to read my post, I still had little to no interest in other people's conversations. It wasn't that the lives of others didn't interest me. I just always had my own thing going on and when you fill your time with gossip, there's really no room for anything, shall we say, more diverting.

Okay, since you ask: I was teaching Pierre how to swear in English. Because he'd asked me to. Naturally, my mother, armed with suspicion, intrigue and only half the conversation, decided that I was thrusting vulgar language at a sweet, innocent French boy – either to perturb or captivate him.

Why I'd started thinking of Pierre and our letters on that particular stormy afternoon, I couldn't tell you. All I knew for sure was that my mother was wrong and it was about time she knew.

"Yes, I know," Marisa giggled. "No, I think it's a wonderful idea. Of course, I'll need to talk to him first but..."

I made questioning faces at her but, if I'd had any doubt, it became quite clear that Marisa wasn't raised the same way I was; she couldn't have two conversations at once and so I waited and finished my drink.

I should point out – I don't *need* a drink to recover from conversations with my mother. I just – always seem to have more of them when I've been speaking to her.

Pure coincidence.

"That sounds like it could work. I'll get right on it," Marisa promised. "Okay, Carole. Love you, bye."

I mean, really.

It wasn't as if my mother couldn't cope with a case of the sentimentals. It was just that, if she had to have it, she'd rather it was in the same room as her. She'd never cope over the phone. I giggled to myself and wondered if I was a monster.

I took the phone from Marisa and put it back in its charging cradle. "So, what's happening?" I asked.

She topped up our drinks. "We're having a party."

"We are?"

"We are." She sounded pleased, a particular kind of pleased. It was as if she had a secret.

Not that kind of secret. Behave yourself.

"Why, exactly, are we having a party?" I asked.

"For our anniversary."

I counted quickly in my head. "You're either late, early, or thinking of the wrong person."

She took my hand and kissed it. "Now, you mustn't be upset."

I chose that moment to stare weakly at a ceiling tile.

"But your mother was wondering if Gary – you know Gary who does the calligraphy for the wedding invitations? – she was wondering how he was and..."

"Why? She's never met him. Why would she bother to ask after a man she's never even met?"

Marisa frowned.

"Don't look at me like that. She's up to something. She must be."

"So suspicious!" she replied, shaking her head.

I lowered my voice. "Oh, God. What's she planning?"

"Well, your mother was just wondering if... and I think it's a pretty good idea... if we had a party, it might just give certain people an opportunity to meet. Nothing formal, just a few friends, some sliders, maybe a cocktail or two. Because you know as well as I do, internet-dating isn't for everyone. I mean, it's *supposed* to be, but..."

"Hold on." I held up my glass to make my point but Marisa filled it while I was trying to find the words. "Hold on. My mother – wants to fix Gary up – with someone." I paused. "Gary with the stubble who doesn't wear socks."

"That's him."

"Well, who does she want to set him up with?" I asked.

"No one in particular," she sounded defensive. "Not specifically. But if there's a spark then, who are we to argue with…? Okay, it's for your sister."

My eyes almost fell out of my head. "Where does she get these ideas?"

"Well, technically, I was the one who first mentioned Gary to her but…"

"Why must you meddle?"

Marisa curled her lip. "She was going to do this anyway. At least, with Gary, you know what you're getting. He's a calligrapher. He's hardly going to push your sister into some kind of pyramid scheme or sell her an ostrich farm."

"Online dating really didn't work for you, did it?" I arched.

"I'm here now, aren't I?"

See, if I'd even tried to imagine a scenario where my sister would be inveigled into the arms of my girlfriend's co-worker, I would have thought it was either destiny or, more likely, laziness that had brought them together. Instead, there would be a party, with all the work of a party, followed by face-singeing embarrassment and my sister's sudden entry into a convent, or kismet and fireworks – leading to double dates, movie nights and couply rubbish for the rest of our lives.

For a moment, I wondered who would get custody of me in the inevitable divorce settlement.

Marisa ran her fingers through her hair. It used to be a pixie cut but she was growing it out. But whether cropped and coiffed or short and shaggy, it was an old trick. Unfortunately, it always worked. "I reckon it could be kind of nice if Kelly and Gary made a go of things. Think of it."

"She's my sister. I really don't want to."

"It would give you a bit of company if he and I had to work late. We could all go skating together and..."

"Skating." It should have been a question but it came out flat as a pancake. "When have we ever been skating? When has either of us shown the slightest interest in skating?"

"Maybe we just weren't at that point in our relationship yet. But now, we can be," she said.

See, there's nothing I enjoy more than adhering to a stereotype so, naturally, when Marisa suggested we move in together within two months of meeting, I pulled the key off my chain before giving it a second thought. But I couldn't help but think that the whole Kelly and Gary thing was moving too quickly. It was barely a suggestion before I saw them falling apart. It would be painful and acrimonious, but in that moment, Marisa's eyes were drifting and I could tell she was planning their honeymoon.

My mother would have already named the first child.

At that point, Gary and Kelly couldn't know how much of their lives was being organised for them, but I was confident that by the time the streetlights came on, golfing trousers and entry to the Masons would have been arranged.

It's probably time to tell you a little bit about Kelly. I know a lot about her. As the baby of the family, I'd spent my whole life studying my sister. She was five foot six, slim enough to hate, and she had the clearest skin imaginable.

For a time, in my mid-twenties, I had truly appalling skin. Really. For just over three years, I had something along the lines of eczema, some kind of rash anyway, which started directly over my left eyebrow and ran diagonally down to my chin. In effect, it cut my damn face in half. It was itchy and bumpy and, as the first thing people saw of me, restricted my social life to people who'd lost their glasses, and terribly forgiving types who had their own flaws that made them hard to look at.

I spent a huge amount of money – really, money I didn't have to waste – on skin creams and face packs, lotions and miracle cures and, although it calmed down from time to time, it wouldn't heal. I suppose I should be ashamed that it took me every ounce of three years to realise I should see a doctor. I suspect it's because I faked all kinds of injuries to get out of PE as a kid that I maintained an unbearably high opinion of doctors. I wasted so much of their time, I'm surprised I didn't find my way onto a list. Anyway, it didn't occur to me to make an appointment for something as small-time as my face until I'd spent a couple of hundred quid on cream.

Anyway, once it got to the point that the tears running down my face felt like razors slashing through the skin, I called the surgery.

Bingo-bango, one blood test after another, and I was told that my liver function was normal, which I never doubted. I mean, I abuse the thing but not enough to kill it off. I was very nearly proud. My kidneys were fine. My calcium and haemoglobin and a whole bunch of other things I can't remember now were excellent. But my iron level was a little low and my folic acid was almost non-existent.

After a couple of months putting spinach in everything that didn't run away, and taking vitamin B9 supplements, my face went back to normal, but it would never be as clear as my sister's. But, as I told myself for three solid years, if you've got the personality, it doesn't matter if your face looks like it could be read by the blind.

And as it went, my terribly exciting blood tests and my bathroom full of lotion forced Kelly into going for a check-up. And, shocker, she too was afflicted by the family standard – the word that could replace the flat-line tone in the world of romance – fibroids. So dull, so pedestrian, so many of them.

I've had regular ultrasounds since I was twenty-eight. Presumably, my sister's done the same since her results came through. As much as we're close, we've never needed to talk about what our lady-bits might be growing while we're – chatting on the phone, sitting down to dinner, watching box-sets on Netflix – whatever we're doing, the fibroids grow, they swell. They require a regular inspection if only to ensure they're not planning to rise up and enter parliament.

I took, quite swiftly, to referring to mine as 'the gremlins'. Apparently, the other expressions I chose were inappropriate and/or offensive to people on passing buses. My gremlins kept me watching my figure. They made me wonder if I was getting a little thicker round the middle while they made themselves comfortable on my sofa-like womb. They made me wonder if every angry word, every rise in the blood, every bloated moment, was due to my hormones going out of whack while my stupid body cared for what it must have thought was a baby. Stupid body.

We never talked about it, so I didn't know how things were for Kelly. We would talk about other things to avoid it. I thought, if it worried her, she would find a way to sneak it into the conversation.

'*Did you see* Come Dine With Me *last night? Was it just me? That second couple was never a couple. By the end of it, they were barely friends. Anyway, what if, by the time I'm ready for babies, my uterus is so stuffed with growths that there's no room for an egg to divide? What if my hoo-ha resembles nothing so much as a Christmas turkey when the stuffing explodes?*'

I mean, she probably wouldn't do it like that but...

As far as I understood it, until the gremlins were big enough to own property, neither of us was in danger. Unless, of course, pregnancy was a real consideration...

Don't get me wrong. I know damn well that, as a lesbian, it's not as if I checked my ovaries at the door – the desire for family is universal, it has nothing to do with sexuality – but I wouldn't know how to tailor my jokes for an underage audience.

In any case, as the younger sister, it would be unseemly for me to spawn first. So, it was down to Kelly.

I've never been a coward but I wouldn't want to be exhausted and covered in sweat and other excretions at the moment my mother realises she's a grandmother. I'd want to be there with the camera, taking snaps as she begs the birthing partner (whoever they may be) to train the child into calling her 'Gan-Gan' like the Queen, or 'Bunny' to make her feel like she's still got it.

Of course, before any of that could happen, Kelly would want to be settled and happy in her own life.

At the time Marisa and my mother were sorting out the details of an accidental meeting, Kelly had her own flat. She had a good job and a decent bunch of friends, any of whom could be roped in to be aunties, uncles and godparents at any time of the day or night. She drank green juices and took care of herself and, ultimately, her skin deserved to be passed down to the next generation. That, or it would have to be preserved in a frame.

All she was missing was the sperm and it's not as if you could get it in a shop.

I tried very hard not to take the blame. But with my relationship flourishing and Marisa's general disinterest in other people's lives gelling so easily with my own, I was blindsided when she started listening to my mother.

I found myself feeling grateful that my girlfriend had no brothers. I couldn't quite imagine how long it would take for a relationship to blossom between partners who were also brother- and sister-in-law.

In some ways, it might have been easier to manage a crush on a particularly attractive cousin.

At least, an out-of-town cousin.

Having spent a lot of time watching my own face, looking out for any blister-like intruders, I already knew what it was going to do before I started speaking. I was making a small 'o' shape with my mouth, which would sprout all manner of lines once I got comfortably into my forties, and I'd lowered my eyebrows, so the lines would have a marvellous trench-like furrow to go with them.

"Hold on," I said, releasing the tension from my mouth. "When is this party we're having?"

"Next week," Marisa breezed.

It was quite sudden when the thought popped into my head. "Are we hosting it?"

"Of course," she said. "It's our anniversary."

"Well, it isn't," I huffed.

She smiled and slid a takeaway menu my way. "Did you want Chinese?"

See, while I'd been watching Marisa's business expand over the past eighteen months, she'd watched my desire for sweet and sour chicken balls do the same. She knew damn well I couldn't protest about much of anything when I could practically smell the prawn crackers.

But in the quiet moments, between the telephone order and the ringing of the doorbell, it hit me: we were having a party.

I'd never been much of a one for hosting. She knew this. It was the first thing I said to her, in fact, when she mistook me for the woman who'd booked her for the retirement do. Once I'd finished laughing, of course. Marisa could do it all day, every day but I'll tell you what I told her – I'm an excellent guest. The consummate guest. I've never enjoyed the idea of random people scattered around my home, getting lost, maybe going through my drawers while choking back the drink that I'd had to pay for.

I mean, it's perfectly possible to love your friends without paying for their liver damage. Isn't it?

SEE, IF I'M HONEST with myself, I don't find other people half as interesting as I find myself. If only I'd remembered that, I could have stayed out of the mess and saved everyone a lot of trouble.

However, since everyone else was having a pretty jolly time of it, I suppose I felt a little – left out. So, one thing and another, Gary and Kelly were a couple and I was the one who suggested the camping trip.

At various points along the M3, I watched myself in the vanity mirror and wondered how I had lost my mind so completely. Between Gary, filling up the back seat of the Volvo, peeking out from underneath his acoustic guitar and struggling to find the right chord, and Kelly, squishing herself into the far corner, her face pressed and pale against the window, my tilt-and-flip attempts at map-reading paled into insignificance. I was just surprised we were still talking when we arrived at the site.

As the mock-Tudor houses gave way to an endless stream of gorse bushes and their tiny buttery flowers, all I could think about was the futility of boy-girl stuff.

I didn't want to think about it, obviously, but it's often the way of things. You do everything you can to think of something else, but the same slippery image finds its way into your mind. And it just seemed so bizarre: girl has to pretend to enjoy it more than she does so that boy doesn't get upset. Boy has to tell himself he enjoys it less than he does, or he risks short-changing girl. I couldn't think how they managed it.

Anyway, my sister and the calligrapher had been a thing, with hopefully very little in terms of bedroom-related pretence, for eighteen months. Marisa and I had just gone over three years and so, naturally, the New Forest seemed like a good idea.

And then we got to the campsite.

An imposing, rather new-looking, five-bar gate was opened by a grizzled old man with a fisherman's hat and a face like an old tree. He smiled, revealing very few, rather yellow teeth, and proceeded to tell us that we'd made a good decision: that camping was the ideal way to test a relationship prior to marriage.

I had assumed he was talking for the benefit of the straights. It caught me off-guard to find him looking directly at me. Then again, I wondered if perhaps he had assumed I was one of Gary's harem. The most marry-able one, maybe. It supplied a momentary boost to my confidence, about which I was to feel pretty lousy for hours to come.

Having found our adjoining pitches, Gary made a big show of being able to reverse the caravan and park up in one smooth manoeuvre. After a nine-point turn, caused entirely by the relative bumpiness of Hampshire, apparently, the handbrake groaned and a breath puffed out of his mouth.

In the meantime, I'd spread the tent out flat across the grass, straightened out all the poles, and lined up the pegs beside the rubber mallet from the camping shop. I'd had a crack at it a few times in the flat. Not trying to impress anyone; I could just imagine trying to read the instructions in the pouring rain, and watching the book of words disappear in a sudden gust of wind, closely followed by the supine tent, and possibly, my girlfriend. As it was, the weather was fine so most of my imaginings were off the mark in any case. I couldn't help but feel rather annoyed about that.

We couldn't set a real campfire because we were right in the middle of the Forest and there's only so much danger a girl's heart can take when she's on holiday. Still, the four of us spent a good amount of time outside mine and Marisa's tent, gathered round the mini gas ring, the kettle whistling, smoking joints and trying not to giggle. I didn't much fancy sharing a smoke with the man from the gate and his small collection of rotting teeth.

It was a good weekend. Marisa and I spent much of our time tent-side, while the other two, if only for the sake of sleep, had to adjourn to the caravan if only occasionally. There was nothing of note to pull us into their space, aside from the chemical toilet, which lost its allure with astonishing speed.

Really, if you want to make the whole family uncomfortable to the point of gagging, share a chemical toilet for a weekend, I dare you.

Anyway, beyond choking on the potent mix of weed and leaking gas, and sneaking off to the caravan after an ill advised dinner of baked beans, there were other highlights. I brought a penknife and ate all my meals with it. Even in the case of the beans, I punctured and ate them, one at a time, from the end of my blade. Marisa had a spork, largely because I was the one who took her shopping and we decided between my knife and her spork, we'd look like a professional class of campers.

Gary and Kelly had spent a few days wandering round Millets, and had bought a brand new set of travel cutlery. It weighed almost nothing and had bright pink handles – like, shocking pink, bubblegum pink – and yet, we still managed to lose at least two spoons, which will probably be found by a team of archaeologists in a couple of thousand years, somewhere south of Brocklehurst. I doubt the pink will have lost any of its potency, but I wonder what they'll think of the people who used and then lost them.

I suppose, as a holiday, it was more fun for Marisa and I than it could have hoped to be for Kelly and Gary, but my sister forgets that I grew up with her. She could have roughed it, if she'd wanted to. However, the holiday was cut short due, in no small part, to the absence of Egyptian cotton. It was a silent understanding, reached as we washed our plastic plates in slow-running, tepid water – whatever else they were, my sister and the calligrapher were hotel people.

Kelly had rolled onto a spider on the first night and scared the life out of Gary when she stood up in her sleeping bag and a little brown carcass spilt off the pale blue nylon. *'That would never happen in the Premier Inn,'* he told her.

Having convinced Gary that, with the spider's death, he was no longer in peril, we went out to dinner on the Saturday night at a local pub. Kelly was determined the leave early the next morning, no later than six, she said, in order to miss the traffic. Gary said nothing. Marisa knew better than to get involved. Unfortunately, I didn't.

"Now, just hang on a minute!" I cried. "I thought we were having pudding."

Marisa closed her eyes and wrapped her fingers round my wrist. Even from across the table, I could see she was willing me to keep quiet.

And yet, "What?"

She took a sip of her lager top.

"Do they not have sticky toffee pudding, is that it?" I asked. "Because I'm happy with ice cream, you know me."

"Right, well." Marisa cleared her throat. "If you'll excuse us, Charlie and I need to powder our noses."

I'm ashamed to say, I didn't catch on at all. "I don't."

"Trust me, you do."

"Since when do you speak for my bladder?" I asked.

"Sweetness," she said, barely masking her irritation. "Don't you remember all the coffee you drank back at the caravan? And this is, what, your third pint? Surely..."

"Ohhh," I smiled, the penny finally dropping. "I understand. Of course. *I need to go to the bathroom now.*" I suppose I winked at Gary although, to be fair, it was more a blink that went wrong. "Don't wait up," I mumbled.

As we made our way along the path, towards the pub's front door, I snaked my hand about her waist. She gasped.

"Oh, for God's sake," Marisa whispered. "Try and control yourself, will you? Can't you see they're falling apart?"

"Who are?"

"Your sister and Gary."

"Oh, I see." I held the door open for her. "Did you fancy the sherry trifle or the fruit salad?"

"Aren't you even a little bit upset?"

As we got to the Ladies' room, I shrugged. "Well, it's a shame, but if it isn't meant to be then it isn't meant to be."

"But we're to blame!" she wailed.

I gawped at my reflection in the mirror. "How d'you work that out?"

"We put them together," she replied, over the wall of the cubicle.

"We bloody well didn't! I didn't even want the sodding party. You know how I feel about parties."

She started humming to herself to cover the sound of peeing. If we hadn't been arguing, it would have been quite thoughtful of her.

"So, are they breaking up now?" I asked.

"Well, how should I know?" Marisa said nothing for a moment. Then, "She knows she can talk to you, if she wants to, doesn't she? I suppose she could go to your mother, if she was desperate but – she can't be that desperate, can she?"

"I think you're getting ahead of yourself," I said, searching my reflection for blocked pores and nose hairs, although I'd never speak to her about such things. "If she had problems, Kelly might talk to me. *Might*, I'll underline, because she knows I'm not great with these things. But she wouldn't go to Mum. She started all this nonsense, not us.

"Anyway, Kelly's hardly likely to speak to me now, when I've spent half the evening battling linguine. I understand, of course. It's hard to take emotional advice from someone who's ever so slightly spattered with puttanesca sauce."

"Okay," she sighed. She didn't sound defeated, so much as exhausted, as if we'd been married for a few hundred years.

As we walked back out to the picnic table, the moon shimmered in the velvet sky and the stars came out one by one. Gary was already standing by the car. Having paid for dinner, it was clear we would have to forgo pudding, as he turned the key in the ignition.

"Everything all right?" I asked, like an idiot.

"We're fine," Kelly huffed. "We just need to talk through some things."

And that was it. The whole thing. Whatever was happening was none of my concern and that was just fine. Of course, it couldn't last.

───※───

RATHER THAN TINKER too much with Kelly's problems, I found myself headlong in my mother's. It was like a Greek tragedy.

"Charlotte, my love, have you ever been to a divorcing?"

I clamped my mouth shut. Eventually, I managed, "I'm sorry?"

"Excellent. I'll explain it, then," she fizzled. "What it is, when a couple is breaking up, instead of separating out their friends and possessions, and getting the dog to run between them in a quiet, dismal sort of way, they have a party."

"A what?"

"Like a wedding reception, with cakes and photos. Perhaps even speeches. And they toast the relationship, even as it ends. So, have you ever been to one?"

"A reverse wedding reception?"

"Yes!" She sounded almost hysterical. "It makes more sense, I suppose, if the couple has actually had the wedding, but we can work around that."

I couldn't help myself. "It sounds revolting."

"Oh, good, so you understand it."

She chuckled.

I didn't.

"Anyway," she went on, "how would you feel about hosting one?"

I couldn't speak.

"With your Marisa's background, I'm sure she could organise something appropriate inside an afternoon, but it would be a lovely gesture, really supportive, if you were to host it for your sister."

"Are you serious?" I howled. "You want *another* party?"

"They're depriving me of a wedding, Charlotte. After all the work I've put into this relationship, I might never be the mother of the bride. Can you imagine what I'm going through here?"

My heart was in my throat. "Kelly and Gary are breaking up? Definitely breaking up?"

"Of course," she puffed, clearly fed up with me. "It's all decided. Please try and keep up."

"I knew they were having a bit of a hard time of it but... shouldn't Kelly be the one to tell people?"

"Well, you're not *people*, Charlotte. You're family."

"Thank you," I choked. "But shouldn't Kelly be the one to...?"

"Oh, be fair, darling. She's beside herself."

I could barely speak. "And so you want a party."

Her voice went very dark. "I have two daughters, Charlotte. Two, and neither of you has given me an event. See, in theory, that's the best thing about daughters, my love – daughters give you events: Sweet Sixteens, and End of Term parties, leaving dos, weddings.

"But my girls have given me no events and it's not right. No, it's not right. I've given all my adult life to you two. You've given me heartache and worry and more wrinkles than I can count, or even see all that clearly. I've had to contend with dropouts and druggies and lesbians and that man who sold your sister's bed. But I can live with all of it. I can even do without the wedding, as long as you can give me a reception."

I didn't know what to say.

"Oh, just so you know, darling," she concluded, "it's pretty common practice to compliment the mother of the bride so, try and work it into your speech, all right?"

※

RATHER THAN TAKE MY mother's word for it, I decided to call Kelly to be certain that a) she and Gary were definitely finished, and b) she could cope with a party to honour my mother.

"Oh, that," she said, casually. "We just – weren't compatible. I'd rather not talk about it. You don't mind, do you?"

"And the party?"

"Apparently, we're getting a chocolate fountain."

The real problem was that I couldn't remember the last time I'd been to a party where something didn't go horribly, abysmally wrong.

In my experience, something always ran out: the wine, the toilet roll, the guests. Sometimes, the music was too loud, making proper conversation impossible. If the food was supposed to be hot, it was soon discovered to be cold to the touch and inedible from being fingered by half a dozen guests. If it was meant to be cold, the heat of all those heavily-perfumed bodies would soon see it bubbling in a quiet corner of the room. From time to time, just to mix it up, a hostile ex would wander in to make a scene, or someone with one of the less fashionable allergies would dig into the dip before disappearing in the back of an ambulance.

From what I'd seen as the partner of a party planner (try saying that three times after a bucket of margaritas), by the time the first guest arrived, the host was usually just shattered enough to hand over the keys to the house and call it quits. The only way they could avoid the myriad worries and thoughts of catastrophe – was to not host the party in the first place.

You understand, of course, that the consummate host is not and never has been a carefree, happy individual. She might look all gloss-cabinets, bleached teeth and well-behaved hair but, underneath the shimmering surface, she is a crazy-eyed, dribble-chinned control freak who has spent hours of her life folding napkins into waterfowl, and matching wines to the drunks she is expecting. After an especially large party, she can be expected to have a nervous breakdown and join the rubber sheet brigade within the month.

Please don't misunderstand me: it's no great shakes being a good guest either. You have to work out a considerate and original gift, you must compliment the décor even if the carpet is so wildly patterned it's like walking across a migraine, you must ask after the family and pretend to listen to the inevitable monologue about little Timmy's piano recital and the Labrador puppy who, although firmly attached to your leg, recently won a good citizen award.

No. Parties, generally, should be avoided.

And yet, of course, despite this accumulated knowledge, I found myself preparing to host a second party for reasons I didn't completely understand.

And as my sister made various sounds down the phone, I made a list inside my head of all the idiots I'd have to invite. It seemed the sort of thing where friends, both old and new, would be expected to make an appearance. It was effort enough not to stare at the people I knew from school – the boys who'd gone prematurely bald, the girls in belly-binding underwear, pretending they could breathe. It was hard to consider conversation with people of that sort, especially when all I could think was how they'd pretend that their teasing and name-calling was all in good fun because we were fourteen. The suggestion being that their adolescent harassment made no odds to my fourteen year old heart.

But, naturally, they would all be there. It seemed my mother had a guest list and my girlfriend had already drafted the email. They'd all be there. Smiling. Asking after the years in between. Watching my sister break up with her boyfriend.

She was still talking...

"We just wanted different things, that's all. When did Marisa tell you?" Kelly asked. "Have you known this whole time?"

"H-how long is *this whole time*?"

"It's got to be... six months, maybe."

I made a mental note for some time later. When I'd forgotten to put the recycling out or couldn't be bothered to do the washing up – it would be a useful tool to have in the back pocket. Marisa knew. She knew and didn't tell me.

Unless, of course, she did.

It could be hard to keep up and sometimes, I didn't even realise I'd tuned out until she asked a question.

"What kind of things?" I asked.

"Huh?"

"You said you and Gary wanted different things..."

She sighed and suddenly I didn't need her to say it.

"You'll... you'll never guess who I saw in the High Street yesterday," I rushed. "You remember her from sixth form, the one who worked at Robinson's? Her with the teeth?"

"Oh, my God. Not Heather?"

As my sister rattled on for a few minutes about Heather Whatever-Her-Name-Was, scanning her brain for pertinent details about the half-forgotten girl –

"She used to make a lot of friendship bracelets, didn't she?" Kelly remembered. "What were those things she gave everyone at the end of year party?"

Crabs, but I didn't interrupt.

I was thinking about how unfair it was that men could have babies right the way through to the grave, but women were stuck with a tiny window of fertility, before the eggs began to harden and the uterus fell.

Nothing against fellas, you understand. Not my style, but that's almost irrelevant. People who actively despise whole swathes of the population – you know the types, they usually spew out their venom across the cheaper sort of newspaper – what they're really saying is they hate people. All people. They'll let out a little of the sickness by rattling on about a whole gender or colour or faith, but really, they hate all of us. Luckily, you can see the bastards miles away. Hatred like that does something to your face.

No. I don't blame men for their almost boundless fertility. It's nature I blame.

Kelly had gone quiet.

"So, you know there's going to be a cake, don't you, Kels?" I hurried.

"Oh, spare me! What kind?"

Those women who needed something other than themselves to live for, something small they could dress up and worry about for the rest of their lives, had – what? – a dozen years: to grow up, to learn to be a proper adult with a working understanding of home insurance, council tax and APR, to become financially and emotionally stable, to find someone with whom they could share values, attraction and conversation enough to keep them in at least *polite* contact for the rest of their lives – and even then, they'd have to have the ability on their side. I wondered how other women coped with the fleeting nature of bodily maturity and an absence of willing sperm. Perhaps they just took all the pregnancy vitamins all the time. Just on the off chance. All it would take was one clever little sperm and hips at a conducive angle, and the whole world could change.

She'd stopped talking.

"Mum wanted to go with fruitcake," I told her. "For the sake of tradition."

"Eugh."

"I know."

But if nature were to throw a few pitfalls in the path, there might be a low-sodium diet, loose boxer shorts, the giving up of every single one of life's most entertaining vices, endless supplements, fertility treatments, meetings about sterility and sperm-washing, Kegel exercises to keep the uterus standing to attention – the list stretched out all the way to menopause.

"I hate fruitcake," Kelly whined. She's my sister and I love her, but she whined.

"Anyway, I think I've talked her into chocolate. It doesn't really matter. I'm the one who's making it. By the time she realises I've done my own thing, it'll be too late to change it."

"So," Kelly shuffled, clearly wanting to get off the phone. "When is this stupid party anyway?"

"You know, you could do me a favour and refuse to come," I told her. "Then, if you want cake, I can bring you cake, but none of us will have to deal with visitors and their perfume and the noise and mess of it all."

"No, it'll be fine," she breathed. "You know she'll just keep on about it 'til it's done and Gary's pretty keen, for some reason." Kelly chuckled to herself, "Maybe he thinks he'll meet someone special, eh?"

"Fuck him." It fell out of me while I was trying to work out how old my sister actually was. *She was six when I was born,* I thought. *That was right. So that would make her... Jesus. She couldn't be thirty-four!* I remembered there was a doctor on daytime TV who'd referred to a thirty-four-year-old woman as *'an older mother'.* Honest to God, an older mother. I couldn't believe my ears.

"Charlie!"

But I was wrong. In that moment, I knew I was wrong.

My last birthday had been one of gin and tonic all day long. Much of that week was a blank. I'd missed a year. She was thirty-five. Thirty-five! Hardly the end of everything but, God, she'd lost so much time.

We all waste our lives with the wrong people, of course. Only occasionally, but it's unavoidable. Some people don't show their true selves until it's too late. My sweet, unfertilised sister might have wasted the best of her ova on a go-nowhere relationship.

"Charlie? Are you still there? I asked you when the party was."

Part of me, a part I didn't much care for, couldn't blame Gary. A father who didn't want to be a father was no father at all. Actually, the only person to blame in this whole sorry mess was my mother. Our cysts, my rash, all our extra bits came from her side of the family. She was the one who pushed Kelly into a relationship that might have seemed easy but was, as it turned out, doomed. The quick slip-slide into marriage and the unavoidable army of kiddies were all her idea. Her latest mistake, of course, was sitting back and waiting while absolutely nothing happened.

"Char!"

"Sorry. Yes. I'm here," I shuddered. "Are you all right, sweet?"

"I'm fine," she said.

She was devastated.

"Did you say it was *this* Friday?" she asked.

"No." I thought for a moment. "No, next week, maybe the week after. Whenever the eighteenth is." I was barely paying attention anymore. From the moment I started thinking about my sister's ovaries, it was too late. I needed a drink.

∞

WHEN MARISA GOT HOME from work that day, I was practically crouching at the door, waiting. Every muscle tensed, every thought frantic. It had taken most of the afternoon, but I'd got myself organised.

Marisa liked a cup of coffee when she sailed in through the door. A tiny little coffee in a special espresso cup. I couldn't contain my excitement. She was due in at six. The kettle clicked at half past five. I needed those last few minutes to get my wording right.

"Hey, button," she said, bustling past me with a bag of groceries and chucking her keys into the bowl beside the door. "How was your day?"

"We have to cancel the party," I said.

She put the bag on the counter top. "What?"

I adjusted my face and smiled thinly. "I mean, how was *your* day?"

"Hang on..."

"Oh, well, if you insist," I said, "I'm worried about Kelly."

Marisa took small breaths before saying anything else. "What's wrong her?"

"She wants a baby," I said.

"We've talked about this, button," she blinked. "There's no point telling me what to get when I've already been to Tesco."

"What?"

"What?" She frowned. "Did you say she wants a baby?"

"I'm sure of it."

"I don't know where I'd get one of those," she huffed. "Why would you think I could get one at Tesco?"

I handed her the coffee cup and glanced at the ceiling. "I can't be certain, of course, but I think that's what the problem is. She was forever putting Band-Aids on her teddy bears and cradling next-door's cat when we were kids. Don't think the cat much liked it but she's a born mother. And now... she might never get her chance."

"Oh, my God!" she gasped. "This coffee is freezing."

"It's a Frappé. Isn't it? It's the style."

Marisa glared at the cup. "It's got a skin."

"Has Gary said anything?" I asked. "At work, I mean, has he said anything about a baby?"

"You're sure Kelly wants one? You couldn't have been mistaken?"

I took a deep breath. "The party is a terrible idea. Kelly will never get through it. She could barely speak to me today. We can't do this to her. Putting her in a room with all those wankers from school, and Mum, and Gary, and – pour it down the sink if it bothers you that much – and a bloody fruitcake, it'll break her heart."

"If we cancel…" But she didn't say anything else. She was doing complicated maths in her head, trying to work out how much she was going to lose on the deposits she'd already paid out.

I set the kettle going and did some calculations of my own.

"What if…?" I began and changed my mind.

"Go on."

"What if I got rid of the wording on the cake? What if we just have Kelly round for the evening, cancel everyone else and just have Kels, a cake and a bucket of booze?"

"What about the ice sculpture? I suppose we could still have it but it's a bit…"

"Yeah," I nodded.

"No. It's a terrible idea."

I looked at the lino. It needed replacing. Funny how you only notice these things when life is too complicated to let you do anything about them.

"Are you all right?" she asked.

"I'm okay."

"You're not," she said.

"I don't know what to do," I admitted.

She nodded to herself. "We have the party."

"But…"

"We have the party, we make it special. We make sure Kelly has something to smile about."

"Stripper?" I asked.

Marisa shook her head. "We invite everyone. We get people waiting at local bus stops. A huge crowd. No expense spared. We'll need flowers. Lots of them. We make it all about her, and how wonderful her life is going to be without..."

"Hardly without. There's Christmas and birthdays, and Easter. Mum's always been keen to keep the family nearby at Easter."

I couldn't have known then that one of us was barking up the wrong tree.

THE PROBLEM WAS, AS it always had been, we didn't talk about things. We're not good at it. Not like Americans. When we're hurt, we just carry the pain around with us until we're able to make jokes about it, or we go completely round the bend. Those are the only options. There is no in between.

But I'll say again: I did not push my way into the drama. I was invited.

I shouldn't have stayed.

The party would be enormous. So big, in fact, that no one would ever know exactly who was to blame for everything that went wrong. Because things would go wrong, of course. It was all planned. Marisa had her own stuff going on, but I could be quite meticulous with the details when I put my mind to something.

If she wanted fruitcake, she could have fruitcake... but not in our apartment. And when the time came to piss all over the parade, I'd be there with the watering can because I'm classy like that.

I had everything straight in my head. We'd have the party. I'd decorate the *chocolate* cake with something a little bit... not obscene. No one said obscene. But something that my mother would never approve of and, ultimately, she would never know. We'd lie and say that the caterers were double-booked. Something like that. Words would be had and by the time she realised what was happening, it would have already happened.

It was as I undressed that night that I saw the awful truth. Only six years older than me but it would have been worse for Kelly. As I took my shirt off, I saw it. The droop. It was like the fall of Rome.

Of course, it occurred to me that sleeping in a bra and double-checking all the windows and doors might keep my breasts in the house overnight, but then tiredness hit me like a truck. I could barely keep my eyes on my notepad.

"Are you going to turn the light off, or not?" Marisa asked.

"What's this?" I smiled. "Do I hear the sparkling tones of a better offer?"

"Actually, I'm shattered. Can it wait 'til later in the week?"

"Of course." Not accustomed to being turned down, even on the point of falling asleep, I went back to my notes.

A few minutes passed in silence.

"See you in the morning, button," she said.

"When?"

She frowned at me.

"When, later in the week?" I asked.

Marisa thought for a while, batting the idea back and forth behind her eyes. "I can probably manage Wednesday..."

"Well, only if you can fit me in."

I closed my notebook on the words 'Cake Decoration' and turned out the light.

※

SEE, REVENGE IS A HUNGRY beast. You can't just keep it as an idea. You must feed it. You have to be creative. You have to tend to and look after it, cherish it. It's not something to pick up on the way home from the pub like a bunch of apology freesias. Real revenge takes commitment. I was thinking about it as I stood on the balcony, pretending I didn't want a cigarette.

The days had skipped past, the party was on the horizon, and Kelly had finally left Gary's flat. I think it's fair to say that it was ill advised for her to move back in with Mum, but with Marisa tied up with all her last minute flapping and screeching down the phone, Kelly couldn't have come to our place. A silence had developed between us.

I'm not suggesting for a moment that my relationship was on the rocks. You have to talk for a relationship to be on the rocks. But it was nothing to worry about. It was always the same in the handful of days before a big party – Marisa would go to some secret place inside herself, somewhere I couldn't reach her. She'd stare into space for extended periods, wondering what she'd forgotten, how many people would die due to her crudités, how extensively she'd be sued.

I'll admit, I was beginning to worry. Two days before the party, or three as far as Mum was concerned, Marisa sat up straight on the sofa, bolt upright, like she'd been wired into the National Grid.

"I'm meant to get the rest of Kelly's things from the flat," she said.

"Well, I can do that."

"No," she hurried. "No, don't worry. I've got it. I'll be back... I don't know. Later. And check the board for me, will you?"

And she was gone.

I pottered around for a while. I rearranged the magazines on the coffee table. I counted the teabags in the caddy. I looked, albeit briefly, at Marisa's big white board.

Catering – great big tick. Excellent. Off to a good start.
Drink – double tick.
Ice sculpture – tick.
Chocolate fountain – question mark. Slightly worrying.

Cake – *tentative tick.* I wondered if I should take the hesitation personally. And then, I saw it.

Flowers – *'Button, would you mind?'*

I rolled my head from one shoulder to the other and decided it would be unseemly to have my first cocktail before four. Since there was time to place or check the order, it wasn't as if she'd told me which, I could go to her favourite florists and do whatever it was I was supposed to do. After returning from such a trek, I reasoned, I would have earned my first strawberry daiquiri.

I steeled myself, ironically enough, with my mother's words. '*Order in advance. Even if they might live for days, have them delivered on the morning of the party. And no tulips. Don't* make *me explain.*'

I took a look around before saying a word to the pinafore behind the counter.

Roses seemed wrong.

Violets were trite.

Peonies looked like sad old men.

Carnations were for salesmen.

Lilies were for funerals.

Tulips were unnecessarily sexual.

Gerberas made Marisa sneeze.

Lilacs.

I seemed to remember that Tallulah Bankhead had said something about lilacs. Maybe it was about falling in love. Oh God, that would be wrong. "*...It's the eyes, don't you know and sometimes the smell of lilac.*" I couldn't remember how it started.

Having landed on lilacs, I moved over to the counter. It was only when the woman looked up and smiled that I remembered what Tallulah had said: it was about everyone being basically bisexual, but in much more classical, gritty language.

Gawd bless Tallulah.

"Ah!" the woman announced. "You'll be here to confirm the flowers. For Friday, isn't it?"

"Umm," I dithered.

"You work for Marisa Wilson, don't you?"

"Certainly feels like it," I murmured. "What did she settle on, in the end?"

She ran a finger down the order form and announced, "Tulips. How nice."

"Pervert."

"I'm sorry?"

"I said, *'Perfect'*. See you Friday."

"HEY THERE, GARY," I pushed for what I thought was probably a smile.

"What are you doing to your face?" he asked.

I couldn't say I was completely sure, but I didn't feel the need to explain it. "Anyway, I've brought a few bits from Kelly. Think she must have been in a bit of a hurry when she packed."

"Actually, I'm pleased to see you," he said.

"Well, the flowers are sorted and..." My face crumpled. "What did you say?"

"There are a few bits of Kelly's still in the bedroom. Thought you might like to – collect them up for her?"

I frowned at him. Pointedly. "Didn't Marisa come over this afternoon? I thought she was doing all that stuff."

He held the door open for me and ushered me in. "Thing is, she got most of it but I think she might have been a bit upset."

"Really?"

"Well, she was clearing her throat a lot but she looked a bit, I don't know, tearful when she left."

"Right," I said. "Well, I'll talk to her when I get home. Obviously. We do talk, you know. So what did she leave behind?"

He led the way to his bedroom and opened the door. "I won't go in, if you don't mind. It's strange. I never thought it would come to this. I mean, I love her and everything but, sometimes..." He heaved a sigh that might as well have been a fridge-freezer. "Sometimes, things just don't work out the way you think they will, you know?"

"I do. I understand. But I really don't want to be talking about this. It's weird and I want to go home."

He breathed for a moment. I wondered if he was going to cry.

"Thing is," he said, "it's in the... in the bedside drawer. Don't make me say it. It would be wrong for me to take a look in there. I mean, she probably already took it with her but... what if she didn't? But it would be terribly wrong for me to check." By means of explanation, he added, "I'm her ex, now."

My mouth fell open. "If you're talking about what I think you're talking about, I'm her sister."

"But you're a woman," he insisted. "It won't mean the same sort of thing to you. For me, it's a symbol of failure. For you, it's just equipment."

"Right," I said. "Go and get me a bin liner. For your information, it's just as uncomfortable, if not, more so, for me. But, whatever. All I'm going to do is turn the damn drawer upside down into the bag and fling it at her when I get the chance, all right?"

When he came back with a full roll of bin bags, he hesitated.

"Has... has Marisa got a problem with me?" he asked.

I was getting tired of the whole damn thing by this point, so I said nothing.

"When she was here earlier, she hardly spoke to me. And then, with all the coughing and – she shut the door on me, you know. Came in, threw her handbag on the bed, shut the door and started coughing. I know it's awkward, with Marisa and me working together, but does she blame me for the break-up?"

"Probably," I shrugged.

"What?"

"You can't blame her for being uncomfortable. We're all uncomfortable. This is an uncomfortable situation. Anyway, I've spared you the worst of it. Mum's coming on Saturday, so at least you won't have her to deal with."

He smiled weakly.

I took the hint and left the door open.

"I suggest you stare at the wall for a tick, while I take a look at this drawer." I opened the first black bag, grasped the drawer handle and looked at the ceiling. I'd always said I should have been a ballerina. My choreography was exquisite. Sadly, my audience had fled to the sitting room.

"*Oh, and thank you, Charlie,*" I mocked. "*So good of you to help me with this delicate situation even though it's none of your business and you could be at the exciting end of a cocktail by now, Charlie.* You're very welcome, Gary."

As it happened, her bedside drawer only contained a bag of worry dolls and some travel magazines. I hadn't meant to look, but they spilled out of the bag almost upon entry. I glanced around. The art on the walls was noticeably his: all unnaturally posed wild animals and motorcycle parts. The stack of books on the floor consisted of crime dramas, some new, some with cracked spines. Even if Kelly could be forced into a crime drama, she would never abuse a book in such a way.

I put my head around the frame of the small en-suite. Only one toothbrush. Blue for a boy. Her monogrammed towels had gone. The bathroom cabinet had small circular patches on top where the colour was lighter – all her creams and potions, cleared out. I wondered if I should ask Kelly, being older and more experienced, if there was some kind of cream – for the droop. I decided against it on the grounds that she was newly heartbroken. A sagging chest, if she hadn't already noticed it, would just be another problem in her life.

Back in their bedroom, I checked the wardrobe. It didn't seem likely that she would have left anything but... no. Just suit after suit in shades of black and grey, and rolled ties and belts on a couple of tilted shelves.

That was it. All memory of my sister expunged from the room. Even the smell in the apartment had changed, from honeysuckle and vanilla to something more musky, fusty, not Kelly.

"All done?" he asked, heading back into the hallway.

"As far as I can see," I said. "If you find anything, would you...?"

"Yeah." He paused. "See you tomorrow night, then."

"This is weird, isn't it?"

"So weird," he said.

AS I CAME THROUGH THE door, I called out. "Flowers are sorted. Gary thought you were upset."

I didn't know where she was. It was only her keys in the bowl that told me she was home.

"I said Gary thought you were upset, darling."

Still no sign of her.

"He thought you'd been crying," I went on.

Still nothing.

"Did you, maybe, want to talk about it?" I asked.

"I think I've done something a bit silly," Marisa said.

I DIDN'T KNOW WHAT to say. Well, you don't, do you? When your girlfriend goes a bit – I'm sure there's a kind way of saying it but – insane, and you're left to pick up the pieces, it's really rather unfair.

Calls were made. Kelly was informed, and thus instructed not to answer the telephone under any circumstances. During the course of the call, Mum, tragically, found out about the date change and cancelled all her plans in order to boogie on down along with everyone else. The only thing to calm poor Gary the calligrapher was the promise of a handful of my beta-blockers and an early morning visit from me with a scrubbing brush.

When I got to his apartment, I held the list in my hand and prepared for the worst.

The damage had to be fixed and immediately because we couldn't have the party without the groom-to-have-been. And, of course, we couldn't cancel. People, as it turned out, would not understand. It was too late and we had to proceed or bring doom upon the planet. Or something like that. Marisa was very keen on the old hyperbole in the early mornings.

As much as she should have returned to Gary's apartment, head in hand, apologies abounding, and fixed the whole sorry mess herself, Marisa had the fairy lights to untangle so… it had to be me.

As I pulled the sea bass out from underneath his mattress, and looked into its cold, dead eyes, I caught sight of Gary, lurking in the doorway.

"Sorry about this, Gary. I don't know what came over her."

"Hmm," he managed.

"Maybe it's menopause." I chuckled. Alone.

"Least you know what'll happen to you if you ever get on the wrong side of her," he said.

I glanced back at the list she'd given me. "How's about you nip out, eh? Get yourself a coffee? I'll soon have this lot sorted."

He hovered for a moment.

"Of course," I said. "I understand. Do you want to bung me over another bin liner? Think this poor sod's going to have to be double-bagged."

"I'll tell you what," he began. "I'll just make some coffee here. Can't really go out. Not like this," he gestured to his boxer shorts.

"Of course. Did she cut holes in all your trousers, then?"

"Oh, she didn't cut holes in them," he said, his voice rising.

"Oh, I thought...?"

"No. She cut them straight across the kneecap."

"Ah." I didn't know what to say. "Don't suppose you've got any shorts or dungarees, have you?"

"Not ones that haven't got chilli sauce in them," he replied.

"I'll have a coffee, if you're making one," I said, trying to sound perky.

As he shuffled off, I glanced down at item number two. Luckily, she'd only cut the buckles off half of his belts. An attack of conscience stopped her from shredding his silk ties.

Poor Gary had already learnt not to trust anything in the ensuite. He hadn't recognised the smell of oven cleaner in his shampoo bottle, but he'd certainly noticed, a little too late, the puncture marks in the top of his tube of toothpaste. Invisible to the naked eye, it had taken only the humblest squeeze in the middle of the tube to push pale blue gunk over his thumb and forefinger.

Eventually, she'd explained the coughing. Not distress, nor seasonal ailment, she had hacked her lungs up to cover the sound of torn paperbacks. She hadn't gone so far as to split each book in half. No. What she'd done – she had carefully and meticulously torn out the last four pages of every book in his bedroom.

Gary was humming in the kitchen. I stood at his side of the bed and pulled out the cabinet. Just as she had promised, there was his mobile, underneath the pine. It must have switched itself off at some point in the night but Marisa was adamant, she had got through to the talking clock in Sao Paolo before hiding the handset. His bill would be astronomical. Their relationship was clearly at an end.

I began to wonder how easily she thought she could learn calligraphy.

Marisa had tried, lord knows why but she'd tried, to justify what she'd done by telling me about the things she had stopped herself from doing.

She hadn't reported his credit cards stolen.

Which, of course, made her a saint.

The only reason she hadn't done it was he hadn't been stupid enough to leave his cards unguarded in the bedroom.

She hadn't logged into his Facebook and started dangerous, lusty conversations with strangers. I was so proud.

She hadn't placed his obituary in the paper.

I wondered how I'd never seen this side of her before. But then, of course, it hit me. I couldn't have seen this side of her before because, until Gary and Kelly, we had lived in our own little bubble. A bubble of two. This madness was just a symptom of the melodrama into which we had been so viciously sucked.

I tossed the black sacks into a wheelie bin out back and slurped the coffee quickly. Gary had been shaking his head for a few minutes before he spoke.

"So, Marisa's crazy, huh?"

"She," I struggled. "She's a very passionate woman."

He pouted. "Passionate as a box of frogs."

"Yeah," I sighed. "Couldn't help but notice, you've got a lot of Frederick Forsyths in your bedroom. You must tell me what you think of 'The Fox'. That's his latest one, isn't it?"

"Oh, I haven't read it yet, but I'll let you know."

He'd never know the ending, of course. And so, I left him.

TWINKLY LIGHTS HUNG from the exposed beams in our apartment. Having gone a little overboard with the reed diffusers –

frankly, anything more than one is both extravagant and stinky – I'd turned the balcony into an outdoor scent room. I had the feeling the neighbours might not speak to me again but that was no great loss.

My mother was doing circuits of the room, smiling sadly and imitating a zip pulled across her mouth – as if, whatever it was, she couldn't talk about it.

The party was into its second hour when Marisa pulled the cheese puffs out of the oven and the doorbell rang. She was red in the face and angry-eyed, so I did what I had to do: I went out to the scent room for a cigarette.

As I inhaled, I saw a blur that looked like my girlfriend rushing towards the door. Sour mood notwithstanding, when I heard the voice, I kind of wished I'd been able to practise proper adult behaviour. I would have had a better view.

"Hey, Riss. Thanks for doing this," Gary breezed as he pushed past her.

I could only imagine what was happening to her face.

"Presumably...?"

"Kelly's been here since the start. Obviously. It's what you expect from the people whose party it is," she spat.

"And Carole?"

"She was here this morning," she couldn't keep the exhaustion from her voice. "She's had the hairdresser over twice."

"I suppose I should say 'hello' to a few people, eh?" He was so close to escape.

"You've got your speech ready, haven't you?" Marisa asked.

"Of course," he smiled. As I caught sight of him, he was leaning in towards the centre of the snack table. "Ooh, are these mushroom?"

Marisa's eyes had gone wild and kind of bulgy as she headed towards me. "Give me a drag, will you?"

I shrugged and handed her the cigarette.

"Do you think we've cursed this place now?"

"Huh?"

"In having a break-up party here, are we doomed?"

"With a party? No, I don't think so."

She smiled.

"We were doomed from the moment we introduced them."

She was quiet for a while.

"Are we going to talk about this?" she asked.

"Not tonight," I said.

"I saw what you wrote on the cake."

I giggled.

"*No one Needs Your Opinion, Carole*? She's going to hit the roof, you know."

"Too much?"

She didn't miss a beat. "No. Regardless, what does it matter?"

Marisa didn't say anything for a while. My cigarette was almost out. The night was getting chilly. I might have escaped back into the music and the heavy push of people, but then she spoke.

"It's you who wants the baby, isn't it?" she asked.

Suddenly, there was no air.

In the middle of the room, Gary pulled my sister to his side and tapped a spoon against her wine glass. "Ladies and gentlemen, if we can have your attention for a moment, please..."

The Desiccated Ingénue

I CANNOT UNDERLINE this enough: it's not a midlife crisis.

I know what you're thinking.

She's up and mentioned it straight away. She's getting all defensive when I'm just sitting here, minding my business. Of course it's a midlife crisis. What else could it be?

Well, I'll tell you.

It's an epiphany.

Oh, yeah, that's what it is.

I know. Because I looked it up.

While the rest of the world has been moving on up, rushing about, focussing their attention on what they want, applying for mortgages, getting engaged, married, divorced, having babies, parent-teacher evenings, weekend visits, getting their steps in and whatnot, some of us have been… Well, there's no other way to say it – some of us have been thinking.

Not dithering. Not festering. Just working things out, getting our ducks in a row. It's hard to say quite how it sneaks up. Because by the time you've put it into words, you've aged again.

You certainly can't explain it to young people. One day, you turn around and you're just too old to get the coffee. It's like, one day you're learning to contour your makeup, and the next, you're too old to be the trophy wife.

I remember when I was a kid – Sundays used to last for weeks. Christmas seemed to come around every few years, like that extra day in February – although, of course, we had none of them. Not in those days. Leap years were like Halley's Comet; spend an extra few minutes in the shower, working on your bikini line, and you'd miss the whole thing.

Now, I can't imagine how we've got back to July so quickly.

I see myself ageing in the mirror. The strain on my bones, and the shape of my buttocks and thighs, further proof of time and flesh spiralling out of control. I know. I'm in danger of sounding like the only things holding me together are varicose veins and rain bonnets.

But it's not like that.

I stopped to smell the roses when I was seventeen, looked up from the petals, and I was wearing a homemade, 'Kiss Me, I'm Thirty-Eight' badge. And I don't know how it happened.

Last thing of any note was school.

I was a very able pupil. An extraordinary number of options opened up to me. I was built for learning. I had a phenomenal memory, the skill to keep up with lessons, and a devotion to homework that I kept to myself for fear of broken bones. Although not altogether popular with other children, people like me remember being loved by form tutors, violin teachers, librarians, headmasters, substitute teachers; the list goes on and gives us something warm to think about when the nights grow dim.

My inner child has thrust her hand up in the air. She's waving, biting back the answer, fit to wet herself, such is her desperation to stand up before the class and explain the riddle that is me.

I'm too old to get the coffee.

It's a thing: the older you get, the more you learn. The more you learn, the more you realise how little you really know. The more you recognise your limitations, the less desirable narrowing the field even further becomes. This understanding, at least in my experience, seems to kick in around the second year of university, when you're already a specialist in your field. And so, of course, it's too late. Second year of cryptozoology and all I could think about was how I didn't know a thing about the Great Fire of London or the Salem Witch Trials or *Fame*, the TV series.

Anyway, the fact of the matter is this: I did my A-levels. I went to university. I followed the path. I realised how little I knew. Felt bad about myself. Got my degree, and prepared to begin the life of my choosing.

Of course, nothing is ever that simple.

I suppose I was twenty-two – thereabouts – when my mother suggested I should apply to become a runner for TV personality and DIY guru, Timber McRae. She thought it would be brilliant. Frankly, it was the only idea of hers that I'd taken seriously in years, and it was prompted entirely by the fact that she wanted me out of her house.

Apparently, I become rather annoying after twenty-odd years.

Anyway, with no cryptozoology work available and no gofer jobs popping up in the Classifieds, I settled on visiting my aunt Irene twice a week.

Aunt Irene didn't even know who Timber McRae was, which made me feel better about being passed over for a job that didn't exist, and most of our afternoons included a solid five minutes' speculation about the relationship problems of people on commercial television. Frankly, it seemed, I'd had a narrow escape.

I never went to Irene's house without a book. Having shut myself in the heavy wood and dusty smells of libraries for a good number of years, and having little to say to her otherwise, I read to her. Biographies, history books, the occasional bodice-ripper. She'd have me read right up to the slightly saucy scene, and then, Irene would have me turn the corner in, and flip the pages on until we got to something lighter – some problem with the staff or a letter from the vicarage. The naughty passages – with gamekeepers, tennis instructors and buttoned-down housekeepers – were meant for a time when I was out of the room. A fact, about which, I am still grateful.

Anyway, in really no time at all, I moved into my aunt's house, getting out from under my mother's roof and feet. I became Irene's narrator and entertainment. She occupied a precious space in my little world. She became my champion. We read about the great moments in history. She introduced me to some of my favourite authors. We gossiped and giggled about famous people who we'd never meet because, even though it might look to be the other way round, *we* were better than *them*. And then, she up and died on me.

I cut my hair. Grew it out. Cut it again.

I caught up on the soaps. Not much to report there. When the ratings are falling, they chuck in a lesbian. When they're sure nobody's watching, they pop in a baby-swap story.

I tried online study, which is to say, I enrolled on a number of courses I've yet to – actually start.

I suppose I got a bit bored just reading to the houseplants and, with money getting a bit tight and no desire to sell Irene's house, I took up a series of temping jobs.

They didn't really work out. It's hard to cultivate meaningful relationships with workmates you'll only know for a few days before one or all of you disappear over the horizon and into another drip-dry office with an angry note on the microwave.

I had a crack at dating.

That didn't really work out either.

To begin with, I couldn't quite get the hang of the whole swipe right-swipe left thing. I still don't know which direction signifies an interest. Anyway, I wound up matching with a right load of nutters.

There was one, I thought, that might have been a bit of all right. Long blonde hair, faux leather trousers, bit younger than me but nothing disastrous. It was after dinner when it all went wrong. She asked me what my safe word was. I thought she was joking. Told her, the only sensible safe word was *stop*, and I laughed. She didn't call again.

So, I sat down, had a little word with myself. *Que Sera Sera*. Gotta love a bit of Doris. If it was meant to be, it would have been. Maybe it loses something in translation...

See, because I know what my trouble is. Although I don't really think of it as a problem but... Okay, here it is: I can cope with other people's intimacy right away, but that doesn't mean I'm ready to share my own.

A lot of people will, I suppose. Maybe some people find it easier getting to know someone when they're horizontal and upside down, but not me. Anyway, since my dates tended to involve fat chips, curry sauce, and a full and heated discussion about whether or not we'd stolen the profile pictures of dead people, they rarely graduated into second dates.

I'll say this: it's hard to cram a whole relationship into one meeting.

Luckily, I was trained by Irene. As long as I've got romance novels to come home to, I'll be fine.

Anyway, getting back to my original point, I had an epiphany. I knew suddenly, and totally, exactly what I needed to do.

As they're supposed to, my epiphany came out of nowhere, but I suspect I'll remember that moment for the rest of my life.

I was just sitting on the pier, eating a prawn cocktail sandwich that, quite honestly, tasted like it was on the turn. Rather than pitch it into the nearest bin, as anyone else might have done, I just ate faster. There was logic at work. But as I was looking out at all those purple, grey waves and the white slashes of gulls floating on the cloudy blue air, it struck me.

When you're young, *young*-young, you get all the mucky jobs because you're too inexperienced to complain. In my late thirties, I was too mature to face the slow and steady rise through the ranks, with every station learned through good, honest toil. But I was old enough to fake it. Not for me the life of the desiccated ingénue, but I was pretty sure I could pretend I knew it all, if required.

Also, if we really boil it down (and I rather think we should), I had a huge amount of experience. I'd worked, occasionally for *days* at a time, in offices, in shops, in a museum gift shop, various cleaning jobs, bit of newspaper stuffing. Nothing too taxing, but lots of it. I'd encountered all manner of people – at some distance, none of them too close, but I'd made what might be termed 'a study of humanity'.

And do you know what all that amounted to? Life experience.

I knew people.

Not people with influence, of course. I'd had no days with Timber McRae, but I knew what made people tick. I knew a lot about the jobs that people didn't want, the people they didn't need in their lives, the things that got them all worked up, because I'd seen it during my office days. I'd watched it on commercial television. I'd read about it with Irene.

Now, you might suspect that such an understanding would lead me into a life of beer pumps and stale ale smells. It did occur to me as a possibility, but then I realised, as a barmaid, I would have to be relatively sober in the face of other people's secrets. I'm not a complete simpleton, so no part of that idea held any allure for me.

I did go to the pub because, what am I, dead? But I didn't take a job behind the bar. I went to work in the small lounge, with the faded red sofas and the low-slung tables, and made myself look as ethereal as possible.

I don't mean headscarves or fistfuls of silver jewellery. I'm no mystic, psychic, patchouli-person. I don't carry the waft of incense in my wake, and I know nothing of runes or cards or pendulums. *Pendula?* I just couldn't think how an agony aunt would dress – in real life. When she looks down from the newspaper columns, she usually has big glasses and a wide range of cable-knit cardigans. But real life included summer and she couldn't dress that way in July.

Anyway, after messing around for half-hour, holding up turtle-necks and slinging them back on the bed, I settled on a loose blouse, jeans and flip-flop combination, and headed over to the pub. I reckoned it would be better to sit and get a feel for the place, given that I'd never actually crossed its rubber-matted threshold before, and slowly work my way into the day-to-day life of the place.

Okay, fine. I'm stalling.

You got me.

Some people would calling it setting the scene but...

The fact is, I kept up the pretence of work. My heart was never in it. I didn't earn much but it was enough to stay on top of the bills. And okay, I couldn't quite afford the luxuries like holidays and road tax, but I spent my evenings in the pub.

When a person has a bit of a drink, they lower their guard. We all know this. The inhibitions come sprawling out across the carpet and before long, you'll hear all kinds of things. The sorts of things that would usually only be told to a priest. It's at times like this that you become very grateful that the bar is still in service. Some secrets can only be absorbed and borne with copious amounts of gin.

I suppose, in all my agony and defeat – the principle feelings that come with grief – I developed a bit of a thirst myself, so the pub became my natural habitat.

Having been born in a second-class carriage at Lime Street Station, I could have been a born traveller but actually, I've just never felt attached to any particular place. Except Irene's house. The train was holed up at the station when I made my presence felt. There was no hanging about in those days. When a baby was to be born, she was to be born. And so I was. Didn't even get out of the carriage or, at least, that's how the story goes. It's probably a mess of lies, but a romantic nature allows me to believe it.

I was no sooner weighed and washed, than we made our way home to Skeggy. Growing up on the sand does something to the mind, so they say. Having lived near the water, I couldn't bear the idea of being anywhere else. Salty and cold, I was cursed with lifelong youth. I say cursed, but I know it's supposed to be a blessing. It isn't, but I know it's *supposed* to be. Having always had a young face – not a beautiful one, but it was youthful – I suppose I thought it would never change. Like there was a painting of me in an attic somewhere, doing all the ageing for me.

I'm not looking for compliments. I'm not one to dangle the hook of – *I'm not beautiful* – and wait for you to protest. The hell with that. The beautiful people take too much for granted. They're idiots, the beautiful. No, given the choice, I'd sooner be plain.

Plain, mark you, not repulsive.

Getting back to the point, we moved east. A little south as well, but mostly east. I was eight, maybe nine – old enough to remember, not quite old enough to recall the exact date. We came to Cromer, just down the road and across a bit from Aunt Irene. She was getting older and Mum had this notion of writing up the family history and thought it best to get it right from the horse's mouth. As it goes, Mum and Irene soon discovered they couldn't stand being in the same room together – Irene didn't care to be compared to a horse and Mum didn't fancy explaining herself – so we spent some years finding other reasons to have moved.

All people really know about Norfolk is that it's very flat. Being flat, it's worth noting, it's also very windy. There's nothing to get in the way of the frosts, which come straight from Russia and end somewhere in the bones. So, okay, from Liverpool to Skegness to Cromer: I am a woman of many parts. All of them watery.

If I track it back, gaze into the mists of time and root around for the source, I think I gave my first opinion, unsolicited of course, when I was around five years old.

My nana was wearing court shoes, highly polished, beautiful sheen, with a little kitten heel. Perhaps two inches high, nothing outlandish, but she tottered. She was only a little woman, you see. Little women don't walk, they totter. I watched my podgy little reflection in those black and shiny uppers, and I asked her: 'Aren't those shoes too tall, Nana? What if you fall?'

It was barely an hour later when they wheeled her into Casualty.

And when the neighbour boy was climbing the apple tree that leaned from his side into ours, I told him: 'There's moss on that branch, Christopher. Be careful you don't slip.'

I warned him.

Before you think the worst, I should explain. He didn't fall and break his neck. Not even his collarbone, arm, pelvis, back. He didn't break any part of himself. But there was a crunch when he landed. A terrible sound, I don't think he ever recovered from it. He came out of it better than the cat, of course.

I didn't say much of anything for a while after that. None of my advice had been especially insightful but, in some slight and childlike way, I suppose I wondered if I had spoken the danger into being. The power of suggestion is a terrible thing. I know now that my advice was only common sense stuff, but as a child, I clamped my lips together, tried to think happy thoughts and ignored the world around me.

It couldn't last, obviously. Slipping into my teens, I couldn't stop myself. I blame the hormones. Like every teenager since the breed was first discovered (sometime in 1967), I longed to mix it up, sneer at the world and tear it apart, make it new, make it better, make it mine. To do all of that, I'd have to say something.

There was a whisper in the locker room, a room that smelled of cheap body spray and unadulterated feet, that one of the girls had a crush on the English teacher. I tried to tell her – doomed from the start. From before the start, in fact, since he only knew her from the split infinitives that peppered her essays on Shakespeare and Yeats.

She didn't listen. They never did, back then.

It didn't take long for the poor, harassed, lantern-jawed Mr. Peel, becoming more fraught and haggard with every lesson, to call in Mrs. Dwyer, the deputy head, and words were had. Joanna Maguire couldn't chase the crimson from her cheek for the better part of a fortnight. That was after she came back, of course. Joanna's parents came for her, some pretence, something about a stomach ache, and then she sobbed into her pillow for a few days, waiting for the gossips to find another target. They didn't, you know. They never do.

I said nothing, barely nodded a hello to her in the assembly hall. It was after she threatened to splash my supposed secrets across the bathroom tiles that I decided to go off, somewhere, anywhere, for college. But my secrets were never secret. Not back then.

I continued my observations of mankind from the canteen. I learnt the little ticks, the hints, that come across through body language and a flicker in the eyes, a brief dilation, a quivering lip. And I kept it to myself. I could see the disasters on the horizon, but I gave no warning. People have a tendency to trash the messenger on the cubicle walls.

It was only after Irene died that I knew I couldn't stay quiet any longer. I realised, because it's not as if I'm stupid, that there was a chance my words would fly straight into a windowpane, leaving a streak of red to slide and sputter down the glass, but it was my risk to take.

You see it sometimes on social media. Someone, who you know to have a brain will inexplicably repost some holier-than-thou piece about how children don't respect their elders, their grandparents, teachers, a whole swathe of society, like, a massive proportion of the people they see each and every damn day. And when you get into the post, you realise that these children who are, of course, to blame for every single thing that's ever happened, were born in the eighties and nineties. The 'children' are pushing forty and, if they are responsible for anything, it's because they're the adults.

And it occurred to me: I am an adult. My words carry almost as much weight as I do. My opinion might be invaluable to someone. Some anonymous someone who I would doubtless find at the pub.

And so, no more stalling, I went to the Lamb. Pretty soon, the random drunks became my drunks, and I went from plain old Esther Moody to the Sage of the Sands.

In the beginning, I sat back, a Bloody Mary in one hand, a loose bar mat in the other, and all I did was tap along to whatever was on the scratchy-sounding radio, waiting for a problem to fall into my lap.

Most of the customers kept to themselves. Not unusual, I suppose, given that they didn't have the first idea who I was. It was harder to overhear their troubles when they mumbled into the beer foam and hummed a mournful, almost acoustic version, of the theme tune to *Cagney and Lacey*.

I don't know when every tune had to go all soft and floaty, and kind of despairing, but there it is. Every advert, every sad scene in a soap opera, has to have a hollow-voiced acoustic version of some hip-thrusting disco classic. Sometimes, these things creep up on you. Like menopause or alcoholism.

Anyway, back to the bar. I couldn't tell which one it was, but one of the regulars had a particular weakness for ginger biscuits. There was no question of it. The tang and spicy smell pervaded the very wallpaper. I started leaning back into the upholstery and glance around the room, examining the drinkers, quietly suspecting each and every one of zing-addiction.

I had only been going to the pub for a week and a half before I came in useful. It's a delicate line, I'm sure you understand. Sometimes, people don't actually *want* advice. They want to hear themselves talk so they can work it out for themselves. They might not even know what's bothering them until they hear it scramble out of their mouths between belches. Some people, I can tell you now, get outright offended if you take a breath deep enough to suggest a comment on the way. Still others, poor souls, have no idea that they actually need help.

We had the usual selection of drunks: the slur-speech buffoon who laughs at jokes he hasn't told, the erudite, functioning alcoholic with an attaché case and the breath of a dead gerbil, the sleepy drunk who sprawls out on the bar like it's his brother-in-law's sofa, the loud-mouth sputtering single nonsensical words every few minutes before settling into silence, and the common collection of kids, knocking back shot after shot of brightly coloured sugar and hurling it back over the pavement on the way to the kebab house.

I'd grown used to thinking of myself as a mentor long before anyone actually spoke to me. We all do what we can to make it easier to live with ourselves. So, naturally enough, when the shout came out across the bar:

"*Oi, darling! What do you say? Should Barney leave his missus or not?*"

I wasn't even sure if I was the 'darling' he was asking but I didn't hesitate.

"Depends," I said. "Do you think she can find anyone better?"

A sound came out of his mouth, like he was chewing on wet toast.

"I'll take that as a 'yes'. Probably best you hang onto her, eh?"

There were a few chuckles. It may be worth mentioning that we'd all had a drink but I suppose it went to my head – not the vodka. The acceptance, the feeling of belonging.

Still, that was how it all began, and over the following days and weeks, more questions came my way. Trivial stuff mostly, nothing you wouldn't find on the cheaper brand of morning chat show.

'*Wife wants a new Ford Mondeo, but I think I might be gay, what should I do?*' – that type of thing. But then, one day, quite unexpectedly, Thing came and sat with me.

When I was first introduced to him, the nickname did worry me a little. A lot, really. Thing – it's hardly a term of affection but, as it was explained to me –

"We call him Thing but really, it's just short for Thingummy. Thingummy Bob, really.

"When he first started coming up, we already had four guys called Bob. The first one was taken at face value and, as such, called Bob. The second one arrived a few years later but he was a skinny-wristed thing; there was no chance he could usurp the original Bob. Thus, he became Bobby. It was only a few weeks before the third one crossed the threshold. He kind of looked like a deviant, so we called him Bobert. And when Thing here showed up, wanting to stick with Bobby, we convinced him that Thingummy Bob was better. He's a little," he pulled an imaginary dishcloth back and forth through his head, "but he's basically harmless."

'Thingummy Bob' Stimpson was a sweetheart. He was tall and soft, with bright blue eyes and a gentleness that belied his forty-odd years. And he smelt of ginger biscuits. Thingummy was equal parts kind and worrying. You'd leave your children with him, but you'd phone up every four and a half minutes, just to check.

"Can I buy you a drink, Sage?" he asked.

"You know me," I said, although, realistically, he didn't. "They say people are seventy percent liquid but that doesn't sound like enough, does it?" And even though I was dumbing down my usual conversation, I could tell I was talking over the top of his head. I made a mental note to watch that.

He raised his glass with a toast, "God bless my wife's husband. He's had a hell of a time."

I smiled, "I didn't realise you were married, Thingummy."

"Oh, I'm not. It's just something my dad used to say."

We sat in silence for a time.

"I know what people say about me," he said. "I know they think I'm a bit..."

"Oh, I'm sure they don't think you're..." I said.

Turned out, neither of us was going to say it.

"They think I'm slow."

"I'm sure they don't," I fluffed.

"When I walk in the room, they whistle *'If I Only Had A Brain'.*"

I couldn't think what to say. "It *is* a catchy tune," I tried.

"I didn't do so well at school," he went on. "Can't be that though. That's so long ago, it's best forgotten."

I found myself nodding because it was easier than disagreeing so early in the piece.

"And I still hang around with Tommy Sideways. I suppose that could be it. You won't have met him, I don't suppose. Doesn't come in here. He's not allowed."

"Oh?"

"No, he's a vicious bastard," he smiled.

I steepled my fingers. It seemed like the right thing to do.

A few drinks later, the lounge cushions were dented with the remnants of us, and a forest of empty glasses filled the table.

"I knew Tommy at school," Thingummy explained. "He picked on me a bit. Made a game of it. He'd see how hard he could punch me, or how long he could hold me under the water in the boys' toilets, before I passed out."

"God, Thingummy. That's awful."

"He was just joking," he shrugged. "It was harmless stuff. Kids' stuff. But, when we got a bit older, he changed. Got a bit cosier with me, on account of I could drive, and the ladies used to like me. I was a handsome bugger back then.

"So, Tommy used to come with me out on the town. I wasn't great at knowing when the girls were flirting with me. You never know when people are just being nice. And they always went home with Tommy, anyway. I never understood it. They'd sidle up beside me and lick their lips. Some of them would touch my arm and throw their heads back laughing, although I'm not sure what they were laughing at. Maybe they were making fun of me, but it didn't seem like it.

"Mostly, I kept to myself. They didn't smile so much with Tommy as they did with me, but I suppose that's because they were serious about him. There were a few times, in the mornings, when he'd come to the worksite, grinning from ear to ear, telling his tales. He'd tell us the girl's name and what she looked like, and I'd try to remember her face, but it was gone.

"And then, the weekend come and we'd go into town again. I'd not see the girl again. Never thought much of it truth be told."

I didn't want to ask, but I had to. "What did he do with them?"

He looked like a lost child. "I don't know."

"You never asked him?"

"You really don't know Tommy, do you?" He took a big slurp of his pint. "You can't just ask him something like that. Grabbed me round the throat once, headlock-like, only reason I knew how long I'd been out for was the theme from *Channel 4 News* was playing. Must have been an hour. There was a gap between *The Simpsons* and the news. Nothing there. Just a blank. He was just sat in the corner, watching me. God, he laughed."

A shiver ran across the back of my neck.

"Thing is – Tommy's gone a bit quiet lately. I don't like it. He's never so bad as he is when he goes quiet. Something's upset him. He doesn't usually stay that way for long without something slipping out."

"Don't you have other friends?" I asked.

"Course I have, darling." He paused and tapped my arm. "I've got you."

My heart sank.

"So, what happens when Tommy goes quiet?"

"Usually, it means he's working on a plan."

Nope. I thought it was already worse, but there was a darker place.

"Doesn't that frighten... I mean, are you safe, Bobby? Do you need me to call someone for you?"

"No, you're all right, darling. He's a mate. He'd never do anything lasting to me. That'd be his lifts all dried up."

I took a sip of my drink and realised what was missing. "So, did you want advice about something, Thingummy?"

"I want a wife," he said. "So I'd have a reason to stay home."

I took a breath but couldn't think what to do with it. It was true, Thingummy Bob wasn't like other people. It wasn't that he was slow, although, of course, there was that, but he was an interesting guy. It was like – you know when you were a kid and you'd play a forty-five record at a thirty-three setting? He was like that: the tempo was off but there was something fascinating about him.

Frowning, I couldn't tell if his desire for a wife was a direct flirtation with my ring finger. His eyes were so gentle and his smile so confused, there could be no doubt: it wasn't a threat. It seemed unlikely, with all he'd told me about his head-flushing, girl-disappearing mate, he would threaten me when he'd been on the receiving end of so much.

Just in case, I switched from Bloody Marys to plain tomato juice, which is and always has been disgusting and inexcusable. The barman smiled and shook his head. He leaned across the bar and whispered quickly.

It seemed Thingummy and his stories of Tommy Sideways were pretty well-known, nothing to worry about, the sort of story that fades into the background. But if I'd known then what I know now, I would have gone with my instincts and the hell with anyone who'd suppose I was paranoid.

Anyway, I got myself settled, with my own little nest in the lounge bar. And in the ensuing weeks, I made myself comfortable, indispensable.

And then she walked in.

I knew, you see. It was as if I'd already seen the film and the same scene was flashing before my eyes.

It was as if I was disappearing.

You could call it resentment, perhaps even jealousy. You'd be wrong, but you could call it whatever you wanted. The fact is: when Rachael McDonnell turned up for her first shift behind the bar, all gold name necklace and aubergine lipstick, I might as well have vanished.

It would be fair to say that we didn't get along straight away. I was just on my way out for a breather when the door swung towards me, splashing my blouse with tomato juice and bending my cigarette at the filter, and there she was: thick blonde hair, smiling eyes and whisper-thin, purple lips. She wore a pair of dark blue jeggings and a t-shirt with a sparkly logo that made me want to vomit. *History – make it or be it*. On a barmaid, for God's sake. I swear I'm not a snob.

I'm clearly not a snob because, while Rachael was all philosophy-tits, I was in a three-day-old blouse with, I was disheartened to note, spatters of last night's gravy, enough tomato juice to suggest an aggressive nosebleed, and an inexplicable pigeon feather.

Naturally, my friends and former audience flocked to her. She wore a balcony bra. We didn't find that out until her second shift, but it was there, lurking just below the surface, like a family secret or a venereal disease. They couldn't get enough of her and her polyester-mixed, double-D profundity, and I found myself alone.

And that was the way of things for a good old while. They stared at Rachael in all her sparkly newness. I sat in my corner and took discreet sniffs at the contents of my blouse. Somehow, no one needed to talk. They shed their problems like damp umbrellas at the door.

With nothing serious to chat about, they took to telling Rachael how pretty she was. Even Thingummy Bob started brushing his teeth again. It was disconcerting.

I decided to view it as a holiday. Even when you love your job, even when it's a job you're actually paid for, everyone needs a break from time to time. I didn't go so far as feeling grateful to Rachael for giving me a break. Not at all. Frankly, she was a trinket. A shiny little bobbins, little more than a distraction. I should have felt bad for her, being all surface, no substance, but she was too smiley to pity.

Of course it couldn't last. A perfect silence never does.

One by one, they returned to me. Their problems were no richer than before. My insight was hardly earth shattering, but I went back to feeling useful. I could almost forget that Rachael was still standing there.

When she came to the table, with the tray announcing her bust, I began to notice that she hardly looked at my fellow drinkers. I wondered, for a moment, why so many of her looks were reserved for me, why they were lingering and pained. There was a question there. Something she needed, but I shrugged it off.

I assumed it was advice she was after. It seemed unlikely to be anything else. When a woman, stained with last night's dinner, walks alone into a bar, she doesn't imagine that anyone thinks anything of her. And, let's face it: a woman who isn't a hundred percent on finding her own mouth with a fork is not someone about whom anyone thinks wicked and delightful thoughts.

It was somewhere round her second month working the bar. Everyone, or so it seemed, was taking their drinks out to the beer garden. The middle of spring, the primroses were out, the air was damp but not too cold and I found myself alone in the bar.

Rachael went to say something, so I headed for the door.

A small crowd had gathered around the back corner. It took me a moment to find a gap but then I saw him. Thingummy had been crying. His voice was thin, his words uncertain. They came out in a stammering rush.

"I don- I don- I don't want to talk about it!" he yowled. "Just le-leave me alone."

I ignored his words because I didn't suppose he meant me, and edged a little closer. I slid a hand upon his shoulder. He shrugged it off but turned and looked at me.

"Smoking shelter?" I asked.

"Smoking shelter," he said.

In truth, it was little more than a birdwatchers' hide, but it served as a dry place in the winter when the ornithologists took an evening off, it was less exposed than the picnic tables, and at smaller risk of lightning strikes than the thinning poplars at the edge of the garden.

I handed him my lighter as we settled on the chilly bench. Figures of drinkers slid and sloped between the tables, their voices lifting from occasional words to a dull rumble.

"So, what's happening?"

"I can't," he said.

"Well, that's all right. We can just sit quietly, it's fine."

"Tommy," he said.

"Did he do something to you?" I asked. Straight out. Like a hero.

"No, it's just... He... Can you keep a secret?"

"Of course, I can." I might as well have buffed my fingernails. Instead, I lit my cigarette.

"Well, how are you for money?" he asked.

I'll admit I didn't know how to respond to that one. "Well, I –"

"Only, I don't think I can *keep* splitting it, but if you're really pushed, maybe..."

"I'm struggling to keep up here, Bobby."

That made him smile. It was only small but I saw it.

"What it is, I came into some money, you see. Uncle died."

I took a breath.

"No, it's all right," Thingummy rushed. "He was old. And ill. Still, Uncle left me some money and – I didn't mean to – but it just sort of slipped out. Now Tommy's in a huff with me. Says it's not fair. He's got no uncles, you see."

I took a drag and thought for a moment. "It can be dangerous lending money to friends, Bobby."

His eyebrows shot up.

"Well, not *dangerous* dangerous, but I can't think anyone's ever loaned money to a mate without losing their money and messing up their friendship."

Okay, I watered it down, but introducing Shakespeare, when Thingummy had already been upset, felt like a step too far.

He let out a half-laugh, half-gurgle. "He doesn't want a *loan*, darling. He wants me to split it. Straight down the middle. Fifty-fifty."

My mouth dropped open. I only noticed because suddenly my cigarette was on the floor.

"He says after all he's had to put up with from me, it's the least I can do. Besides, I'd still have five grand. That'd be enough to fix up the bathroom, I reckon. Course, I'd have to keep living with the damp patch in the kitchen, but that's not so bad. It's only growing at the moment 'cause I've had the heating on. I suppose I could just switch it off for a while. See if that dries it up a bit."

He waited while I rolled another fag. I don't suppose it occurred to me that I could roll and listen at the same time.

"Before I came here, Tommy told me he could just take the lot and no one would know. Either he'd keep me quiet or he'd have rid of me, but there'd be some changes round our way. Not sure what he meant by that."

I shook my head. "I know he's your friend," although I couldn't think why, "but friends don't give each other thousands of pounds. They watch telly and talk about their problems. They have a laugh and commiserate with each other. They make plans, they have things in common. They chat."

"So, what should I say to him?"

Rachael appeared with a drinks tray and a smile which fell as soon as she realised she was intruding. She handed over the drinks and didn't even wait for our protestations that she'd brought the order to the wrong bench.

Thingummy took a sip of cloudy cider and winced.

I don't know where the thought came from but: "Would he believe you if you said you'd lost it?"

He took a long drink of cider and made a face.

"Lost it where?" he asked.

"I don't know," I admitted. "On a horse. Or a bus."

He leaned in and whispered, "You can't bet on buses, darling."

My smile was brief. "Would he believe you, though?"

"Probably." He rubbed his chin. "He's always saying I'd be lost without him. And that I couldn't find my arse with both hands. And that I'd have been put in a home if it wasn't for him. He says he'd do anything for me, but... *I lost it on a bus.* Yeah, I think I'll say that, then. Thanks, Sage."

Once we were back in the main bar, I realised I should have left before my third drink. I certainly should have left before my fifth. But with the weight quite visibly off Thingummy's shoulders, he smiled and winked to the girl behind the bar and I couldn't keep my eyes off them. Thingummy had clearly lost his heart.

At closing time, completely certain that I should be tucked up in bed with my hot water bottle and my Sudoku puzzle book, the barmaid edged towards me. I didn't realise how tightly I was gripping the bar until I tried waving and couldn't move my hands.

"Can I ask your advice?" Rachael asked. "Only, I hear you're the one with all the answers and I could really use some help."

"Sure," I slurred with a smile. "What do you need?"

"Thing likes me," she confessed.

"Who?"

"Thingummy Bob."

"Oh," I replied. "Okay, then."

"No, I mean, he *likes* me."

"Fine."

Total silence.

"Oh," I realised, "and that's a problem. I see."

She didn't seem convinced.

"Because – you don't like him?" I suggested.

She looked at her shoes and shook her head.

Thankful that my gift had not deserted me, I asked, "Have you tried telling him?"

"I'm sorry. I shouldn't be bothering you with this. I'm sure I can handle it. It's just, there's something about you…"

My eyes widened.

"You remind me of my mum."

And, just like that, I couldn't be doing with giving advice to barmaids anymore.

"You're right, of course," Rachael sighed. "I should just try again. Maybe he needs to hear it more than once for the message to get through. It's just, he was saying how he'd like to take care of me, *like a little doll* and – I don't like the sounds of that. He says he'd treat me well and – I'm nineteen, you know. I'm not looking for anything serious."

"But you think he is?"

"Yeah."

"Tricky." I would have said more but a burp burst inside my throat and made my ears pop. For a moment, I thought I might be dying.

"He said his mate would want to meet me too, but he'd…"

"Mate? What mate?"

"I think he said John."

I took a breath.

"Might have been Tom. Whatever," she took my empty glass. "He had a funny surname."

"Sideways?"

"That's it. Do you know him? Am I being mean? Should I give it a chance, see what happens?"

The screaming inside my veins was just an echo for the screeching inside my head. *Get away from him. Tell him you're not interested. Enter a convent. You can't meet Tommy Sideways. Change your name. Move to another town. Get a new job. Run. Run far, far away and don't come back.*

What – I said – was, "It's probably because you're new. I'm sure he'll get over it. When's your next shift?"

"It's Wednesday today, right?"

"All day long," I smiled, though, truth be told, I wasn't sure.

"I'm on Monday, Wednesday, Fridays for the moment, so Friday."

"Okay then." As if I needed her whole diary! "When you see Thingummy on Friday..." I started.

"What if he's not here?" she interrupted.

"If you're open, he'll be here. So, when you see him Friday just – ignore him. Give him the weekend to lick his wounds and then, on Monday, I'm sure everything will be back to normal."

When Friday came, Rachael duly shuffled off to the kitchen every time Thingummy approached the bar. Old Lil served him, humming an earworm that had been bothering her for days, and coughing into the crook of her elbow because, as she insisted, she'd 'been raised right'.

"I don't know what to do," Thingummy frowned. "She won't even look at me, Sage."

Seen through the bottom of a pint glass, his sadness stretched into a distorted, yellowing, hall-of-mirrors pout.

"I know you don't want to hear this. Frankly, no one wants to hear this. But if she was the one, do you think you'd have to try this hard to get her to notice you?"

He belched. "I don't get it. Tommy gets all sorts of women to – not just look at him – they go home with him! I know because I'm the driver. And okay, sometimes he has to help them, with doors and stuff, but no one ever blanks him."

"How do you mean, he has to help them with doors?"

"Well, you know, darling. The usual. He'll give them his arm to get up stairs. Open the car door for them. Gentleman-stuff."

I nodded, relieved.

"And he'll lift them into the back seat sometimes."

A muscle in my jaw started to jump.

"And he'll let them sleep in the car. Some people, you know, they'd nudge a person to wake them up, but Tommy lets them have a kip. Some people have to have a conversation to get through a car journey. Not Tommy."

"And you drop him home, have I got that right?" I tried to sound nonchalant. I didn't sound nonchalant. Luckily, Thingummy didn't seem to notice.

"Yeah, well. He's only up the road from me, so it's no trouble. So, I'll get him to his place and just wait, with the engine idling, while he collects his new girlfriend from the back seat."

I tried to think of what to say but it was clear he had no idea what was going on.

"I don't know why it is he attracts the sleepy ones. I suppose everyone has a type. Thing is, Tommy's type could be any shape, colour, age, but they always fall asleep. I told him," he chuckled, "he should work on his small-talk. He gave me a slap for that one."

I sipped breaths while I thought about what to say.

"So, you think I'm barking up the wrong tree with Rachael?" he asked.

"I think so. Sorry about that," I added. "But it might have been a bit awkward: if the two of you ever had a falling-out, this is your local and her workplace, how would you cope with seeing each other?"

"Yeah, I suppose you're right." He lit a cigarette. "Tommy says a woman likes a take-charge kind of guy but that's not really me, is it?"

"Well..." but there was no right answer to that. I lit a cigarette. "Do you think, maybe, it's time to cut the cord with Tommy? It doesn't sound like he treats you very well and you deserve a mate who takes care of you a bit."

He grinned. "I know what you mean, darling. As it goes, Tommy knows he's not always the nicest guy. He's said he'll make it up to me, though. He did suggest I point Rachael out to him sometime and he'll use his – whatever, his gift – to work out how I can get her to fall for me."

"Oh, Bobby," I managed.

"No. I don't like the idea of him catching sight of her, to be fair. If she got together with him, that'd be worse than her ignoring me.

"Well, I should be heading home, Sage. Have a good one."

And with that, he was off.

IT'S STRANGE HOW, SOMETIMES, you can walk into a room and just get the feeling that something is horribly, horribly wrong.

"... And if you're not going to bother showing up to work, young lady, you'd best call and let us know! I'm sure you have lots of important young-person things to do but some of us are missing *Emmerdale*!"

"What's going on?" I asked one of the guys at the bar.

"Rachael's skiving. Old Lil's just leaving a message."

"... There are plenty of other young women round here who'd love your job. Sage!" she called out. "Not as young as she was, of course, but she could do your job, no problem."

"So, where is she?" I asked my fellow barfly.

He just shrugged.

"And if you're not here Wednesday, don't bother coming back!" Lil shrieked. "Although, of course, we'll want the t-shirt back. Okay. Call me when you can. I accept apologies in the form of whiskey or cash."

I spent much of the evening chewing on my cuticles and ignoring my drink, waiting for Thingummy to come in. The clang of the closing bell shook me from my reverie.

"Righto, that's all, folks!" called Lil. "You've all got homes to go to. And if you haven't, don't make me hear about it now. Night-night, then. See you tomorrow."

"Have you seen anything of Thingummy?" I rushed as she pushed me towards the door.

"You missing your little friend? Not to worry. I'm sure he'll be in tomorrow. It's rare he misses a night, but he never misses two."

But he did.

And the word went round the bar three times – Tommy Sideways hadn't been at work in several days. All that was left of his caravan was a burn mark in the ground and an angry drug dealer.

Thingummy's house, aside from the fungus in his bathroom, was deserted, his important papers rifled through, his bank account overdrawn. Rachael's mother hadn't seen her since the Saturday night she'd gone out on the town.

It's not as if it's my fault.

But, you know what, even if it was, it's not as if I've come out of this completely unscathed. I've had to deal with the police and their questions. I've had to deal with not knowing whether Tommy ran off with Rachael as well as Thingummy's money, or if he took both of them and the cash, or if either of them was fully conscious at any time. That's a lot to live with, you know.

I try to remind myself that I don't have all the information. It's quite possible that Rachael and Thingummy Bob bumped into each other in town, blushed furiously, lost words, and bonded over their awkwardness from different directions. Maybe Tommy Sideways was a figment of Bobby's imagination. I like to think the money was real. Maybe, in a different environment, they fell in love and Thingummy's taken Rachael on a world-cruise.

It's not impossible.

But I don't really believe it.

No nineteen-year-old wants to go on a cruise, world or otherwise. Not the sort of nineteen-year-old who wears slogans and aubergine lipstick.

I can't help but think – I would never have found myself in this predicament if I'd gone to work for Timber McRae when I was the right age to get the blasted coffee.

Author's Note

BIG OLD THANKS TO EVERYONE I dedicated these stories to when they first came out.

In order, they are:

'A Can of Worms: A Short Story of Love and Lies' for Louise Underwood,

'It's The Landing That Hurts: A Short Story of Disaster' for Debs Kerr,

'Desperately Seeking Spinach: A Short Story of Obsession' for Catherine R.,

'If This Were A Swedish Film, We'd Already Be In Love: A Brief History of Fiona' for Sam Herbert,

'Love Letters To The General Public: A Little, Widespread Romance' for Tania Romaine,

'The Good In Goodbye: A Short Story of Revenge' for my mother, Jo – she would have known the character of Carole was not based on her, but she'd want you to know that, too.

And *'The Desiccated Ingénue'* – a bonus story, written for this collection – which I'll dedicate right now to the authors who've shown me such unfailing support and friendship, especially, but not limited to: Anstey Harris, Andrew Shanahan, Glenn Quigley, Zarina Macha, Kerri Davidson, Eugene Francis-Williams and Dario Ciriello.

Boring Bit About Reviews

YOU ALREADY KNOW THIS but reviews really help readers find books. People rarely get my name right, so the odds of someone stumbling across my books are pretty small. So, if you could spare a minute and a line or two of text on Amazon or Goodreads, I'd really appreciate it.

Thank you for your time, dear reader. It means the world to me.

You can find my other books here: https://amzn.to/2EvIhLQ

And if your book club wants to send me any questions, you can contact me via my website at:

www.petrinabinney.com[1]

With many thanks, PB

---

1. http://www.petrinabinney.com

About the Author

Petrina Binney is from 1980s south London. Daughter of a nurse and a carpenter, she spent much of her childhood writing stories to bring into school for whatever the eighties English equivalent of 'Show and Tell' was called. She spent her teenage years avoiding all manner of naughtiness, instead writing copious amounts of self-indulgent poetry and reading multiple Brontës and Daphne Du Maurier. Since late in 2017, Petrina has written and published several volumes of the Sex, Death and Dinner series, and learnt to speak about herself in the third person. Petrina spends the majority of her time in Devon, with her dogs, drinking with older gentlemen and awaiting international notoriety. Read more at https://www.facebook.com/PetrinaAuthor/